LIVE FROM THE UNDERGROUND

LIVE FROM THE UNDERGROUND

CORINNE WASILEWSKI

MANSFIELD PRESS

Copyright © Corinne Wasilewski 2015
All rights reserved
Printed in Canada

Library and Archives Canada Cataloguing in Publication

Wasilewski, Corinne, author
    Live from the underground / Corinne Wasilewski.

ISBN 978-1-77126-089-3 (paperback)

    I. Title.

PS8645.A82L59 2015   C813'.6   C2015-906196-2

Cover design and typesetting: Denis De Klerck
Cover Images: Shutterstock
Author Photo: Teri Young
Copy Editor: Stuart Ross
Proofreader: Eva H.D.

The publication of "Live From The Underground" has been generously supported by the Canada Council for the Arts and the Ontario Arts Council.

 Canada Council for the Arts   Conseil des Arts du Canada    ONTARIO ARTS COUNCIL CONSEIL DES ARTS DE L'ONTARIO

Mansfield Press Inc.
25 Mansfield Avenue, Toronto, Ontario, Canada M6J 2A9
Publisher: Denis De Klerck
www.mansfieldpress.net

In memory of my mother, Annie

PART I

SPRING 1980

The cathedral was already packed when we got there. We weren't late—twenty minutes early in fact—but Varsovians were coming to Mass earlier every week. People who hadn't darkened the door of a church in years were suddenly staking out seats front row centre while the faithful vied for second-rate pews in the back. Faithful or curious, we had come for the same reason, to hear Priest Kowalski; one-of-a-kind Priest Kowalski with brass balls under his pristine white gown.

I am not one of the faithful so I suppose that puts me in the group that is curious. To be honest my faith in the Church has been on the wane since First Holy Communion. The instant I tasted the body and blood, I knew something was wrong. I'd expected a flavour rich and delicious, something more in line with my nine-year-old fondness for sugar and chocolate; say an Oranżada drink and hazelnut torte. Instead, I was eating cheap wine and corkboard. And the Church has been serving me up one disappointment after another ever since. Jesus may have walked on water and rose from the dead, but from my experience, being Catholic offers no real advantage. It hasn't bought me blue jeans at the Pewex or a one-way ticket to America. It hasn't changed złoty to dollars. It hasn't toppled the Communists.

Can Priest K turn things around? I'm rooting for him from the cheap seats. There's no question he's different from the priests we've had before. He's thin as a shoestring, does a wonderful diving header in the goal box, and doesn't wax on ad infinitum about humans as scum and earth as our due as he reclines in a cushy chair with his jowls flapping like a St. Bernard with its head out a car window.

The other priests saw life as an endless round of Hail Marys and Our Fathers, but Priest K says life is about abundance and freedom. He talks about the kingdom of heaven coming to earth and he talks like he means it, his gaze certain and his hands jabbing the air. He could be full of shit, too, but so far I don't see it. Truth be told, I'm excited. It feels like Poland is on the brink of great change. Any day now I think Priest K's going to lay out the blueprints, distribute the shovels, and start us digging the foundation.

The weather forecast had predicted rain, and people entering the cathedral had umbrellas tucked under their arms. I held mine like a walking stick, touching the tip to the floor on alternate steps as I followed my parents down the main aisle. No bench had room to accommodate all three of us, so I laid claim to a vacant seat near the front while my parents settled into a bench on the aisle.

It took a moment for my eyes to adjust to the gloom. Light in the cathedral is poor at the best of times, worse with no sunlight coming through the stained glass. I stared at the rood and tried my best to ignore the theatrics going on around me. The remaining seats filled up quickly and within minutes it was standing-room-only with the crowd pushing forward to fill the aisles.

A nervous energy filled the room. The place seemed less like a church and more like an airport...or a barnyard of chickens competing for corn. Unfortunately, the rooster beside me kept winging his elbow into my ribs with each glance at his watch. I was ready to retaliate with a good prod of my own when the room turned en masse for Priest Kowalski's grand entrance. Anticipation turned quickly to grumbling, however, when the ones sitting down couldn't see past the ones standing up, and the only solution was for the whole room to stand, good seats or not.

Priest K was his usual unassuming self, his gaze fixed on the altar while he calmly walked to the front. There's nothing flashy about him. I think he sees himself mostly as a mouthpiece, as a modern-day John the Baptist calling out in the wilderness. He's the house built on rock, the tree planted by the stream.

The other men in the processional were anxious and shy. No two were in step and the one with the cross drifted from one side to the other all the way down the aisle. The group reminded me of Moses and a slightly drunken band of Israelites passing through the Red Sea, albeit Priest K was more of a Clint Eastwood-like Moses, right down to his steely green eyes and half scowl. Perhaps he carries a pistol under his cassock, I wondered, and couldn't hold back a smile.

Then the organ blasted the opening bars to the first hymn and we all straightened up, squared our shoulders, and exchanged quizzical glances with the people beside us. It was the first time I'd heard the national anthem at Mass, but it was an excellent strategy and exactly like something Priest K would think up. From the very first word, our voices surged to the rafters with a power like to blow the roof off.

Poland has not yet perished
As long as we are alive.
What outsiders have seized
We shall win back with the sword.

March on Dąbrowski
From Italy to Poland.
Under your command
We shall join the nation

The singing grew more passionate with each passing verse. By the end of it, only the men were singing; the women were drying their eyes on their kerchiefs.

This is probably as good a time as any to introduce myself. My name is Darek Dąbrowski. No relation to the Dąbrowski in the song, however. He was Jan Henryk Dąbrowski, an eighteenth-century Polish general who, more often than not, found himself leading Polish troops in faraway lands because Poland had, once again, been conquered by foreigners. Good, old Jan Henryk—he devoted his existence to the liberation of Poland, but, never did live to see that glorious day.

My family Dąbrowski has its own share of heroes. Take one Stanisław Dąbrowski, for instance, who died defending his home in the first Mongol invasion and was thereafter known as Stanek the Brave. His was a gruesome death to be sure, precipitated by an onslaught of arrows, the first one of which implanted itself in my ancestor's chest while the horsemen were still mere ants in the distance. Stanek was strong, though, and built like a bull and through sheer willpower alone refused to yield to his injuries. Still standing as the archers approached, but, with arrows projecting from most major organs and all of his limbs, he struck the ground with his hoe. The front-line Mongols perceived this as an act of defiance and sliced off his head as they galloped past. The Mongols that followed stampeded his body, beating it into the earth with the hooves of their horses. So complete was the mixing of flesh, bone and soil, that, later, with the danger past, Stanek's family found it impossible to separate his body from the earth, although they tried very hard, having salvaged every flour sieve they could find for the job. In the end they admitted defeat and left the body right where they found it. Only laid down some shovels of dirt overtop.

My great-grandfather Jarosław is one of our more recent family heroes. He was a farmer by trade, most of his land devoted to rye, with a small plot for vegetables to feed his own family. In addition, because of his shrewdness with money, he had managed to secure one milk cow, two goats and a coop full of chickens. Among the people of his village, Great-Grandfather was considered nothing short of a success. All the more so because he had four hardy sons who helped work his fields.

To Great-Grandfather, it seemed nothing could go wrong. Even the weather had been giving him her full cooperation for several years by that time. Then, in 1939, when he least expected it, Great-Grandfather's world fell apart. The Germans invaded Poland. It wasn't long before a military truck pulled into the farm and demanded Great-Grandfather render a portion of his harvest to sustain the Third Reich. Great-Grandfather refused. He had a wife, four sons with wives, and twenty grandchildren to feed. He had no food to spare for German gluttons. "If you value your life you will do as you are told!" said the officer. "Asshole!" said Great-Grandfather. Then, before my great-grandfather knew what was happening, the officer drew his pistol and shot him in the head.

Priest Kowalski stepped up to the pulpit and the congregation sprang to attention. Those with glasses took them off and wiped them clean while the rest angled their heads for a better view. "A reading from Paul's letter to the saints in Ephesus, beginning with chapter 5, verse 8."

"Glory to you, Lord."

"'For you were once darkness, but now you are light in the Lord. Live as children of light and find out what pleases the Lord. Have nothing to do with the fruitless deeds of darkness, but rather expose them. For it is shameful even to mention what the disobedient do in secret. But everything exposed by the light becomes visible, for it is light that makes everything visible.' The Word of the Lord."

"Praise to you, Lord Jesus Christ."

Priest Kowalski closed the book and pressed the cover to his lips. "My dear children, my heart rejoices to see you here today because I have an important message to deliver, a message that comes straight from our Lord above, a message that offers courage and hope.

"I look at you, my friends, and I see men and women, boys and girls. I look more closely, and I see tired husbands and exhausted wives, hardworking fathers and mothers trying to raise and support their families. The Party calls you workers and students, and this is true, as far as it goes. But it doesn't go far enough, does it? Certainly, you are workers and students. But you are more, much more. Think. Do you know who you are? Can it be you have forgotten? Has your true identity become a distant memory?"

I looked around the room and tried to pick out the Communists. Certainly the man beside me with the clothes of a farmer but the hands of a bureaucrat; also the middle-aged man across the aisle who kept fiddling with the buttons on his trench coat, a coat with bulging pockets, one of which, incidentally, looked as though it held a tape recorder.

"Let me remind you. You there, tram driver, butcher, steel worker, mother, father, sister, brother, you are not who they say you are. You are the children of the Most High and He is your Father. We are heirs—heirs of God and co-heirs with Christ. Believe me when I tell you God wants to liberate you from your bondage and bring you into the glorious freedom that is rightfully yours as children of God. It is not God's plan to harm you. He wants to make you prosper, to give you hope and a future, to bring you back from captivity.

"Our Father urges us to freedom, but we linger in our chains. Why? Because of fear. Our oppressors are masters of intimidation. They count on our weakness and rule us through fear. My dear friends, God wants us to count blessings, but we number our fears instead: fear of losing a job, fear of losing a promotion, fear of not having a daughter or son admitted to university, fear of imprisonment, fear of humiliation and ridicule. And so we do what they want and give voice to their lies. And every step we take down that lonely, dark road leads us further from the truth. We forget our true nature, and the truth fades away until it is no bigger than a pinhole of light in the darkness.

"Listen to me. It is time for the children of God to come home. You are light in the Lord. Throw off the yoke of slavery and live as children of light, shining like stars in the universe."

Mrs. Majewski in front of me sucked in her breath with the sound of one drawing up drink through a straw. She had lost her entire family in World War II—three sons in the Warsaw Uprising and a husband when his plane got gunned down by the Germans. I knew what she was thinking. She could see Soviet troops moving in from the east. So could I. There was a certain, grim inevitability to it—like school in the morning.

I glanced over at my father, who was leaning forward in his seat and hanging on Priest Kowalski's every word. He held one of my mother's hands on his lap and was stroking her fingers with his thumb. A few seats beyond him was a classmate from school, his face flushed bright red and both his hands in tight fists, which he held by his chest. No surprise there. Tomek was always ready to fight; give him a time and a place and he'd be there. He'd go to the Communist Party headquarters right now if someone wanted him to; take down the first official that came out the door, pound his head into the cement until it was soft as a rotten tomato. And then he'd switch his father's Fiat 125p for the official's Rolls-Royce.

Idiot, I think. I'm not a pacifist exactly, but, I think there's a right and a wrong time to fight, and Poland mostly picks the wrong time. Maybe, I'm just a coward and lack the guts to be a hero. Or maybe I'm just tired of the never-ending shit. I like to think there's a better way.

"We are children of light, but, we are also Poles, and these two strands of our being entwine to form a single cord that cannot be divided. In our hearts, we hold fast to the two: our beloved Poland and our faith in the body and blood of Christ." He held up his hands and joined them together, fingers locked tight. The congregation loved this gesture. The entire room was cheering and clapping. Most of the women and more than a few of the men had tears streaming down their cheeks.

"We know the road to freedom is paved with pain and suffering, but we also know that the Lord is with us and that we need not be afraid. Remember, Christ died to set us free. We pray to the Lord."

"Lord, hear our prayer."

"Heavenly Father, for so many centuries you surrounded Poland with the glow of power and fame and protected us with the shield of your care, but we have grown weak and turned away from you. We forget we are your children, children of light, and for this we ask your forgiveness. Restore us unto yourself and give us the courage that comes from above. Fill us with a holy discontent and make our hearts long for freedom. For thine is the kingdom, the power and the glory, forever and ever. Amen."

After Communion, I waited outside the church for my parents. It was starting to rain, just spitting really. I dug the umbrella into the ground between my feet and prepared myself for a long wait. It can take half an hour for my mother to make her way to the door because she's strategizing every step of the way: exchanging favours, giving compliments, extending special invitations to the state-owned fabric shop where she works so a lucky few can preview a new shipment before it's put out for the public. These "tactical manoeuvres" are probably my mother's most time-consuming work, but, also her most profitable.

My mother came out of the church alone.

"Where's Tata?" I asked.

"He has a meeting," she said, head down, retrieving a cigarette from her purse.

I looked at her with narrowed eyes. "What kind of a meeting?"

"A group of men are meeting with Priest Kowalski: Pan Gorski, Pan Nowak, Pan Pawlak...." She lit the cigarette with trembling fingers.

They all worked at Warsaw Steelworks with my father. The blood drained from my face and pooled in my shoes. "I'm staying, too," I whispered.

"No, you're not."

I don't always do what my mother says—often I don't even

hear her—but this time her tone of voice demanded my attention. I stood tall with my chest pushed forward and tried to sound convincing. "Mama, I'm not a baby anymore. Look at me. I'm almost a man. You heard Priest Kowalski. I want to stay, too."

I pulled on the door, oblivious to that left hook of hers until it was too late. Her fist hit my jaw, driving my head into my shoulder. I turned on her furious, not from the pain or humiliation, but because she'd let my father go. "You should have stopped him!" I cried. "You should have made him come home!" Her eyes filled with tears and I studied her face, completely bewildered. "What is it?" I asked, but she wouldn't say. As the rain turned to a downpour, I handed over my umbrella and walked home alone.

I live in a city whose streets and squares are named after the heroes of uprisings, wars, and revolutions. The names change depending on who's in charge. Right now, our streets are named for Communists. Before that, the streets were named after heroes of the 1920 war with the Bolsheviks, and before that, a range of czarist dignitaries. A word to the wise: should you ever visit Warsaw and get lost, do not, I repeat, do not ask directions from anyone old enough to be your grandmother. Do so and you will assuredly spend untold hours wandering the city, searching for streets that no longer exist.

I live downtown on Dzielna at Marchlewski, the same Julian Marchlewski who was in cahoots with the Bolsheviks back in the twenties. Ours is an ugly, grey block beside Pawiak Prison. There are no prisoners now—it's a museum—and every day I pass its gates, I tread the same ground as the 37,000 inmates executed by the Nazis in World War II.

When I was a child, I was forbidden to dig in the garden. No search for buried treasure, no holes for marbles, no tunnels for toy cars or trains. Hell, just dragging the toes of my shoes through the weeds was enough to banish me inside for the rest of the day.

My protests did nothing to sway the adults in the block, who on this particular issue maintained a strong and united front. "You don't know what you might find" and variations of that theme were repeated over and over again with no further explanation. Their subtle threats kept me in check until the summer I was ten, when my fears were pushed aside by a new and powerful fascination with heavy equipment. I was particularly fond of the machines with big buckets that dig up the earth.

One hot Saturday afternoon, I attempted the formidable. I sneaked my mother's silver salad spoon out of the flat and started to dig. The soil was hard and progress was slow, but my dedication to the task unwavering. I gave absolutely no thought to what I might find or to the cramps in my legs or the blaze of the sun on my back. My intent was pure action and the thrill of exposing that which, until now, lay underground.

I couldn't have gone any deeper than fifteen or twenty centimetres when I found something white and glistening in the dirt. I wiped the object clean with my fingertips and rolled it around on my palm. It had smooth, flat sides that tapered to a single edge and a disturbing similarity to my baby teeth, which I saved in a matchbox under my bed, except it was bigger and one side was coated with a veneer of gold. I closed my fist tight. This was what I'd been warned about. This was a bad find. I dropped the tooth back in the hole and covered it over as fast as I could. Then I threw the spoon in the bushes to conceal the evidence.

From that day forward, my entire life changed. My eyes had been opened and suddenly I saw Warsaw for what it was, not only a city of old squares, cathedrals, and Communist tenement blocks, but also for what lay beneath: a city of corpses. Streets and neighbourhoods that I had previously known as quiet and empty were now inundated by ghosts.

At night, I lay in bed with the blankets over my head and a transistor radio plugged in my ear. It was no use. Nothing blocked out the screams from Pawiak Prison—screams and the stomp of boots on gravel, sometimes gunshots and the smell of charred flesh. And the incessant barking of dogs. One particularly violent night, I crept to the window and looked out. There, hanging from the dead tree in front of Pawiak, were the bodies of five men. I yelped and closed the curtain. When I looked again, they were gone, presumably cut down and buried. The ground showed the marks when I checked the next day.

Suddenly my walk to school took me past Jews with yellow stars on their jackets. Most sat on the curb, shoulder to shoulder. Some slouched against lampposts or slept beneath trees. Some paced the same stretch of street for hours on end, eyes fixed on the ground as though missing some piece of themselves that they yet hoped to find. They all looked to be starving, with skin stretched over bone and dull, blackened eyes sunk deep in their skulls. I often saved my bun from breakfast and tossed it to a little girl who, every day, sat spinning a top under the same giant willow. The bun was never there when I walked home from school.

It was rare to see a German, but, when I did, he was often at the former railway siding where the Jews had been loaded into cattle trucks and deported to Treblinka. I'd pummel him with stones if I thought he wouldn't see me, but I never pushed my luck. I never ventured close enough to kick him in the balls. Once I saw a group of Germans. They skulked the streets in a pack, dark shadows in their high black boots. I turned and ran the other way.

As I've grown older, the ghosts have dropped from sight. They live on in my mind, though—a generation of ruthless judges who make constant pronouncements on my life. To them, I'm always guilty: guilty for standing in food lines for bread; guilty for wiping my ass on strips ripped from the

People's Tribune; guilty for shitting; guilty for puking; guilty for not being dead.

When I can't stand it anymore, I lie on my bed and listen to Bruce Springsteen. I think about skyscrapers and Ford Mustangs, and, I dream about living in America.

❋ ❋ ❋

AUGUST 14, 1980

After supper is over and the dishes are done, I leave for the Old Town where I meet up with friends at the barbican. We share a few cigarettes, if someone's lucky enough to have them, and then, at sunset head down to the river. We throw rocks in the Wisła and listen to the whine of sirens carry over the water from the other side of town. On a truly memorable evening, someone—usually Elżbieta, because her father belongs to the Party and she's always trying to make up for it—pulls out a bottle of vodka and we pass it around. Tonight, when the bottle is empty, Elżbieta scribbles on a scrap of paper and shoves it down the bottleneck. She screws on the cap and lobs the bottle in the river.

"Hey! Elżbieta! What'd you write?" I say.

"Yeah," the others join in. "What's the message in the bottle?" We tease her relentlessly.

She lifts her head to look at me. Her nose is running and her eyes are glassy and red. "It's an SOS, you asshole. It's a fucking SOS." Elżbieta is our very best actress. She lifts her fists to punch me, but I grab her wrists and kiss her on the mouth. She pushes her body against mine, and together, we topple to the ground. We don't have much time before the police make their rounds, barely enough time to work my hand under her blouse, but for a little while at least, we feel like we're alive.

Meanwhile, my parents are at home. They sit in the room that is a combination living/dining room by day and bedroom (mine) by night. My father sits at the table and reads, his stovepipe arms braced against the table, while my mother occupies the couch that doubles as my bed. She pulls the phone onto her lap and starts job number two. The notebook she keeps in her handbag comes out, and then her black and red pens. She thumbs through the book's well-worn pages. It's a ledger of private arrangements set up alphabetically by name, with each page divided into two columns. "Services Rendered" are listed down the first column in black, and "Services Received" are listed down the second column in red. It looks simple enough on paper, but in real life it's a complicated system that requires incredible versatility and smart manoeuvring. My mother is a master.

The first thing she does is record the day's transactions. The colleague at work who introduced her to a farmer who agreed to sell her ham gets recorded in the red column. The woman down the hall for whom my mother hemmed a skirt for free gets marked down in the black column. After that, my mother runs her fingers back and forth between the columns to see from whom she's owed a favour. Once that is established, she lights up a cigarette and picks up the phone.

"Hello, Krystyna. It's Teresa. How are you? I'm fine. Andrzej and Darek are doing well, too. How is Ewa enjoying married life? I still can see her on her wedding day. She looked so beautiful, so elegant, and that dress—it was perfect. I was so pleased to find you that beautiful material. Satin is so scarce these days, and did you know I had to snatch it right out from under the nose of Mrs. Dudek? I told her the material had been put out by mistake, that it was actually a special order for the daughter of the Minister of Culture." She tips back her head and laughs, the ash hanging menacingly from her cigarette. "If there's one thing life's taught me, it's how to think on my feet." She listens, then, deftly orchestrates a quick draw on her cigarette, before tapping the ash into a dish.

"Oh! Krystyna! The pleasure was all mine. It's just lucky I happen to work in a fabric shop is all. But now that you mention it, there might be something you can do. Our TV is on the blink. Wavy lines run across the bottom of the screen as soon as it's turned on. I'm afraid it's only a matter of days before the picture's gone completely. Then what will we do in the evenings? Stare at each other until we go crazy? I'd love to get a colour TV, but, how could we manage it?"

"What's that? Ewa's new husband sells televisions? I didn't know! You would? Oh, Krsystyna, I'd be so grateful. You have no idea. I'll wait for your call, then. Thank you so much. Good night." She hangs up the phone and writes a few lines in her notebook with the red pen.

I get home at eleven o'clock—a few minutes before Radio Free Europe for Poland airs from Berlin. By this time, my mother has moved on to job number three and is busy cutting out clothing patterns or stitching together garments on the sewing machine. I tuck in my shirt and walk in on my father fiddling with the knobs of the radio. Reception is always hit-and-miss. Sometimes the transmission is jammed, and you can't hear a thing. Even on the best of days, static is a problem, but my father presses his ear to the speaker and says he can make out the words if my mother and I remain absolutely still. That means no talking, no eating, no moving, no breathing. And absolutely no using the bathroom. I sit on the couch and try to hold back the piss.

It's hot in the flat, and my father wipes his face with a handkerchief. Meat prices have been soaring all summer. Rumour has it our country's meat has been detoured to Moscow because of the Olympics and Poland is ready to explode. Everyday Radio Free Europe reports on the latest strikes and my father repeats them to my mother and me in a breathless voice: railroad workers in Lublin, glass workers in Lubartów; the Electrical Works at Wrocław, the textile workers in Łódź, 20,000 workers at a helicopter factory in Świdnik, and on and on it goes. This is not the kind of information that gets printed in the official newspapers or carried on the evening news. Officially, Polish men and women are happy and productive workers who sleep like the dead and smile all day long.

My father looks up from the radio, his face flushed with excitement. "Seventeen thousand workers from the Lenin Shipyard have gone on strike! They've barricaded themselves inside the plant and refuse to come out. The people of Gdańsk are sending soup and bread over the top of the wall, and the workers are sleeping beside their machines." He shakes his head in disbelief. "Poland's most important seaport shut down—nothing coming in and nothing going out."

"There goes our television," says my mother, her foot pumping the treadle of the sewing machine in a fury.

✷ ✷ ✷

MAY 1981

The shipyard in Gdańsk lay in siege for almost three weeks. Then, much to everyone's surprise, the Communists capitulated and Solidarity was born. I held my breath and waited for what was sure to come next, but Radio Free Europe made no mention of Soviet tanks rolling in from the East. Still, I refused to get my hopes up. How could we Poles reach the outskirts of the Promised Land without any resistance? And with no loss of life? It sounded too good to be true. I was sure the Soviets had some secret plan of action they would implement at just the right time, with dire results for us all.

My father was of a different opinion entirely and glowed with unchecked optimism. He was convinced that with a little more faith and persistence, Poland would enter a place where people earned a fair wage and store shelves were packed with bread, butter, and sausage. He assured me that life, liberty, and justice would be part of the bargain as well.

Eight months later and still we wait. Life, as we know it remains the same and food shortages have become routine. Aspirin, sugar, cigarettes, and matches are available on an irregular schedule and never at the same time. My father jokes that God is giving Warsaw the opportunity to rid herself of every vice so she can enter sin-free through the gates of the Promised Land. The strategy seems to have worked on my mother, at least, who has renounced her addiction to tobacco. She had to either use the stove or chain-smoke to keep her cigarettes alight, neither of which she found convenient. Regrettably, for my father and me, abstinence has done nothing to improve her overall mood. As for the alcoholics among us, who wants to indulge with no Aspirin to temper the subsequent hangover? A more difficult vice to overcome, apparently, as half of Warsaw walks the streets with pounding headaches.

My father won a seat in the regional Solidarity elections, and he's hardly ever home now. When he is, all he does is sleep or work on articles for the trade-union periodical. Our flat has become a sort of warehouse with posters, leaflets, and newspapers piled up on chairs and tables. My mother hates the mess. Even worse, she hates the stench. The smell of ink fills every room of our little apartment. Now that it's warmer, she opens the windows. But in the winter, she said we'd wake up one morning, all three of us, asphyxiated.

"You're neglecting your family," my mother tells him. "We should come first. You should be helping us."

My father pounds his fist down on the table. "What am I doing, Teresa? What in hell am I doing?" When she doesn't stop nagging, he stuffs work in his briefcase and leaves, slamming the door on his way out. He doesn't always come home at night.

Still, we got through the winter. The days are longer, and the crocuses and tulips have already bloomed. After school, we walk through the Jewish cemetery, Elżbieta and I. I thread poppies through her hair and tell her everything will be all right.

She laughs at me like I'm a lunatic and runs ahead. "Everything is all right. It was always all right," she calls. The flowers slip out of her hair and get trampled underfoot or shredded by the wind into bits of scarlet ribbon. Everything I tell her is a lie. I feel as though I'm lying in a freshly dug grave, my limbs jutting out at odd angles, my mouth full of dirt. The people on the ground throw down their roses. They wipe their eyes and wring their hankies. No one dreams I'm still alive, my heart pumping blood, my lungs drawing in air. No one reaches down an arm to haul me out. Then the shovels dig in, dirt and stones shower down.

✳ ✳ ✳

DECEMBER 11, 1981

My father left for the Solidarity National Congress in the morning. The train ride from Warsaw to Gdańsk is four hours. It was my father's first trip to the Baltic—not that the Baltic in winter holds much appeal. Still, I could tell he was excited. He couldn't sit still, and, while I sat at the table and ate my soup, he paced back and forth between the couch and the bedroom, where my mother had the ironing board set up. She was pressing his clothes: two shirts—one white, actually more of a grey, and one blue—and a navy suit shiny from ironing.

He laid the pieces in a suitcase that was big enough for his entire wardrobe. The few articles of clothing, together with his t-shirts, and underwear, barely covered the bottom. My father said super, more room for all the books and papers he'd bring back from the Congress. Then he laughed a big laugh and winked at my mother who didn't so much as glance up from her work.

After the ironing, she made him a parcel to take on the train: sausage, bread, and a thermos of tea. He put the food into the outside compartment of his suitcase and zipped it shut. When he stood, his face was solemn as he searched the flat for my mother. His eyes settled on the closed bedroom door and he sighed deeply, before turning to the calendar. "Here's the number of the hotel if you need me," he said, and scribbled across the empty boxes at the end of December. "I'll be home Sunday night. The train's due at midnight." He took his coat from the closet and put it on while I watched and wondered whether my mother's retreat to their room meant she was boycotting his departure. My father stood in front of me with his hands on my shoulders, the weight of his arms even heavier in their sheepskin sleeves. "Listen to your mother while I'm gone." I nodded. My father is almost forty, but the ropes of muscle that cross my long limbs have none of the power conserved in his stubby fingers or in the thick bundles of muscle that creep beneath his skin. I struggled to stand straight and meet his gaze. He pulled me close and put his mouth to my ear. "Don't forget: you're the man of the family while I am away." He gave my shoulder a sharp squeeze and I winced with pain.

My mother opened the bedroom door. She folded her arms and stared at my father through eyes heavy with mascara. She had put on the cream-coloured sweater he gave her last Christmas, the one he called his favourite, and had decorated it with a string of pearls. Her lips were painted red.

"Goodbye, Teresa." He bent down to kiss her lips, but she turned her face away at the last minute. "Don't be angry," he whispered, and then gave her a loud smooch on the cheek.

"Be careful," she said. After he left, she stood in the window and watched through a crack in the curtains. He was taking a bus to the train station, and the bus stop was on the other side of Marchlewski. She stood there for several minutes—after the time he would have disappeared from sight and long after the time I should be gone for school.

"Don't worry," I said. "He knows what he's doing."

She didn't answer, but her hands flitted between her hair, her pearls, and the cuffs of her sweater like butterflies buffeted by the wind. If there'd been any cigarettes in the house, there's no question she'd have smoked the whole pack.

※ ※ ※

DECEMBER 13, 1981

I woke up to a room dancing with colour. Shards of ice on the window scattered the light, splashing rainbows on the floorboards and walls. I yawned, pushed my feet out the end of the blankets in a leisurely stretch. For a moment I felt lucky, then I remembered that my father was in Gdańsk and I felt a misery that even a perfect summer day would be hard-pressed to erase. I rubbed my stiff neck and threw my legs over the side of the couch, bracing myself for the cold, wooden floor. I had overslept by an hour. We'd be late for Mass if I didn't hurry.

It was unusually quiet, both in the flat and outside on the street—the muffled quiet that comes with heavy snowfall. I pulled on some clothes and walked to the window. The ground was covered in snow, but nothing remarkable, certainly not enough to explain the empty streets or the eerie stillness that pervaded the neighbourhood. On a typical Sunday, my mother would have been up for hours already: had her breakfast, tidied up the kitchen, finished some sewing, and been in the bathroom working on her hair and makeup. With no clemency for a lazy son, she'd have click-clacked across the floor in high heels, let the teakettle whistle for minutes at a time, slammed cupboard doors, and rattled the cutlery as though it were midday. That being said, I knew this wasn't a typical Sunday and I couldn't help feeling concerned as I searched our tiny flat for a clue as to where my mother might have gone.

I found her in the bedroom, the pent-up heat hitting me like a sweltering day in July as I opened the door. She was perched on her bed with a transistor radio in her hands. She wore the same clothes as yesterday, the fabric criss-crossed with wrinkles, and, her lips moved softly as though saying a prayer.

"Mama, what is it? Are you all right?"

She didn't answer. I had a feeling I could yell directly in her ear to no effect. Then I realized she wasn't praying, but talking along with a voice on the radio. "Our country is on the edge of the abyss. Achievements of many generations, raised from the ashes, are collapsing into ruin. State structures are no longer functioning. New blows are struck each day to our flickering economy. Living conditions are burdening people more and more. Not days, but hours, stand between Poland and national catastrophe."

I heard the speech through to the very end. The Prime Minister was declaring a State of Emergency. Poland was at war. I waited for the shock to set in, for the onslaught of panic. Instead, I felt incredibly calm. The worst thing I'd ever imagined had happened and I was still standing, still lucid and strong.

The speech started up again from the very beginning and I knew that my mother had been listening to the same tape repeating itself all night long. I pried the radio out of her hands and pocketed the batteries. "It's propaganda and lies. Don't believe it," I said.

My mother, hunched like a stone on the edge of her bed, continued her litany without Jaruzelski. She spoke in a monotone, her dull eyes fixed on a place in the wall where the plaster was cracked in the shape of a horseshoe. My father had tried to patch the spot more times than I could count, but she would never let him. She said it was good luck.

I kneeled in front of her. "Listen, Mama. It's me, Darek." I squeezed her hands as hard as I dared. She didn't flinch, didn't so much as blink or whimper. I decided to try a different approach. "It's time for Mass. We have to go." I grabbed her wrists and pulled her to her feet, but she was dead weight dragging us both to the floor, so I eased her back down on the bed. Sweat dripped off my forehead. I wiped it away with my sleeve. The temperature in the room was thirty degrees, maybe more, and I was feeling dizzy. "Let's get some fresh air in here," I said, and went to the window. The frame was seized, but, I worked it side to side and up and down until it finally gave way. I opened it all the way and then stuck my head out the window and gulped the cold air.

My mother shivered and reached for her sweater, clumsily fished her arm about for the sleeve. As I turned to help, something rumbled outside, soft at first but growing louder. The walls and floor shook and the dishes in the credenza rattled. A crystal glass fell off a shelf and shattered in pieces. Tanks! Goddamn fucking tanks! A whole army of them barrelling down Marchlewski.

"Tata!" I ran for the calendar and then to the phone. The line was dead. I checked the cord and fiddled with the switch hook. Nothing. I stood there, helpless, the receiver dangling from my hand as my mother walked in the room.

She scuffed across the floor in her slippers and made straight to the TV, the new one she'd finagled through her private connections. Her skin was an eerie pale, almost translucent in the sunlight. I held my breath as she switched channels. General Jaruzelski had commandeered every station. Staring out through the screen in his big, thick glasses, he was the only show in town. "Our country is on the edge of the abyss…"

"That's enough!" I yelled, at my mother as much as at Jaruzelski, and yanked the plug from the wall. The picture collapsed to a silver dot and then went black.

"It's a war and he's in Gdańsk. I'll never forgive him for this. I'll never forgive him for leaving me alone!"

I know you're supposed to love your mother, and nobody's perfect except for Christ, but, at that moment I hated her. I hated her with every fibre of my being, and it made me sick even to look at her. I grabbed my jacket from the closet. "I'm going out."

"Close the window," she said. "I'm cold."

✳ ✳ ✳

There was a roadblock at Marchlewski: six or seven Polish soldiers milling around an armoured personnel carrier with guns slung over their shoulders. They stamped their feet and rubbed their hands together as though following protocol, while spirals of cigarette smoke circled their heads. Otherwise, the street was empty—no passersby, no cars, not even a stray dog. I walked the other way—one block west toward the river and then north to Miła Street; my destination—Pan Nowak's flat. He hadn't been invited to the Congress in Gdańsk, so I was sure he'd be at home.

At supper one night a few months back, my mother had said Pan Nowak would never go to the Congress, invitation or not. How could he with his wife pregnant and due to deliver the very same weekend? A smile flickered across my father's lips when she said this, but it was hardly noticeable, especially as he ducked his head for a spoonful of soup at the very same time. My mother saw it, though, the same way she sees all the details of my father's existence—from the state of his fingernails and the holes in his socks to the number of hours he sleeps in a night. She threw down her napkin and stormed off to the kitchen. For several long minutes, we endured a steady barrage of banging pots and slamming drawers. My father carried on with his meal as usual, even taking the time to sop up the final drops of soup with his bread before taking his dirty bowl to the sink. With my father in the kitchen, the banging gave way to a murmur of voices and then to my mother's soft cry. When my mother and father emerged, my mother's eyes were slick with tears, but her smile was genuine and she carried a box of fruit jellies high in the air. She set the box on the table with an exaggerated flourish, and with, what was particularly striking to me, no regard for the dribbles and crumbs that remained from our supper.

My mouth watered. Who knew how long she had been hiding this treat and for what occasion? I lifted the lid and we each took a piece. Actually I took two, a red and a green, melting each one on my tongue to prolong the sweet pleasure. Later, when I looked in the mirror to brush my teeth, my tongue had turned a muddy brown.

I approached the corner of Miła with caution. Two policemen stood in front of Pan Nowak's building. The one facing me had his head down and was writing studiously in a notebook; the other was scanning the street. I retraced my steps and found some bushes in back of an apartment block one street over. There, I took off my jacket and hid it deep in the branches before returning to Miła at a run.

The policemen stepped forward as I approached. The one with no notebook held out his hand. "Your name, please."

I slowed down and then smoothly transitioned into that classic runner-recovery stance: head down, back bent, and chest heaving. "Darek Dąbrowski," I panted.

"Show us your papers."

"I don't have them. No pockets." I pulled at the hips of my track pants for proof.

They eyed me suspiciously. "You're not supposed to be out today. Don't you listen to the news? We're at war!"

I shook my head in feigned ignorance. "I don't understand, sir."

The other officer cut in. "He's just a kid. We're wasting our time."

"Get going then, quick, before I change my mind."

I gave them a nod and then jogged straight up the walk and through the front doors into Pan Nowak's building. His flat was at the top. I took the steps two at a time and knocked on his door. No answer. I knocked again, this time with the butt of my hand and twice as hard. "Please, open up! It's Darek Dąbrowski." Swift footsteps advanced to the door, then, paused while the person inside inspected me through the peephole. After what seemed like forever, the door opened.

"Quickly," Pani Nowak said. She closed the door and fastened all the locks—the lock in the doorknob, one chain, and three deadbolts. I followed the easy swing of her hips to the living room, where she motioned me to sit down on the couch. She eased herself into the chair across from me and sat there in a slouch with her stomach looking ready to explode. Her body accommodated the pregnancy as best it could: her legs splayed to make room for her stomach and the deep curve of her breasts pushing up into the V-neck of her sweater.

"Is Pan Nowak here?" I struggled to maintain eye contact, fascinated by the lushness of her body, its hardness and softness, and the fullness of her lips.

She shifted her weight in the chair. "He's been arrested. The police came for him in the night." She stated it as a matter of fact, but, her eyes were bloodshot and her hands trembled.

I closed my eyes and slumped back on the couch.

"What will become of us?" Tears ran down her cheeks as she wrapped her arms around the hard mound that was her baby.

I got up and walked over to the window. The police were still out front. "I'm sorry for troubling you," I said.

She heaved herself out of the chair and ushered me to the door. "Better you leave by the fire escape at the back," she whispered, and pointed a finger to the end of the hall.

I took her hand and raised it to my lips.

"Look at you," she said, pulling back her hand to caress her perfect belly. "You've grown into a man."

I felt the pressure to say the right thing, a single valiant word or a decisive phrase. I looked her in the eye and opened my mouth, but the right words escaped me. What I really wanted was to lay my head down on her breasts and feel her soft body against the hard edge of my face and the comfort of her arms around my shoulders.

✳ ✳ ✳

APRIL 1982

Christmas came and went with no word from my father. We assumed he'd been arrested and jailed, as had so many of the Solidarity leaders who went to the Congress. If he'd been killed, wouldn't someone have told us? For a few weeks, we figured no news was good news.

Then, in January, we got a letter, and, four weeks after that, another. It became a monthly ritual: my mother and I huddled at the kitchen table, our heads bent over a sheet of paper, our faces creased in concentration. We go through the same routine every time. First, my mother examines the envelope—always a standard-sized white envelope with a Gdynia postmark and CENSORED stamped across the front.

"Open the letter," I'll say, but she will not be rushed. It's torture to watch as she selects just the right butter knife out of the drawer and carefully slides it through the seal, as though it is a crime punishable by death to break through anything other than the glue.

Then, sometimes for close to an hour, we are squinting at my father's handwriting, struggling to make it out. "Why won't he print?" my mother complains. "I tell him every time." We pass the letter back and forth and take turns reading it aloud until we're certain we've exhumed the last trace of meaning. By that time, we have the letter memorized, and we'll recite sections from it for the next week or two, sometimes during conversation but not necessarily in the proper context and sometimes just to fill the silence. "Don't worry about me, I am comfortable. Don't be afraid, I have courage," my mother might say on her way out the door in the morning. "Although your legs might be tired, you must keep to the course. You must run to the end. You must never stand still," I might say after a Saturday spent in food queues all day. Sometimes we laugh. We could just as well cry.

This letter is his latest:

My darling Teresa,

It has been a long, harsh winter, but I do believe the worst is now behind us. Signs of spring fill me with hope. The tree outside my window is a mass of buds and the sunshine through the glass feels warm on my face. The nights, of course, remain cold, but this too will pass. Time and patience are on our side. Believe me when I say, it won't be long now.

Resurrection Day is almost here. Light a Paschal candle for me, sweetheart. Set me a place at the breakfast table. Give me a wedge of blessed egg and accept my best wishes.

My most tender thoughts are with you both.

Your loving husband,
Andrzej

My mother folded the letter and returned it to its envelope. "Why didn't he tell me he was cold when he wrote back in January? Does he think I don't care?" She went to her bedroom and came back dragging their down comforter in one hand and the box she keeps for fabric scraps—now empty—in the other. She folded the comforter into a misshapen bundle and stuffed it into the box. I cannot dispute my mother's efficiency. She tucked in the flaps and wrote my father's name and the address of his internment centre on the outside. "Do you think one is enough? Maybe I should send two." I glanced up to find her eyeing the drawer beneath the couch that holds my bedding.

"Mama!" I said. In the midst of her activity, I had pulled out my father's letter to read again. "He's coming home, that's what he's saying. This letter has nothing to do with being cold. He's saying he expects to be home in a month's time."

"What?" My mother snatched the letter from my hand and read it again, slowly this time, her lips mouthing the words. "I don't know how you figure that. All he talks about is the weather and being cold at night and then the bit about Easter at the end. He might be coming home next week or not at all for all he writes. To be honest, this letter tells me one thing and one thing only: on March 30th your father was alive and well. He hadn't been executed or shipped to Siberia." She tied the box with string and left it by the door to mail.

My mother is not a stupid woman, not at all. She is shrewd, calculating and successful in ways many are not, but her skill for reading between the lines is sorely lacking.

I, on the other hand, am blessed with great imagination and a strong intuition. Which of us was right and which was wrong, I cannot say, but this fact remains: my father did not return in the spring or the summer.

✳ ✳ ✳

AUGUST 31, 1982

Solidarity turned two years old today. The Communists thought Solidarity would shrivel up and die once they cut off her head. They never dreamed her body would survive, much less thrive; that she'd wriggle underground and sprout a new head. And so she's lived on two full years, and Poles would be marking the date the same way we mark the anniversaries of all major events in our nation—by taking to the streets in droves. Solidarity might be outlawed, but the streets would be packed.

"You're not going," my mother announced over pierogi a few days beforehand. She said one Dąbrowski in jail was all our family could afford and there was nothing I could do or say to make her change her mind. Personally, she had no intention of attending, a point she expounded on for several long minutes. We had to eat, after all, and she wouldn't get paid if she wasn't at work. Besides, she didn't see what point it served. Hadn't my father already proved what opposing the Communists achieves? She set to cutting up her pierogi after that line, wielding her knife as though it were a hacksaw.

I knew better than to engage her in debate. Her mind was made up, but mine was, too, and I could equal her in stubbornness, providing the cause was one I believed in. Please understand, I love my mother with all my heart, but, at that time and in that place, my love for my father was greater than all the love I had for everyone else in the world combined. It had no beginning. It had no end. It burdened my heart like a pocket of tungsten. Priest Kowalski says perfect love casts out fear. If that were true, I'd be much different. I wouldn't worry that my father's being beaten every day; that the secret police are burning him with cigarettes; that he's sick or cold or hungry. I wouldn't start to shit myself at the thought of being arrested at the demonstration. But the idea terrifies me. That's the reason I must go.

Elżbieta insisted on going, too. I didn't bother to ask her why. I knew she didn't care about Solidarity; she pretends to be apolitical if anything. Chances are she was looking for thrills or else hoping for free cake and chocolates. Elżbieta loves sweets and she would never miss a party, except for one of two reasons: the opportunity to attend a superior party in some other location or a serious illness that confined her to bed. And, unlike me, I think she feels invincible with her father a Communist. She thinks that no matter what happens in this life, her father can secure her deluxe accommodation in the next life the moment she passes.

We skipped school and snuck back to her flat as soon as her parents had both left for work. I hadn't been inside her place for months, not since my father joined Solidarity. I suspect her father had outlawed my visits, not that she'd ever admitted that to me. I'd forgotten how much space they had—three good-sized bedrooms and a full fridge with freezer. She led me to the dining room.

"We can't go to a party empty-handed," she said, pushing

the vase of roses to one end of the massive oak table and rolling back the runner.

"I think you have the wrong idea. It's not a smorgasbord."

"I know. It's a demonstration." She emphasized the word *demonstration* as though she was an expert on the subject. "And if you knew anything about demonstrations, you would know that participants are supposed to take placards."

"Oh." I watched her spread sheets of newsprint on the table and then set out paints and poster board on top. I hadn't done art and crafts since kindergarten and had no pressing desire to start again now, but I was impressed with her efforts and willing to make concessions as a result. Also, it amused me to think that Communist money was funding the cost of this project.

Elżbieta knew exactly what she wanted to paint: a tank rolling over the word *Solidarity*, crushing the letters and making them bleed, but below them, new letters rising up, the same only bigger. It wasn't an original design. The very same picture had been showing up on flyers all over the city. Still, that didn't detract from her talent, and her finished artwork put mine to shame. I went with the easiest thing I could think of: a giant P with a W-shaped anchor protruding from its trunk, which took me all of one minute to paint.

"Why did you draw a pretzel?" she asked.

"It's not a pretzel. It's the Kotwica."

She burst out laughing and punched me in the arm. "Never mind, I can fix it." She dabbed her brush in the paint and proceeded to straighten the line of my P and open the arms of my W with long, even strokes. "Better?" she asked.

"If you say so," I said.

She rolled her eyes. "Twenty minutes to dry and then we can go." She busied herself with cleaning off the table. "Help yourself to any Coca-Cola in the fridge."

A great loop of sausage accosted me as I entered the kitchen. Hanging halfway to the floor, its length struck me as immoral, but my mouth watered just the same. I opened the fridge.

Milk, butter, juice, sliced ham, an entire block of cheese, and the crowning glory—a roast beef. I stood there and stared while waves of nausea rolled through my stomach.

"What's taking you so long?"

I turned to see Elżbieta standing in the doorway. She had mousy brown hair, a slit of a mouth, and eyes like a goldfish. She was perfectly ordinary, except for her Levi Strauss jeans, which she wore every day and were bought at the Pewex with American money. I gave the sausage a shove and it swung between us like a noose. "You're a Red, the same as your father."

She laughed, cut off a piece, and offered it to me. "A person has to eat," she said.

"No," I said. "You're wrong. People have to eat—38 million of them."

I refused the sausage and pushed past her to the door. "I'm going."

"Wait for me. I'm going, too."

"No, you're not." I turned and looked her straight in the eye. "Not with me."

She followed me to the door, but I slipped out first and slammed it shut. When she pulled it open a split second later, I was halfway down the hall.

"Who do you think you are, Darek Dąbrowski?" she yelled. "The Son of God?"

A dark object whizzed past my head and landed on the floor in front of the elevator. Sausage. I ground it into the floor with my heel as the elevator doors rattled open.

※ ※ ※

I went to the demonstration alone. I know I took a southbound bus from Marszałkowski Street, but the details are a blur. I remember a boy, my age or older, trampled over my feet on his way to the exit and I kicked him in the heels.

Constitution Square was packed with people. I could see their red shirts all the way from Nowogrodzka. They stretched like a fiery sea between the grim, concrete edifices that hemmed in the square. The driver stopped the bus a block from the square and told us to walk. I clung to the railing with both hands as I went down the steps, two feet per tread like a frail, old woman. My insides were in a free fall and ricocheting off my ribs and my pelvis.

The noise at street level was deafening. I scoured faces for signs of anger or despair, but they weren't visible. Even worry and doubt were surprisingly absent. In truth, the mood was verging on euphoric. I, too, was gaining courage now that I had joined the crowd. The man next to me shouted, "On a day like today anything is possible!" and I wanted to believe him.

We moved down Marszałkowski toward the Palace of Culture and Science. Spectators in the doorways and windows could hardly contain themselves. They clapped and made V signs, hands high in the air. Women picked petunia blossoms from their window boxes and the petals rained down on our heads. The mood was contagious and given adequate space and the talent, I'd have done cartwheels all the way down the boulevard.

A demonstrator pushed a card into my hand. It was printed up with a poem called "The Twenty-Second Demand." I stared at the words, sure I'd seen them before. They were stark and bold, the kind of words that stick in your mind and are a thrill to say aloud. We shouted together at the top of our lungs:

Give over telling us you're sorry,
What guilt for past mistakes you carry;
Look in our faces, weary slaves,
Grey and exhausted, like our lives.

Put back our words to what they mean,
Words which grew empty and obscene,
So we can live with dignity
And work in solidarity.

Four tanks pulled into the intersection up ahead, but we didn't skip a beat. Polish soldiers filed out with smooth, measured movements and lined up shoulder to shoulder across the road.

"Keep marching," someone called. "They won't do anything. Those men are our family, our sons and our brothers."

I studied the soldiers' faces. They were boys, most of them: Polish conscripts with wide eyes and still faces. I watched their hands. Were their fingers inching closer to their guns or was I scared shitless and imagining things that didn't exist? I eased myself into the outer margins of the procession so that, if need be, I could get away quickly. Then I noticed the riot police arrive down a side street. The other demonstrators were so intent on the soldiers that they didn't see a thing. I saw them, though. Their sleek, black figures poured out of the jeeps and armoured personnel carriers like an oil spill. "ZOMO!" I yelled. "ZOMO!" The horde continued to press forward, brushing past me on both sides. They seemed insensible to the danger, and, although I yanked nearby arms and told people to run, my advice went unheeded. I quickly focused on saving myself and pushed my way back through the crowd with the hope of escaping through the rear. No such luck. Scores of ZOMO were already there, their bodies lined up six or seven men deep. As I stood there stock-still, the people at the head of the line broke into screams. I was like one of those Polish soldiers, too scared to move but registering every detail—sun flashing off shields, boots pounding pavement, and the smooth, rhythmic swing of arms and legs.

The riot police spread their arms and fanned out like crows descending on a garbage heap. They had beady eyes behind their visors, and, as I watched, the smell of my own sweat and fear filled my nostrils. One, for whatever reason, chose me. I watched him elbow his way through the crowd straight toward me. I watched the apelike swing of his arms. I watched his face through the shield as he hauled back his truncheon. He had the same goldfish eyes as Elżbieta, the same lank, mousy bangs. The ZOMO was her brother, Tomasz.

The club hit the soft part behind my knees and I folded like a seedling. Red beams coursed through my limbs, streamed down the inside of my eyes, and, when I hit the pavement, red waves emanated from my body like an aura. The blows rained down on my back, my head, my legs; no body part was spared. My flesh absorbed them like a sponge. I was numb and felt no pain, only my ears would explode from the rampage of feet thundering past my head and my heart would explode from the rage.

Tomasz left me in a heap, face down in the street, and I anticipated the grand finale—a bullet to the back of the head or a tank rolled over my torso: either way, a quick, clean finish. But certainly not this: arms hoisting me into the air, slinging me over a shoulder in the same easy manner one carries a coat on a warm, spring day, and taking me away to who knows where. I prayed to God this stranger was a friend.

We travelled what seemed like several blocks, a crude estimate based on the number of times we traversed curbs, because, I couldn't see; my eyes were sealed shut, and when I tried to force them open, only slivers of light showed here and there between my lashes. I thought I might be safe when I heard the sound of water, not the steady stream of a tap left on, but the ebb and flow of living water. Then it hit me: I would be dumped in the Wisła where I would surely sink to the bottom and drown. I opened my mouth to beg for my life, but my voice was weak and the words muffled by my captor's shirt.

The man lowered me to the ground in the same careless way one sets down a sack of potatoes. "Here. Wipe your face." His was a commanding voice, a voice that started deep in his chest and then surged up like a fountain. A sopping-wet cloth was pushed into my hand. I eased myself onto my side and pressed the rag to my eyes. Water poured down my face and into my clothes. I rubbed until my face was clean and then glanced at the rag—soaked through with blood. My shirt and pants were stained red, too.

"Nosebleed," said the same take-charge voice.

I turned to the boots beside my head. My eyes traced a path from the neatly tied bows to some sturdy legs in khaki pants to a tree-trunk chest to a middle-aged face with a beret on top; a Polish soldier, one from the demonstration.

"It looks worse than it is. Scrapes and bruises, maybe a broken nose, but you'll live. Can you stand?" He put out his hand and pulled me to my feet. "You've lost a shoe."

My heart sank. It was the only pair of shoes I had. Broken bones and bruises heal, but where would I get a new pair of shoes? I could hear my mother now, see her picking up the phone and flipping through the pages of her notebook. I tentatively lifted a foot off the ground and straightaway lost my balance. The soldier steadied me with a firm hold of my arm.

"You Andrzej Dąbrowski's son? You live on Dzielna?"

I nodded.

"Come on. I'll take you home."

✳ ✳ ✳

It was still early when I got back to the flat. My mother wouldn't be home for another two hours—three if I was lucky, which I know by now I'm not. I crawled to the bathroom and turned on the water with my chest braced against the side of the tub. I walked my fingers up the ceramic to the taps. My joints were wrapped in adhesive with even the smallest movement creating a tension that was near impossible to conquer. Peeling off my clothes was an epic struggle—blood had fixed the fabric to skin. It took me almost as long to strip naked as it did to work my way into the tub. The water was up to my neck—an obscene measure by any account and more water than I typically use in a week, but the heat eased my pain and I refused to feel guilty. Through half-closed lids, I watched the blood, the fresh red trickles first and then the hard, black clots, lift off my skin and float to the surface. The water turned a rusty red and then to filmy grey. I stayed in longer than I should, until the skin on my fingers was wrinkled and white and it was getting on to the time my mother gets home.

I dried off in front of the mirror, a slipshod job with me holding the towel by one end and dragging it over any part of my anatomy within reach. My body was in full bloom—meaty red roses across my chest and limbs and great lumps of swelling under the skin. I touched a finger to one of the lumps. It was hard, not like rock, but, like an overripe melon. I trembled with rage. I didn't want revenge. I wanted out—out of Poland. I wanted to leave and slam the door so hard behind me the entire country would shake on its foundation. I wanted to go to America, live out the rest of my life in peace and die from a heart attack or cancer. No horrible hero's death for me. Tentatively, I straightened a leg. I eased on track pants and a long-sleeved shirt, these for my mother's sake, because the day was warm and short sleeves more suitable. The less she could see of my bruises the better. Who knows? Maybe sometime today her glasses fell off and got buried under a bolt of cloth. I wanted to spare her undue pain.

I held on to the wall and shuffled to the living room. My body was seizing up. I had to sit down, or, better yet, lie down and not move anything for a day or two, maybe a week, a month at the most. Gingerly, I lowered myself to the couch, knocking over one of my father's bulging files on an adjacent bookshelf in the process. Some papers fell out and slipped under my backside. Shifting my weight to one buttock, I edged them out an inch at a time. The top sheet contained a single poem: "The Twenty-Second Demand." The other sheets were copies of the first. I crumbled the papers into a ball and got to my feet. Shit on "The Twenty-Second Demand"! Shit on this country and its pitiful history! Shit on everyone who lives here who can't see the future because his head is too far up his ass! I took the file, and, clutching it to my chest, carried it to the window where I pushed it off the window ledge. A solitary woman in the courtyard below stopped hanging out her sheets to watch. She raised a hand and waved. "Go fuck yourself!" I yelled. She bent down quickly for a fresh sheet, stabbed a corner to the line.

Meanwhile, the poems fell through the air like flightless birds, drifting first one way and then the other. From six floors up they resembled patches of snow where they lay on the ground. I admired the effect a moment. The straight-edged whiteness soothed my ragged rage.

Completely exhausted, I returned to the couch where I managed to achieve a certain bare measure of comfort by lying on my side and working a pillow between my knees. I blasted Bruce Springsteen to make myself feel better. I fell asleep, but it was a short sleep that came to an abrupt end once my mother got home.

"How did your father's papers get outside?" Her voice shook, but I couldn't tell if it was from anger or fear. I rolled onto my back to find her standing above me, a pile of soiled papers in her hands. These slipped to the floor when she caught sight of my face and she stood there a moment, completely still, her hand hiding her mouth. Then she dropped to the floor and pushed back my bangs, lifted my shirt and let out a cry. I flinched and squirmed out of her reach. "What happened to you?" she whispered. "Tell me." She leaned in close and wrapped her arms around me, carefully, the way one might hold a porcelain vase from the Ming Dynasty.

I pulled away. "Nothing happened." Holding my breath, I forced my legs over the side of the couch and log-rolled to a stand to prove that everything was fine. Ignoring the pain, I tried to simulate a normal gait and not the lurch of a Hollywood zombie. Halfway across the room, beads of sweat broke out on my forehead. I wouldn't make it to the door, let alone to the kitchen, and even one more step was more than I could manage. I grabbed the back of a chair and held on for dear life.

My mother was at my side immediately and, with her as a crutch, I made my way to the seat of the chair where I gingerly sat down and braced myself for her lecture, something about the hardships of life as the wife of a political prisoner and now as the mother of a son who would turn out the same way, a son who risked his life to attend events she had forbidden, a son who lied, and could not be trusted.

She took a pillow from the couch and tucked it in behind my back. "Rest," she said. "I'll make you something to eat."

She came back with an open-faced sandwich, a hot mug of soup, and some water. "These first," she said, dropping two aspirin in my hand and bringing the glass to my mouth. "They'll help ease the pain." Then she secured a small towel under my chin, put the soup in my hands, and perched on an adjacent chair, at the ready should I need her. She watched me intently, as though she could urge the food to my mouth with her eyes. Every mouthful I took softened the worry lines in her face, so, I ate everything, although I was not hungry at all. Then she helped me back to the couch, rubbed ointment on my cuts, and arranged cold compresses on the swelling.

She ate nothing that night. She didn't pick up the phone or her notebook of private arrangements, and the sewing machine sat idle. All evening she moved like an automaton between the couch and the kitchen, changing my ice packs and boiling water for tea. She didn't talk, but the whistle of the teakettle and the spoon tapping the sides of the porcelain cup comforted me in a way words could not. At ten o'clock my mother was still at the table, all alone in the dark. Before I fell asleep, I heard her walk over to the liquor cabinet and select a bottle. After that the only sounds I remember were the slosh of drink and the clink of glass.

❋ ❋ ❋

SEPTEMBER 1982

I never doubted I'd see my father again. Even in the beginning, after the initial hours of shock and despair, I knew he'd be back. I couldn't predict the exact time or place, but, it was sooner, not later. Every knock on the door heralded his arrival. I imagined waking up to find him eating breakfast at the table. He was everywhere I went: reading papers in buses that passed on the street and queuing in lines outside butcher shops.

When the days passed and he still wasn't back, my expectations began to slip. I no longer imagined him around every corner. I still believed he was coming home, but I was willing to concede it might take a while—a more few weeks, maybe a month.

Nine months later, my hopes were pinned on the next season and I told myself for sure my father would be home by Christmas. So, when a knock came at the door on a late Monday evening in September, the week after the Solidarity march, I automatically assumed the worst. It was the police come to carry me away or deliver bad news about my father.

My mother and I stared at each other, she on the couch with her notebook of private arrangements and I at the table with my homework. Another knock, a series of urgent raps to the door. Neither of us made a move.

"Teresa, open the door!"

My mother jumped up, her arms fluttering at her sides like the wings of a caged bird. The notebook spilled out of her lap and one of her hands knocked over the teacup she had balanced on the arm of the couch. She unlocked the door and threw it wide with me looking over her shoulder. My father was there in the hall, hanging back a bit as though he might have the wrong flat or thought perhaps we had moved someplace else. He looked older than I remembered, with his hair mostly grey and his navy suit easily two sizes too large. The jacket sagged on his shoulders like it was sliding off a wire hanger.

My mother flew at him, burying her face in his neck. The comforter he held bunched under one arm dropped to the floor as he took her in his arms. He held her face in his hands and kissed her lips. Tears streamed down her cheeks and over his fingers.

"Take off that shirt and I'll wash it," she spluttered, half laughing, half crying.

"Teresa," he murmured and smoothed her hair with his hand, and then he reached out and pulled me into their circle.

※ ※ ※

The next morning at breakfast my father laid three tickets on the table. "We are leaving Poland," he said.

I grabbed the nearest ticket and studied it closely. "Canada?" I glanced at my father and then back at the ticket. "We're going to Canada?" Sunlight streamed through the lace curtains, pinning scallop-edged blossoms onto the wall.

"Canada?" My mother laughed. She beat her fists on the table and stamped the cracked parquet floor. "I hope the price was not too high. Since the start of martial law, no one is leaving the country."

"Our flight leaves tomorrow."

My mother pushed back from the table and sat with her hands on her hips. "This is true, what you say, Andrzej?" She wasn't laughing anymore.

"They gave me a choice: sign a loyalty oath to the Party or else leave the country." He stood up and pushed his fingers through his lank hair. I'd never seen it so long, all the way to his collar. "They gave me a choice, Teresa. For this I am lucky."

My mother chewed her lower lip a moment and then forced her mouth into a tight smile. "A trip to the West for the family Dąbrowski. Our first vacation abroad. We are lucky, all three of us."

"One-way passports, Teresa. We're not coming back. That is the arrangement."

My mother lost control of her mouth. It drooped at one corner like a torn pocket. She stared at my father, then at me. Her eyes lingered on my arms where the bruises had turned to brown and yellow smudges. She stared at my arms, put a hand to her mouth, and moaned.

"Canada." I rolled the syllables on my tongue. They were quick and light and easy to say. "Canada." I knew one thing about this country and one thing only: it was close to America. I went to the bookshelf and pulled out the atlas. The pages automatically fell open to the United States of America. I gazed with longing at that very great land all carved into neat squares and rectangles; the land of the free and home of the brave. I slid my hand across the page from left to right, from the Pacific to the Atlantic. I touched a finger to Los Angeles, New York, and Chicago. I traced the northernmost border, the thick black line that separated the United States from Canada. Then I found the map of North America. "What part of Canada are we going to?" I asked.

My father pressed his thumb below our destination. "We land in Toronto and then fly to Fredericton."

I narrowed in on the atlas and began to search.

My father studied the book over my shoulder. "Toronto," he said pointing to a large dot in a teat-shaped piece of land that dipped well below the rest of the country.

My heart pounded. Toronto was only half a thumb's length from New York City. I could drive there in a day. I could hitchhike—it was not impossible. Fredericton was more difficult to locate, but finally I found it, too, farther east and even closer to America. "Yes!" I shouted, daring to believe my dream would finally come true. I started packing right away, although, I did not know what I should take.

"Winter's coming," my father said. "Pack something warm."

I packed my winter boots and my sheepskin vest. I packed my long underwear, my coat, and the heavy wool hat and socks my babcia had knit me last Christmas. I packed all my

Bruce Springsteen cassettes. I didn't pack any warm-weather clothes. My plan was to have a Levi Strauss wardrobe by next spring at the latest and a pair of Adidas for after the snow melted and I walked streets of gold.

I tacked a note to the door of the flat the next day when we left. It said:

To Whom It May Concern:

I've gone to America and I'm not coming back.

Sincerely,
Darek Dąbrowski

PART II

SEPTEMBER 1982

Top Ten Facts about the North Atlantic Right Whale

1. Every summer the North Atlantic right whales come to the Bay of Fundy to feed.

2. They come for the plankton. A single right whale eats 4,400 pounds of it each day.

3. Right whales are mammals and feed their young milk.

4. Their bodies are 40 percent blubber.

5. Fully grown they can be sixty feet long and weigh 120,000 pounds.

6. They swim slowly, reaching 9.3 km/h at top speed.

7. They are highly acrobatic and known to breach and tail-slap.

8. They are one of the world's rarest mammals with only 250 left in the North Atlantic.

9. Extinction of the species is inevitable unless humans do something to prevent ship strikes and their entanglement in fishing gear, both being major contributors to their death.

10. Male right whale testicles weigh 1,100 lbs—the biggest in the world—and their eight-foot-long penises also set records.

Both male and female North Atlantic right whales are extremely promiscuous. Not only that, but, they engage in group sex. I've kept both those facts off the list, though, mainly because if word got out we had "immoral" whales living in our bay, that'd be the end of the species right there. In fact, the churches would probably pool their resources and start a fence at the Maine border, wrap it around Campobello Island and Grand Manan and then straight across the bay to Yarmouth. They'd nail big signs to the fence posts that said: "Repent for the Lord is Coming Soon," "Seek Ye the Lord While He may be Found," and for the whales with hearts that have hardened to stone, "Right Whales Keep Out!"

I don't usually deface library property, but I found a page in a science magazine that had a picture of a female right between two males that I had to destroy in the interest of saving the species. She was on her back and the males on their sides, their penises contorted like snakes, stretching up and across her body and then down into her vagina, both of them inside her at the very same time. They were something to see—those brazen penises with their stunning manoeuvres. They reminded me of the tanker truck filling up the underground tanks at the Irving.

I'm not a sex maniac, in case you're wondering. But I do collect facts and I realize that sometimes you have to conceal the facts, or at least limit access, all for the sake of the greater good. I don't call that lying. I call that stewardship of the truth. I also call it risk management—depending on the audience I'm addressing in my head.

But, I'm going off on a tangent. The facts on the official list are just as intriguing as the ones I've omitted. Consider fact number two, for example, and tell me how a creature that's bigger than a school bus survives on a diet of plankton alone. Do you know what plankton looks like? It's mostly small—I'm talking microscopic in size and it's not coated in sugar, dipped in chocolate, or fried in oil, so how does it manage to pack on the blubber? And speaking of blubber, how is such a massive creature so athletic? An elephant can't jump in the slightest, so how is it that a creature the size of eight or nine elephants can spring out of the water like a jack-in-the-box? Which brings us to the biggest mystery of all—fact number one: every summer the North Atlantic right whales come to the Bay of Fundy to feed. How, I ask you, can a creature that's bigger than a school bus, and not just one but hundreds of them, come to the Bay of Fundy each and every summer and I not have a clue, except for I've read it? I know what you're thinking: big deal; who cares? The point is I live here. The Bay of Fundy is my home. Okay, so I can't see the ocean from my window, but, give me fifteen minutes (twenty if I'm pedalling upwind) and I'm there, kicking off my sneakers and cooling my hot, sticky feet in the waves. All right, so I keep my sneakers on because the beach is covered in rocks and the water is cold enough to freeze off toes even in summer, but the bottom line is—I'm there. Give me just ten minutes and I'm at the top of Kelly Hill with a clear view of Fishtail Light and Wolf Island and beyond those the oil tankers out in the bay.

Don't get me wrong. I believe in right whales. I just doubt they're here. I need to see one for myself and then I'll believe. That's why I'm down by the water all summer long. I patrol the cliffs that look out to sea, scanning the waters for some kind of sign. I know what to look for: a V-shaped blow, a flash of shiny black fluke, a crack of thunder as eighty tons of unadulterated whale flesh hits the water in a massive belly flop. I want them to be here. I really do.

I see dolphins and porpoises all the time. They swim just offshore. Their sleek bodies arc across the water as they move in perfectly choreographed lines. Seals, too, lazy as cats, sun on Wolf Island. The uninitiated mistake them for boulders, and it's only when one breaks away from the herd to lumber into the water that one realizes they are animate beings.

I beachcomb for proof when the tide is out. I'm not sure what I'm looking for, but I expect to know it when I see it: a curved length of rib or a plate of baleen; a tree-stump-sized vertebrae. Maybe some poop as big as a pop machine because a creature that size has got to shit big. The usual finds include wet gobs of jellyfish clinging to rock, bright orange fisherman gloves, odds and ends of rope in all the colours of the rainbow, pieces of buoy, driftwood, and, of course, shells galore, rock crabs, eyed finger sponge, skate egg sacs, whelks, sand dollars, sea urchins, and scallop shells with pink peppermint stripes that are just right for mobiles. I thread them with ribbon close to the hinge, attach them to rings, and then hang them in windows to blow in the breeze.

I find lots of stuff, but nothing so far that proves North Atlantic right whales live in the bay. I'm still looking, though, because, if fact number one is correct, then my luck's bound to change. Sooner or later I'll hear a blow echo off the volcanic cliffs and turn to see a right whale rise up from the waves like the peak of Mount Logan, water streaming down its sides in sheets. I'll stand there transfixed, my heart tight as a fist and pounding a hole right through my chest, and all those hours spent watching and waiting will finally be worth it.

I guess I should introduce myself. My name is Eleanor, but I go by Lennie for short. Nobody calls me Eleanor except doctors' office receptionists, supply teachers, and such—strangers, in other words. I like the name Lennie. I like it a lot. But, on formal occasions, I introduce myself as Eleanor because it goes best with Hanson. "Eleanor Hanson" sounds accomplished and sophisticated. "Lennie Hanson" sounds like the name of a racehorse or an heirloom tomato.

I have two sisters and one brother: Michelle, Lucy, and Jude, all younger than me. My mother named us after Beatles songs, but she'd never admit it, not since that evangelist came up from the States and preached a whole week on the evils of rock and roll. The next time the garbage truck came around, her whole record collection went out with the trash. Lucky for Dad, the evangelist didn't talk about country music and so his Tom T. Hall and Anne Murray albums escaped unscathed.

I live on the New Brunswick side of the Bay of Fundy, in the St. John River Valley, also known as the Bible Belt. My town is called Lampeq. It's the rhinestone-studded buckle on the Bible belt.

Lampeq is on the St. John River, but it's also near the sea. This last fact has been downplayed from the very beginning. The founders of Lampeq, the United Empire Loyalists, shunned the sea and built their community on the river where the dark waters of the bay are hidden by trees. I say they were naive. The trees do nothing to keep out the fog and the influx of salt water at high tide. And when you close your eyes at night, the wind in the leaves mimics the roar of the surf to a T.

When I talk about the whales, no one cares. The people in Lampeq are tied to the land, not the sea. They work in the woods, not on the water. They eat meat and potatoes. The only fish that pass their lips comes frozen with Captain High Liner on the box. If I mention the right whales at supper, my father says, "Next year you're getting a job in the summer." If I push the fact that they're almost extinct, he blows up. "Oh! You've got problems," he says. "I've got a car with an alternator on the blink and we need a new furnace, but you're the one with the problems." Then my mother tries to smooth things over. "Does it really matter, dear? I mean, they're under the water and you can't see them anyway."

I've talked to Pastor Martin about it. He says I'm too caught up in the things of this world, that I should have my eyes set on heavenly things. He says God will look after the rights if it's part of his plan. If it isn't, then there's nothing we can do about it. Then he quoted from Matthew to prove his point:

Look at the birds of the air; they do not sow or reap or store away in barns, and yet your heavenly Father feeds them. But seek first his kingdom and his righteousness, and all these things will be given to you as well. Therefore do not worry about tomorrow, for tomorrow will worry about itself.

That's what people do around here—they quote Bible verses to convince you they're right. I could quote from Matthew, too, the passage about the sheep and the goats:

Come, you who are blessed by my Father; take your inheritance, the kingdom prepared for you since the creation of the world. For I was hungry and you gave me something to eat, I was thirsty and you gave me something to drink, I was a stranger and you invited me in, I needed clothes and you clothed me, I was sick and you looked after me, I was in prison and you came to visit me...I was almost extinct and you rescued me.

I could tell him I think God is testing us, that God is the whales and so far we're getting an "F." I know. God is God and he can do anything. I know about the virgin birth, Daniel in the lions' den, the parting of the Red Sea, Peter walking on water, and the feeding of the five thousand with five loaves and two fishes. I know about the Resurrection. But, I also know about the passenger pigeon and the dodo and all the dinosaurs that ever lived. My best guess is God won't intervene. The right whale is doomed unless we humans get off our backsides and do something.

I stared out the window as the plane skimmed over row after row of matching black roofs and immaculate gardens with teardrop-shaped inlays the colour of sand. Skyscrapers glinted in the distance, a straight line of them marching two by two into the sea. And then the plane dipped lower and we were hovering over multi-lane highways that stretched all the way to the horizon. This was Canada. Toronto, to be exact. I licked my lips and swallowed hard to wet my mouth. The mishmash of feelings in my chest was hard to pin down: one part pride, one part desire, but two parts excitement laced with fear. I glanced at my parents who were sitting beside me, my mother powdering her cheeks and applying fresh lipstick, and, my father, forehead wrinkled, studying a newspaper; studying, not reading, because the stories were in English and he doesn't know a word. My heart swelled with love for them both. All three of us deserved to be here and one day soon we would prove it. We would do something great.

But Toronto wasn't our final destination, only a stop on the way to someplace else. I checked my ticket for the name—Fredericton. That shouldn't be so hard to remember. Not when the first part—Frederic—is the name of Poland's most famous composer. He, too, fled Poland as a teenager. I guess a third-rate existence under Russian occupation just didn't appeal to him. He went to France and became "poet of the piano." I was going to Fredericton and who knew what I'd become. I realized immediately that "Frederic" was a sign and Fredericton would be amazing. Toronto was great, but Fredericton would be ten times better. Fredericton would be so brand-new the paint on the houses would still be wet and hot steam would be rising off the asphalt.

This belief sustained me almost until touchdown, when the bleakness of the landscape became irrefutable. We were landing in a veritable forest of trees. Our new home was a wasteland. I glanced across the aisle at my parents where my mother had the window seat. She sat very straight with her hands clasped on her lap and her eyes glued to the headrest in front of her. Then, her right arm a blur, she reached up quick and closed the blind.

Fredericton, too, was only a stop on the way to someplace else. From there we were driven a hundred kilometres south to a little town called Lampeq. Lampeq was not New York City. Lampeq was not Toronto. Lampeq was not even Fredericton.

Lampeq had no skyscrapers, no traffic, no crowds. The houses were plain and almost all painted white, with tin roofs that curled at the corners. A handful showed signs of a glorious past, but you had to look beyond the peeling paint and rotting woodwork to see it; you had to ignore the rusted-out car in the circular drive and imagine a stately carriage instead, its horse pawing the ground, eager to reach the coach house in back. Not that I was interested in history. I'd come here for the future, not the past. I'd come here for the Levi Strauss jeans and the Adidas running shoes. But there was a serious problem. Lampeq had no Levi Strauss jeans, no Adidas running shoes, and the Ford Mustangs were outnumbered by trucks hauling dead trees.

We had come to the end of the world. My mother, she sits in the kitchen and cries.

✳ ✳ ✳

SEPTEMBER 28, 1982

There's a new boy at school. He's tall and blond with wide, wide cheekbones that make him look like a fighter. You can tell just by looking at him that he's not from around here. He's too fair, too tall, too interesting.

I think his is the first immigrant family to settle in Lampeq in a hundred years. I'm not joking. People always choose big cities like Toronto and Montreal over our Maritime towns. We watch their jet trails as they pass overhead. Exotic for Lampeq is when a car with Ontario plates stops at the Irving in the middle of summer. If Lampeq were a flavour of ice cream, I guarantee we'd be vanilla.

"He's from Poland," I said to my friend Sandra in the school cafeteria on his very first day, and pointed my head to where he sat alone at a corner table, unwrapping his lunch done up in wax paper.

She shrugged her shoulders like it was nothing, like Poland was on the other side of town.

"Poland!" I insisted. "You know: the Iron Curtain, Auschwitz, Solidarity..."

She rolled her french fries through the gravy that coated her food like a layer of sludge and then popped them into her mouth one fat riddled blob at a time.

"Remember the candles I put in the window last Christmas?"

"He smells like boiled cabbage and he doesn't speak English." She stopped eating long enough to lick her fingers.

"It was martial law, remember?" I remembered. The clips from the news were seared in my memory: scenes of total chaos complete with smoke clouds, explosions, and riot police. The TV had shown a tank running over a man in the street. He had his arms raised in surrender, but the tank didn't stop, didn't even slow down. Then President Reagan came on the screen. "Light a candle in your window as a small but certain beacon of our solidarity with the Polish people," he said. "Let the light of millions of candles give notice that the light of freedom is not going to be extinguished."

I immediately went to the kitchen, where my mother was busy making supper. "Where are the emergency candles?" I asked and started rifling through drawers.

"I don't think we have any," she said.

I wasn't surprised, knowing my mother, known also as the Queen of Positive Thinking. She doesn't believe in calamity. When the power goes out, she chalks it up to God's will and we sit around in the dark until the lights come back on. I, on the other hand, believe in both preparing for emergencies and accident prevention. That's why I keep my own flashlight and a supply of Band-Aids and batteries in a Pot of Gold chocolate box under my bed. I also have some canned goods and bottles of water tucked away in my closet.

I kept looking until I found them: a whole box in the cubbyhole over the sink, each one bright orange with a tumour-like pumpkin bulging out of its side. I hesitated, but then took two. They were candles, after all, and beggars can't be choosers. I stuck them in holders and lit them with paper towel twisted into a wad and set ablaze on the stove, because another thing my mother doesn't believe in is matches. I put them in the front windows, replacing them as they burned out, and lighting them every night until I'd used up the box. Sandra—surprise, surprise—had no recollection.

When the Polish boy and I crossed paths a week or two later I couldn't believe it. He looked at me like he had something to say, something incredible and amazing. He had piercing blue eyes the colour of water beneath ice.

"Yes?" I moved close to the wall and laid a hand against the cold concrete to steady myself.

"Where is toilet, please?"

"Excuse me?" I narrowed my eyes and zoned in on his mouth. I was sure I must have heard him wrong.

"Where is toilet, please?"

I led him down the hall and around the corner to the men's room. I walked slowly, racking my brain for a way to salvage the moment. At the door, I turned and looked him square in the face. "Solidarity," I said.

He stared at me blankly.

I tried a different tack. "Lech Wałęsa."

His eyes opened wide.

I made V's with both hands. "Victory!"

He grinned. "Zwycięstwo!"

I smiled so hard, my face hurt.

His thumb jabbed his chest. "My name is Darek Dąbrowski." He spoke slowly and carefully, like my life was in the balance and with the right pronunciation he could win my freedom.

"I am Eleanor Hanson."

"My very great pleasure." He took my hand and touched it to his lips, and then disappeared into the washroom. I stood there a moment and studied the back of my hand, my ragged cuticles and my nails chewed down to the quick. I pressed my hand to my lips. My lips were scratchy to the skin, but his lips were soft as a sun-ripened plum.

Now we're not exactly friends, but we always say "Hi." At least I say "Hi." He says "Good day" or some archaic phrase he's picked up in his English-as-a-second-language class. We speak even when he's standing on the fringe of a group of boys, dragging on a cigarette, or I'm sitting in the library doing homework with my friends. Sometimes it's just a wink or a quick smile, never more than a few words. When the moment is over, I wipe my sweaty palms down the front of my pants and pretend I don't care. I've learned not to get my hopes up. That way I'm never disappointed.

If you asked Pastor Martin, he'd say the most important thing about me is I'm saved, which is Baptist lingo and translated means my sins are forgiven and Jesus lives in my heart. The major benefit to being saved is that it guarantees my place in heaven when I die, kind of like insurance or an advance reservation, which is pretty amazing when you think about it and a real load off the mind. Still, I can't help but wonder. If Jesus lives in my heart, shouldn't it have some effect now? Like, shouldn't I feel different inside? Less nervous? More kind? Shouldn't it be easy to do what is right? Sometimes, I wonder if I'm saved at all. I put my hand on my heart. Jesus, are you really in there?

There are other people who'd say the most important thing about me is my looks. I know they're wrong. I'll admit that I'm pretty—a little on the short side, but, at least I'm not fat. And my eyebrows are perfect. I like my hair, too. It's a nice brown with gold highlights. Sometimes I wear it parted in the middle and hanging down straight; it makes me feel as though I'm looking through a curtain—like a modern-day Catherine

Earnshaw spying through the window at the Lintons. Usually I wear it in a long braid down my back, especially when I'm out biking or walking Fishtail Point. Looks are nothing to build a life on, though. Too fickle. A bad case of acne, alopecia, or under-active thyroid and one's beauty is history. I say it's better to be ugly or average at best. It keeps the people around you real.

My teachers would say the most important thing about me is I'm smart. I think they're closer to the truth. Intelligence has got me places. For one thing, it's created a huge gulf that separates me from my peers. Can you imagine the agony I endure on a daily basis as I listen to my friends go on about their amazing new diets, the cute shoes/purse/earrings they saw in Saint John over the weekend, and their difficult decisions around growing their hair out versus getting it cut. "The International Whaling Commission has put a moratorium on commercial whaling," I interject when there's a lull at the lunch table.

They look at me ever so briefly, a glazed look in their eyes. "I think you're from another planet," says Sandra.

"Will they come back for me, soon?"

"Not if they have brains and know how to use them."

As far as I'm concerned, the most important thing about me is I worry. A lot.

OCTOBER 13, 1982

A picture of Darek Dąbrowski and his parents was looking up at me from the front page of the *Gazette* when I got home from school. I set my books on the verandah railing and picked up the paper for a closer look. The picture took up a quarter of the sheet: Darek's mother in a chair with Darek perched on the armrest and his father standing in behind. Off to the side was a table set for dinner with a turkey holding centre stage. Mrs. Dąbrowski was beautiful. She wore a blouse tucked into a skirt that showed off her legs, and her hair hung to her shoulders in loose, blond waves. Everything about her—her hair, her posture, even the solemn expression on her face—reminded me of an actress from some old-time movie. Only her hands weren't movie-star material, but rather great mitts with soft, lumpy knuckles and sausage-shaped fingers. I stared at those hands with fascination. Hers were hands that made bread and canned stewed tomatoes. They knitted, sewed, scrubbed, and cooked. They could probably make fire with two sticks. She was no stranger to emergencies, that's for sure. I imagined she kept a cupboard full of batteries, not to mention a good supply of matches, candles, light bulbs, and fuses.

His father looked altogether different, older and more ordinary with his grey hair cut short so that he was all hollow cheeks and high forehead. His hands looked better suited for office work than hard labour, and I was intrigued by the way they held his wife's shoulders, not the light laying on of hands typical in a family picture or the possessive clutch that boasts to the world that she's his wife and his wife alone. No, his was a firm, purposeful hold, like she might disappear if he let go, drift off into the atmosphere like a runaway balloon.

And Darek, Darek stared at the camera with the strangest look on his face, an expression that was half anguish, half horror, like he was watching his own house burn to the ground. It bothered me—that look—but I couldn't stop staring. My eyes were drawn to it like they would be a car crash or the emptiness at an amputee's shoulder or hip where the attachment would be for an arm or a leg.

"'Polish Family Celebrates First Thanksgiving in New Brunswick.'" My mother had materialized on the verandah with a carton of milk from the corner store.

I turned the page. My mother turned it back.

"'Andy and Teresa Dąbrowski together with their eighteen-year-old son Darek pause for a family portrait before sitting down to a turkey dinner at their new home on Orange

Street.'" She pronounced Dąbrowski with a *brow* as in *eyebrow*. which was wrong, but I didn't correct her. "Does he go to your school?" she asked.

"What do you think?" I rolled my eyes. There's only one high school in Lampeq, so the question was pointless. I steeled myself for what would come next.

"What church does he go to?"

I shrugged my shoulders. I wasn't about to tell her he was Catholic, that I'd seen the whole family come out of St. Gertrude's when I was biking to Fishtail Light last Saturday to pick the last of the purple heather and hopefully see a right whale before they left for the season. Mr. Dąbrowski was saying, "Please to meet you, please to meet you," in a deep, booming voice that carried halfway down the street while pumping the arm of every man, woman, and child within a quarter-mile radius. Mrs. Dąbrowski was clinging to his side like an oyster on the half shell and saying nothing at all.

St. Gertrude's stands on a hill on the outskirts of town. It's less a church than a castle, with its brick exterior, twin steeples, and huge wooden doors with medieval-like hinges. Late in the day, just before the sun drops behind the hills, the stained glass in the windows shines rubies and gold.

If you came to Lampeq searching for the house of God and all you had to go on was looks, the Catholic Church is the place you would pick. My church and the others are all painted white and squat along Main Street like eggs in a carton. They don't come halfway to St. Gertrude's grandeur.

On the other hand, if your search was based on hours of programming, my church would win hands down. We have two services on Sunday and prayer meeting Wednesday night. We have choir practice, baby band, Explorers, Sunday school, youth group, AWANA, and ladies' missionary circle. We have a gazillion Bible study groups, a class on each and every book in the Old and New Testaments, divided according to age and sex.

If you were basing your search on the conduct of its members, we'd win that one, too. All we Baptists do is eat too much, gossip, and criticize others. The Catholics do all this and worse. They go to Friday-night dances at the Legion and play bingo at the Knights of Columbus Hall. They drink beer and smoke cigarettes. They use the Lord's name in vain. They waste money on lotto and play cards to the wee hours. I know what Pastor Martin would say. He'd say Darek Dąbrowski is headed for hell, and if I'm not careful he'll drag me there with him.

"The Pope's from Poland and he's Catholic," said my mother.

"Roman Polanski's from Poland and he's Jewish."

"Oh."

My mother would never say a word against God's chosen people. I set the paper on top of my books and we went in the house.

✻ ✻ ✻

NOVEMBER 15, 1982

My father has never been one to keep his thoughts and feelings to himself, and it is perhaps just a slight exaggeration to describe his personality as part army tank, part bullhorn. Even asleep, his snores rock the house, and an overnight guest would need to wear earplugs to have a moment's sleep. My mother, too, is an extrovert by nature; that is, until now, until we settled in Lampeq. I am the quiet one, and so, these days, when my father goes out and my mother and I are alone in the house, the place is a graveyard. No laughter, no talking; even in the same room we keep to ourselves, each lost in thoughts that, for my mother at least, seem too painful to share.

Today, like most days, I am sitting at my desk when my father gets home. He puts his shoulder to the bloated back door and heaves on it like he's rolling the stone away from the tomb. The doorknob rattles, the wall shakes on its foundation, and then the door gives way. Cold air floods the hall and pushes icy fingers through the cracks around my door. I shiver and push my feet deeper into my slippers. Winter comes early to this part of the world. Snow already covers the ground and the sun is hidden by clouds all month long. The water and sky push on each other, their boundaries blurring into one, and I am caught between the two, lost in a no man's land of dreary grey.

My father stops outside my room, his shadow dark beneath the door. He taps twice in greeting and then moves on to the kitchen. He won't interrupt me when I'm doing my homework. School and books are sacred to my father, and study is an act of worship. To him, education is a necessity of life, and just as vital as food and water. Certainly he considers a university degree more valuable than money. Money comes and money goes, but what is put in your head stays there forever. I have not asked him how he expects me to do well when all of my subjects are in a language I cannot read or write. He does not understand how difficult English is for me, that it might take ten years for me to graduate from high school, that I might be an old man before I earn a degree. To be honest, the language is the least of my difficulties. The problem is I cannot think. My mind wanders constantly, and even in the past ten minutes I have not recorded a single word in Polish or in English. Instead, I have filled the margins of my paper with row upon row of tiny rectangles, the top row always left uneven, like a lower jaw with missing teeth. I draw these boxes without any thought, my hand working of its own accord. But when I study these boxes, I know right away they are the ramparts that surround the Old Town back in Warsaw. I harrumph in disgust. I know what it means. It means I feel vulnerable. Defenseless. A feeling I was no stranger to in Poland, but one I never expected to have accompany me here.

My father is different. He delights in his life here. Perhaps it is not so unusual given the time he spent in detention. Perhaps he would rejoice in life anywhere, even in Russia, provided he was free to go where he pleased. No—now my talk has turned ridiculous.

He has picked up English easily, as easily as the burrs in the woods attach to his clothes. Woodswork is hard, but he seems to enjoy it, takes pleasure in using his muscles again, and it shows in his figure. Two months and his arms and chest have recovered most of their bulk.

Six days out of seven he gets up in the dark and goes to the kitchen to put up his lunch. He stands at the counter in wool socks and long underwear, humming happy mazurkas and slathering butter on bread. Then, after two cups of coffee and a big dish of porridge, porridge because in Lampeq kasha does not exist, he's putting on work clothes and going outside.

A Canadian in a blue half-ton picks him up every morning. Bill is his name. He is younger than my father and performs in a band on Saturday nights. He is the singer. Onstage he wears a black cowboy hat, black shirt, blue jeans and belt with a big silver buckle. I have never seen this band or heard Bill sing, but he showed me a picture as proof of his talent. His legs are spread wide and he's holding the mike like he's kissing a woman. I was too shy to ask, but I think in the photo he wears Levi Strauss jeans. One day soon, when my English is better, I will find the courage to ask where he bought them.

"Billy the Kid," mutters my father six mornings out of seven as he waits in the cold outside on the stoop. I imagine him pulling up his sleeve to check his watch. "Right on time." He is being sarcastic as Bill is consistently ten minutes late, sometimes fifteen. He makes up for it in speed, though, and has a glove compartment of speeding tickets to show for it. Six mornings out of seven, my father throws his lunch bucket into the back of Bill's truck and climbs into the cab. In the beginning, Bill kept his radio on Big Country 97 and played his favourites turned up loud. The whine of harmonica and tired guitar carried all the way to the back of the house, and I'd roll onto my stomach and cover my head with the pillow to shut out the noise.

One day, early on in this arrangement, my father lost his patience. "Kurwa!" I heard him say as he threw his lunch bucket in the back. "Still you are playing this funeral music! My ears! How they suffer."

I uncovered my head and waited for Bill to order my father out of his cab. It was his truck, after all, his gas, his radio, and his trip across town to pick up my father. "Andy, Andy, Andy," Bill said in a laughing voice (all the Canadians have changed my father's name to Andy). "You think you can listen to this music once and then love it forever? No, no. It doesn't work that way. You have to acquire a taste for it. You have to open your heart to the pain and the healing. Give it some time. A few more weeks, a month at the most, and you'll be playing these songs at home."

"Never will I like it, this garbage!" yelled my father. Then all went still, and I could only assume my father had shut off the radio. I also assumed they made the thirty-kilometre drive to the Burdett Woodlot in silence, because, I know for a fact they returned in silence at the end of the day. I was a witness to their silence, as the garbagemen had been and gone, and I was returning the garbage can to the shed when they drove in.

My father is stubborn and tends to see things one way. I do not think it occurred to him that Bill, too, might be offended and refuse to stop for him the next morning. He was up at five, as usual, buttering bread and humming happy mazurkas in the kitchen. He obviously knew Bill better than I—Bill, who indeed showed up, but ten minutes late, as per his schedule. Even more surprising, when my father opened the cab door, I was sure I heard the ethereal notes of flute punctuated by the nasal staccato of clarinet and snare drum. I jumped out of bed and glanced out the window. My father was slapping Bill on the shoulder. It seemed my father had forged his first great Canadian friendship. Now it was CBC Radio One driving out, Big Country 97 coming home.

My father's been cutting down trees for several weeks now, long enough for the water blisters on his hands to have dried up and turned into callous. He comes home with fir needles under his skin, which I pull out with a needle. Once he came home with a gash in his arm wrapped up with a t-shirt. "Are you all right?" I asked.

He removed the blood-soaked cloth, held his arm over the sink, and dumped half a bottle of vinegar over the wound. "Like never before," he said with a laugh.

He is happiest in the morning, before he leaves for work, although it's possible his level of happiness continues to rise as he tramps about the woods all day—I am not there and would not know. But one thing is certain: his mood quickly deteriorates once he gets home. I hunch over my English notes and try to ignore the noise in the kitchen.

"Teresa!" My father lifts the lid on the soup pot: red borscht, not to the calibre of my mother's cooking, but edible. I made it after school, right after I finished washing the dishes from breakfast and yesterday's supper. It was the best I could do with the few ingredients left in the house. I hear the clang of metal on metal as my father serves himself a bowl and then the drag of chair legs as he sits down to eat it. After a moment, he gets up for another. Then the fridge opens and shuts. Cupboard doors, too. My mother was to go shopping today, but failed her duty. My father does not see the challenge this task poses for my mother. I suppose I should not be too harsh a judge. He is not here to see how she struggles to get up in the morning, how she sometimes stays in her pajamas all day and does not dress until after I get home from school.

"Teresa!" My father's voice trails off as he moves from the kitchen to the front of the house. "There is no food in the house."

I imagine my mother sitting in the same position she was in two hours ago when I took her some borscht: slumped in the chair from the Salvation Army that Bill brought to our house in the back of his truck. She sits there all day, unless, she's in bed. She sits there, eyes closed and face pinched as though she has a headache. She gets up for the bathroom, that's all. I open the door of my bedroom to hear what they say.

"Put on your clothes. We're going shopping."

My mother's reply is too faint to hear, so I slip into the kitchen.

"Listen, Teresa, Darek and I are your family, your home. We left Poland. We cannot go back. One-way passports, Teresa. Listen to me. We live here now. Canada is our home."

My mother starts to cry. I cannot hear her, but I know she is crying. The house itself shudders as though sharing her grief. I go back to my room and close the door. I lie down on my bed and stare at the ceiling.

"You have to try, Teresa." My father's voice is firm and leaves no room for excuses. "You will come to like it here if you try."

After a while there are footsteps in the hall, a single tap, and my bedroom door opens. My parents stand there, my father holding tight to my mother's elbow, as though she might try to escape or perhaps slip through the floorboards, as though the draft from the door might blow her away. My mother wears street clothes under her coat. Her blouse is pulled to one side so her neck is exposed. The hollow in her throat is more like a hole, and her collarbone shines white through her skin.

"We are going for groceries," says my father. "Finish your homework while we are gone."

"I will buy us some apples," says my mother in a voice that is almost a whisper.

"Tomorrow when you get home from school you will eat apple cake, yes? Hot apple cake with a nice glass of milk." She slips a hand under her coat to hike up her slacks.

"Apple cake is my favourite." I get up and kiss her on the cheek. Her skin is dry and flaky, her face pale, and her eyes tired and dull. For a split second, her eyes meet mine, but just as quickly she looks away. I imagine she is dreaming of Dzielna Street—our flat with three rooms, her sewing machine, and the colour TV, the bakery where she bought our bread—dense loaves of rye with slits cut in the top. Her eyes run through the lists in the ledger of private arrangements she keeps in her head. She remembers each name, turning it in her mind like a precious stone in her fingers. I watch her with a growing sense of unease. It's like my father and I aren't in the room, don't even exist, the way she retreats into herself and has no interest in the world around her. My father guides her to the door and she doesn't resist. The wind slams the door with a bang.

I return to my English vocabulary words, but the letters squirm on the page, their black lines twitching as though the paper is awash in ants. There will be no apple cake tomorrow. Or the day after tomorrow. Or the day after the day after tomorrow. This talk is only a game that we play. My mother is homesick and I think it is killing her.

I cannot sit still any longer, so I throw down my pencil and go wash the soup pot and my father's one bowl and spoon. Then I go to the front room, the room my mother sits in all day, turn on the lamp, and empty her ashtray with its bank of fine ash. My mother's smoking again, more than ever before. I open the window a crack to let in fresh air. A few letters lie propped against the lamp. I pick them up. There's one to Babcia, one to my mother's sister, and one to her friend from the fabric shop, each envelope sealed and addressed in full, but without any stamps or airmail stickers. The letters are slim—a single sheet each. I hold one up to the light. If I knew what she wrote, I might know what to think, what to do, how to feel, but the paper is folded and the words impossible to read. I consider opening one, have my thumb under the flap, but then decide against it. I'll mail the letters instead and go put on my coat. The post office is closed, but perhaps there are stamps at the drugstore or supermarket. If I have to, I'll walk all the way to the mall. At least I'll feel like I'm doing something, helping out in some way. A part of me knows this doesn't make sense. A part of me knows I could walk all the way to Toronto for stamps and my mother's situation would remain exactly the same. This part of me knows there is only one solution for my mother and it is far away across the sea.

✳ ✳ ✳

MARCH 1983

I shifted my weight in the pew. Varnished to a high gloss, the long oak benches were easy on the eye but a killer on the backside, and the wool collar of my coat was scratching my neck and itching like crazy. Unfortunately, there was no taking the coat off without freezing to death—a slow and painful death by hypothermia. Not that I'd have taken it off even if the church was a sweltering 100 degrees—not with the skirt I was wearing. The one that pinched my waist and pulled tight across my middle before falling in wide pleats down to my knees. The one that made me look at least ten pounds overweight, if not the other unforgiveable option.

It was a baptism Sunday. I shivered and wrapped my arms tight across my body as Pastor Martin led a middle-aged woman down the steps of the baptismal font. I hoped the water was warmer than air temperature—closer to the temperature of the tropical waters sparkling in the giant mural above the font. The woman clasped her hands and pressed them to her chest, her white gown billowing like a sheet hung to dry. Her eyes stared straight ahead, focused on some distant island in that wipe-down vinyl, aquamarine sea. I knew how this moment felt—standing nervously in the water, waiting to be plunged beneath the surface and, more importantly, being raised up to newness of life—your sins washed away.

Pastor Martin assumed an official stance, one arm around the woman's shoulders and the other gripping her hands in a capable way. "Do you, Mary McKenna, acknowledge Jesus Christ as your Saviour and Lord?"

"I do."

"Do you promise, with the help of the Holy Spirit, to love and serve God for the rest of your life?"

"I do."

"Then on this, the confession of your faith, and at your request, I now baptize you in the name of the Father, and of the Son, and of the Holy Spirit."

He submerged her in one fell swoop. She came up spluttering and coughing, water pouring down her face. Her hair hung in wet strands, and the white gown clung to her body, emphasizing her melon breasts and thick thighs. I glanced away, embarrassed. I knew how this moment felt, too—the feeling of disappointment when newness of life turned out to feel no different from the old life I assumed would slough off like a snake's skin and float like scum on the surface of the water.

Triumphant chords burst from the organ pipes as Mary McKenna seized the railing and hauled herself up the steps, water streaming from the sleeves and hem of her robe. The choir exploded into song:

> *Redeemed, how I love to proclaim it!*
> *Redeemed by the blood of the Lamb;*
> *Redeemed through His infinite mercy,*
> *His child and forever I am.*

Not to be outdone, or perhaps as a show of support, the radiator pipes suddenly kicked into gear with a repetitive clanging that sounded like someone had taken a stick and was beating the living daylights out of them. The door at the top of the stairs opened a crack, and an invisible hand pushed through a beach towel. Mary McKenna buried her face in its striped folds and then flung it over her shoulders, clutching it to her throat with one fist as she climbed to the door.

Sandra nudged my leg. I glanced down at the note she'd written in the margin of her church bulletin:

Find a prom dress yet?

I rolled my eyes and shook my head.

A boy descended the steps. He couldn't have been more than seven or eight. The water was up to his chest and his teeth were chattering like a glass full of ice cubes.

"Do you, Peter Phillips, acknowledge Jesus Christ as your Saviour and Lord?"

"I d-d-do."

Another nudge.

Less than four months to prom.

I took a pencil from the pew pocket in front of me, pulled out my own bulletin, and scribbled:

I want to go to prom like I want a hole in my head.

The boy sprang out of the water like a frog, his mouth a wide, toothless grin and his eyes bright marbles. Pastor Martin stepped forward, arms and eyes raised toward heaven. The sopping sleeves of his black robe hung down in jagged points like bat wings. "We have done, O Lord, as you commanded, and still there is room."

> *Redeemed, and so happy in Jesus,*
> *No language my rapture can tell;*
> *I know that the light of His presence*
> *With me doth continually dwell*

I bought my dress in Bangor yesterday.

Under her words she had sketched a floor-length dress, front and back views—with a plunging V in the front and an open back.

Looks sleazy, I wrote.

You mean flirty, she wrote back.

"Sleazy," I said with as much authority as I could pack into a whisper, and then used my pencil to sketch a less revealing sweetheart neckline and shaded in the back.

Pastor Martin must have left a trail of wet clothes in the dark corridor outside the baptismal font and then ducked into the choir room for dry ones—knotting his tie in an all-out sprint—because he was back in the sanctuary before the organ had finished blasting the final notes to the hymn. (Of course it helped that the song had four verses, with the refrain repeating itself over and over again.) Now he was leaning casually against the edge of the pulpit, not even short of breath. "Did you hear the one about the lady on the airplane who was reading her Bible?" he asked, his head on a swivel to take in the whole room.

"No," everyone said.

"Well, the man sitting next to her gave a little chuckle and asked, 'You don't really believe all that stuff in there, do you?'

"'Of course I do,' the woman said, and shot him a withering look. 'It's in the Bible.'

"'But what about that guy who was swallowed by the whale? How do you suppose he survived all that time in there?' the man asked.

"She hesitated, but, for only a second. 'I guess I'll just have to ask him when I get to heaven.'

"'What if he isn't in heaven?'

'Then you can ask him,' said the lady."

Everyone laughed, everyone it seemed, except Sandra and me. Sandra was busy drawing beards and moustaches on the faces in her Sunday-school paper and I plain didn't think it was funny. Call me crazy, but I don't find jokes about someone's place in eternity all that amusing—especially when that place is presumed to be hell.

Pastor Martin strolled to the other side of the pulpit and draped his arm across its velvet runner. "It's easy to get sidetracked with a story like Jonah's, because everyone is focused on the whale. Let me make one thing clear here this morning: Jonah is not the story of a whale. It's not the story of a bitter and angry prophet. It's not the story of a city bent on self-destruction." He paused for emphasis. "The book of Jonah, my friends, is the gospel in miniature. In four short chapters, Jonah tells the story of God's love and deliverance for all of creation."

I watched Sandra open the bulletin to the "Order of Service" and then, with thick strokes of her pencil, cross out everything down to and including "Message from the Pastor."

"The narrator is a master storyteller. Rising action, climax, denouement—all those elements of plot structure that you learned in high school English are there. And as with all good stories—the conflict comes early. Listen to these great opening lines: 'The word of the Lord came to Jonah son of Amittai. "Go to the great city of Nineveh and preach against it, because its wickedness has come up before me." But Jonah ran away from the Lord and headed for Tarshish. He went down to Joppa, where he found a ship bound for that port.'" Pastor Martin looked up from his Bible. "Are you hooked yet? Do you want to keep reading? You better believe it. All those unanswered questions just begging for answers. What made Nineveh so wicked? Why did Jonah run away? What made Tarshish so appealing?"

Well, let's clear up that last question right away. Jonah fled to Tarshish because it was about as far away from Nineveh as he could get in an age with no trains, planes, or automobiles, which leads up nicely to my next point—the story is written in the style of a tall tale. Notice the exaggeration: great wind, raging sea, deep sleep—everything is larger than life. Even Nineveh is described as a very large city, so very large that it takes Jonah three days to cross it. Think about that a moment: a three-day journey—walking, of course. That's at least twenty miles per day; let's say sixty or so miles in total. That makes Nineveh bigger than Fredericton or even Saint John; that makes Nineveh bigger than Toronto." He scratched his head. "Hold on! Small wonder Jonah refused to obey God and went running in the opposite direction. He was probably a small-town boy like one of us." He smiled in that boyish way of his, rocking back on his heels with his hands on the pulpit.

Sandra had flipped over her bulletin and was scratching away with her dull pencil:

Michael McBride keeps looking at you.
I bet he'd take you to the prom.
Want me to ask him?

I refused to look across the sanctuary to where the older teenage boys all shared a pew. I grabbed Sandra's wrist and squeezed it tight. "No!" I mouthed.

"But he's cute," Sandra whispered.

I shook my head vigorously, snatched the paper, and scrawled:

He's not my type.

"Your type ain't been seen 'round these here parts in a long, long time," she drawled.

I rolled my eyes. All I wanted was someone interesting—the kind of person you might get if you rolled Jacques Cousteau, John the Baptist, and Heathcliff all up into one; someone who'd been out of the province at least once (Maine didn't count) and pronounced library with two r's; somebody kind of like Darek Dąbrowski.

Sandra dug her elbow into my ribs and shoved her bulletin under my nose.

What's not to like? she'd written.

I want somebody different, I wrote back.

"Irony is another tool used by the narrator," said Pastor Martin. "When the storm blows up, the sailors—non-Israelites, mind you—come off as more pious than Jonah, the Israelite prophet. They immediately pray to their gods. And where is Jonah? Sound asleep in the cabin below."

Sandra pretended to snore in my ear. I punched her in the leg.

"But there are two things in this story that are not ironic—God's love and God's faithfulness. Jonah is determined to get as far away from God as he possibly can, but he discovers there is no escaping God. God is there even in the depths of the sea. And not once does God give up on Jonah. Not once does God turn his back on Jonah and walk away. Instead, he rescues Jonah, sets him back on dry land, and gives him another chance. And he can do the same thing for you and me, too."

I can't say I found that image of God particularly appealing. Made me think of God as a stalker who asks the same girl out a hundred times and refuses to take "no" for an answer, or, a telemarketer who talks non-stop and won't let you get a word in edgewise until you're left with no choice but to hang up in his ear. I'd rather God keep his distance and wait for me to come to him. And to be honest, I felt a little sorry for Jonah. So he didn't want to go to Nineveh? Who can blame him for that? I wouldn't want to go, either. *Hey, Lennie! Drop everything. I need you to go denounce Nineveh for me. Live and in person. Did I mention it's a city of evildoers trodden with blood and chances are slim you'll get out alive?* I was also annoyed about the whale. Pastor Martin ignored that storyline completely, same as he does the rights in real life. I opened my Bible to the Book of Jonah and scanned for the "whale" parts. There wasn't much, only a reference to a "great fish." How do they know for certain it was a whale? Do whales even exist in the...what was it? Sea of Galilee? Dead Sea? I flipped to the maps at the back and found one labelled "The Prophets in Palestine." Oh—the Mediterranean. I'd never heard of whales in the Mediterranean, but, then again, why would I? It's not like I'd ever been there. It's not like I'd ever been anywhere except New Brunswick and Maine. Make that southwestern New Brunswick, Calais, and Bangor. Sandra was pulling on my arm and I suddenly realized everyone was standing for prayer.

"Our Father God, the apostle Paul has said that neither height nor depth nor anything else in all creation will be able to separate us from the love of God in Christ Jesus our Lord. Merciful deliverance was there when Jonah was at his lowest, and it is still there for us today. Forgive us our unbelief, empower us by your Spirit, and grant that we should bear much fruit. And may the grace of the Lord Jesus Christ, and the love of God, and the fellowship of the Holy Spirit be with you all. Amen."

That was it. Time to go. Pastor Martin walked down the centre aisle to the main doors, which was a sign for the rest of us to collect our things and head out, too.

The cheap pantyhose my mother had picked up at the Metropolitan were sagging in the crotch and slowly creeping down my hips. I gingerly retrieved my Bible from the seat of the pew, bending from the knees instead of the hips, in the hopes of preventing or at least slowing the downward migration of my pantyhose. Then I put my hands in my coat pockets—the Bible pinned to my side by one elbow—and wriggled my fingers around until I had a good grip on the flimsy waistband.

"I think I can get Dad to give me the car this afternoon. Do you want to drive around and listen to my new Billy Idol tape?"

I shook my head. "I've got to babysit plus finish my English essay. It's due tomorrow."

"The *Wuthering Heights* paper? You've been working on that for weeks."

"I know. I'm almost done. 'Love Heathcliff? I am Heathcliff,'" I quoted.

"You are so weird!"

We were inching along the aisle, waiting in line for our turn through the exit, while the fingers of both my hands slowly went numb. I didn't care how much they cost—I'd use all my babysitting money if I had to—sometime this week, before church next Sunday, I was going to invest in a good pair of pantyhose, the kind your thumb doesn't go through when you try to pull them up or feel like a burlap potato sack against the skin.

"There goes Darek-the-Commie—which reminds me, did you know he quit school and got a full-time job pumping gas at the Irving?" Sandra said.

I looked beyond the people ahead of us, out the open door to the street. Men, women, and children all done up in Sunday best were crowding the sidewalk, white clouds rising from their mouths like speech bubbles. Darek Dąbrowski was in the midst of it all, weaving in and out, his no-name high-tops gliding across the icy patches. He wore a navy bomber jacket, his hands pushed deep into the pockets and his bare head bent to the wind. My eyes followed his fast-moving figure down the street. Where was he going? To the Irving? The drugstore? Flemming's Pharmacy at the bottom of the hill opened at noon. I wanted to run after him. Pull a hat down over his ears. Rub lotion into his cracked knuckles. "He's not a Communist," I said.

"Too bad he's going about it all wrong," said Sandra. "Quitting school to pump gas is not the way to fast-track out of this town."

"And since when did you become an expert on Darek Dąbrowski?"

"Since we stopped for gas on our way back from Bangor yesterday. I love his accent. It sounds French."

I rolled my eyes. "You were actually talking to him?"

"Not exactly."

"What do you mean?"

"Dad was talking. I was listening. He's kind of cute close up."

"Sandra," I said through clenched teeth.

"What?"

"Tell me what he said exactly."

"I don't know his exact words. 'You want full gas?' or something like that. You know how he talks."

"I mean about school. What'd he say about school?"

"I don't remember every detail, but he *is* from Europe, remember." She pronounced it *you rope* to annoy me. "You do know Europe, don't you? New York, London, Paris, Munich..." She chanted the chorus of a current pop song.

"What are you talking about?"

"Here's what I'm talking about: Europe on the one hand, Lampeq on the other. Lampeq with a Dixie Lee Take-Out, a Met, and a library; Europe with Harrod's, the Louvre, and Julia Child." She held up her hands and moved them up and down, up and down, alternately, as though comparing the weights of two invisible objects. "Europe? Lampeq? Europe? Lampeq? It's a no-brainer, Eleanor."

"Julia Child is American," I said, rolling my eyes once again, but she had me thinking. *Did Darek really hate it here? Did he hate it so much that he wanted to leave?* A hole opened up in my solar plexus, a hole so deep that I couldn't feel bottom. "You're talking about western Europe. Poland's Communist. At least here he's free."

"Free," Sandra scoffed. "There's only one thing you're free to do in this place and that's leave." She clapped her hands together and then shot one forward complete with sound effects—a rush of air through pursed lips with just a hint of a whistle. "Free people have choices. One shoe store is not free. One ladies' boutique is not free. And there's no place to buy music. No place to buy books. No Suzy Shier, no Le Chateau, no Reitmans, no Pizza Hut, and if you want to get a Big Mac you have to leave the friggin' country."

"Are you and Lennie going across the lines for lunch today?" said Mrs. Lawson ahead of us, turning around.

"No, Mrs. Lawson," said Sandra. "We're just talking."

I liked the way Sandra reduced everything to a matter of buying and selling. As though all there is to life is shopping and fast food when, in fact, she'd ignored the most important thing, how even what we're supposed to think and feel is all laid out for us like clothes for church Sunday morning. "Four banks and ten churches," I said with mock cheerfulness.

"My point exactly."

I shivered as we approached the door and burrowed my chin down into my collar.

"What's up, girls?" Pastor Martin said. He'd switched his authoritative pulpit voice for the joking-around voice he used with teenagers.

I tentatively released my right hand's hold on my pantyhose and pulled it out of my pocket to shake his hand while my other hand dug in deeper, driving the spine of my Bible into my left thigh in a desperate attempt to safeguard my waistband. "Gotta love those whales, aye, Pastor Martin? Here's hoping

83

you never need one when you're out in a boat on the Bay of Fundy."

"Don't you worry about me, Eleanor. I'm right where God wants me to be. No running away or going off course. Which reminds me..." He reached his hand into his suit jacket and pulled out an envelope. "Special delivery from Maritime Bible College." He handed it to me. "Go ahead, open it."

I hesitated, wondering if there was any possible way I could leave the one hand in charge of my pantyhose and open the envelope with my teeth, but, decided against it on the grounds of looking ridiculous, and so went ahead and used both hands, leaving my pantyhose with the miniscule support attained by squeezing my legs tightly together.

"A full-time scholarship?" Sandra said, reading over my shoulder.

Pastor Martin grinned and slapped my back in congratulations. "I'd call that a message from the Lord, wouldn't you?"

"I don't know. I guess it could be," I said, but without his conviction.

"You guess it could be? I know it is." He turned and beamed his Ultrabrite smile full strength on Sandra. "And what about you, Sandra? Have you sent in your application yet?"

"Not yet, Pastor Martin. But I'm thinking about it. I'm giving it a lot of thought. And prayer. It's a big decision—I've never thought so hard or prayed so much. You better believe it." She propelled me through the door and waited until we were out of earshot before saying, "You didn't tell me you applied to MBC! What happened to UNB and our dream apartment? What about all the malls? And those cute guys in forestry—did you forget about them? UNB's got scholarships, too, and you can earn a degree and get a real job after." She put a hand on my shoulder. "Better reconsider, Lennie—chance of a lifetime." Then she slipped into the crowd in search of her parents.

"It's just an offer," I called, straining to find Darek through the jewel-coloured coats and old-lady hats. "I haven't accepted it yet." He was way down the street, and when I finally caught sight of him, my legs broke into a halting run as though my body was determined to catch up with him whether my head wanted to or not. But then my mind kicked into gear or maybe Jesus in my heart, and I shuffled to a stop. By that time my pantyhose were bunched around the top of my high winter boots. I thought about what Pastor Martin had said about the scholarship. When an opportunity presents, does that make it God's will? Or does that make it a temptation to be overcome? Then I thought about Darek and stood there on the sidewalk watching while he started down the hill. First his legs, then his shoulders, and last his head dipped out of sight.

JUNE 1983

I went to the graduation dance with Sandra's boyfriend's best friend Ron who is two years older than me and works in the produce department at the Save Easy. Sandra and Jimmy set it up. I did it mostly as a favour for Sandra because she's my best friend, plus she said she'd kill me if I didn't go. Then there was also the matter of Darek Dąbrowski. It might be my last chance to see him for the rest of my life, and if I missed it I would die. He was still in Lampeq, still at school (turned out his job at the Irving was only part-time), but Sandra was adamant his days here were numbered and I was beginning to think she just might be right. Lately, he did look like someone who hated it here: his arduous treks through the hallways at school, head down, shoulders slouched, and each footstep a chore that seemed to require Herculean effort. And so I was left balancing my selfish need to know a boy who was new and not boring (I use the word *know* in its platonic sense only and not in its Biblical sense because loving one's neighbour is one thing, making love to one's neighbour a whole other ball game. So, for the record, let it be known, I didn't plan to marry Darek—I just wanted to talk to him, maybe walk home from school holding his hand, possibly kiss on the lips, but with mouths closed and no tongue) with his need to get out of a place that was destroying his soul. And then there was God's will to consider on top of all that. It was the thinnest of tightropes.

Ron can't remember my name half of the time and he looks like Ivan Lendl in a pale, malnourished sort of way. But he's not into tennis, he's into hockey cards. He can't get through a conversation without saying "rookie card" once or twice and "mint condition" six times as often. My eyes glaze over the minute he opens his mouth. He wouldn't know a whale if he fell over it. Not unless it was wearing a National Hockey League jersey and had a stick in its flippers.

Ron doesn't exactly like me, either, but he loves an opportunity to wow the masses with his cosmic knowledge of useless data—RBIs, strikeouts, home runs, power-play goals, penalty minutes, blah, blah, blah, blah, blah, and I had tickets to the biggest bash in town, a couple of hundred party-goers who would be a captive audience, at least half of whom would have a partial interest in his trivia.

Oh, I'd had other offers; just not from the only person who mattered—not from Darek Dąbrowski. It wasn't for lack of trying, believe me. Those last two weeks, I went all out. Every chance I got, I gave Sandra the slip and hung out near the smoking pit or on the bench by his locker, trying hard to look cool, like it was normal for me to be all alone with a book in my hands in these abnormal places. I chose the book special for the occasion—*The Joke* by Milan Kundera—the closest I could get to an English translation of a Polish novel, which wasn't close at all because Kundera is Czech. Still, I hoped the fact that Poland and Czechoslovakia were bordering nations might mean the book would catch Darek's eye or even somehow magically pull him to me like a magnet. Unfortunately, it didn't work that way, and Darek passed me by again and again, head down and feet shuffling, fully oblivious to my presence.

Drastic times call for drastic measures, and so, three days before the dance, I decided to take control of my destiny and actually got up and planted myself in his path the minute I saw him coming in from a smoke break.

"Move it, asshole," he said when our bodies collided and *The Joke* leapt from my hands, flew out the door, and took a nose-dive spine-first into the pavement.

"Darek, how are you?" Although I didn't approve of his language, I couldn't help but be impressed with the gains he'd made in English.

His head jerked to attention. "Eleanor! Please, excuse me." He picked up the book, carefully smoothed out the pages, glanced at the cover, and put it back in my hands. "I hope is okay or do you want I buy you a new one?"

"It's not mine," I said, acutely aware the bell for second class might ring any second, and if I wanted him for a date I better get to the point. "It's the library's." I emphasized the two r's in *library* for the sake of his English.

"I will buy."

"No, it's fine." We were in the doorway, Darek holding the door, his fingernails clean and cut square across and his forearm covered in fine, blond hairs, and any second the bell would ring and my time would be up. He stepped back to let me through.

"Take me to the graduation dance," I stammered, my tongue wrapped in flannel and clinging to the top of my mouth like mould on bad peaches.

"Dance?" He glanced at his watch. "Now?" Then he took my hand and pulled me outside, twirled me first one way, and then the other, before letting go to do a pretty good rendition of a Michael Jackson moonwalk.

"Not now," I said, laughing, "Saturday night—at the graduation dance."

The bell rang, cutting off all conversation and causing a major influx of students reeking of cigarettes to come in between us. "I have to go," Darek yelled with a wave, and sailed into the school on the crest of the crowd. "First to learn English and after to talk to a pretty girl."

"Wait! What about Saturday?" But he was already gone. I sank into the brick exterior of the school and slid down to the pavement, scraping my spine every inch of the way. Maybe going to the graduation dance with Darek Dąbrowski just wasn't God's will. Or maybe it was God's will and I'd blown my part. Maybe I'd tried too hard. Maybe I hadn't tried hard enough. Maybe I'd been too shy. Too bold. Too determined to win. If I took this train of thought far enough, I wouldn't be able to move one foot ahead of the other, and so I gave up and defaulted to Ron. The dance was only four hours, four hours out of an entire lifetime. How bad could it be? And Darek would surely be there. That was the clincher; even if he went with some other girl, I could see him and talk, watch him dance from afar.

I wore a shiny pink gown with a sweetheart neckline and short puffy sleeves—the kind of dress I remember Cinderella wearing, the kind of dress I wouldn't buy in a million years. My cousin wore it to her prom three years before. She got it new at JCPenney. She supplied the jewellery as well: a freshwater pearl necklace with matching earrings. The pearls were like little glossy, rippled seeds, the kind of seeds I could see angels picking out of their teeth, if they had seeds in heaven. I had my doubts. How could there be seeds if nothing there ever dies?

"Eleanor! Your date's here," my mother called up from the kitchen the night of the dance. All she knew was that Ron was a Wesleyan and a good friend of Jimmy's.

I was sitting on my bed reading *The Blood of Others*. I finished the chapter I was on—there were only two more pages—then went downstairs.

Ron was clutching a white box in his long, pasty fingers and talking to my mother about pomegranates, whether they still existed or were an exotic Biblical fruit that had become extinct.

It was a topic of conversation only my mother would start up. Much to my relief, his head was bare, and I dared hope he'd left his trademark ball cap with the Montreal Canadiens insignia at home and not out in the car.

Ron handed me the box. Inside was a giant peony-looking corsage that was the same startling colour as Orange Crush. I looked at my dress and then back at the flower. "You got to be kidding."

"What's wrong with it?" he said.

I couldn't believe I was going out in public with this moron. I couldn't believe my parents had agreed to let me go to the graduation dance at all. What about the dancing? The underage drinking? The sex? I should have told them Ron hadn't been to church in weeks, then they might have told me no. Which would have been fine...except for not seeing Darek Dąbrowski.

He reached his hand in for the corsage, but I pulled the box away.

"I'll do it." There was no way I was letting his hands get anywhere near my chest. I speared the pin through double layers of my dress. "Okay, let's get this over with," I said, and led the way to the door.

We went outside and climbed in the back seat of the Impala. Jimmy was behind the wheel and Sandra was fanning herself with an open Duran Duran cassette case. She reached for her purse and pulled out a lipstick once I had reined in my skirt enough to shut the car door. "Here, put this on."

I checked the bottom of the tube and made a face: candy apple. "Forget it," I said, and handed it back.

The dance was in the Lower Lampeq Hall, just two streets over from the Catholic church and kitty-corner to the Knights of Columbus Hall. The parking lot was close to full by the time we got there. Sandra leaned on Jimmy's arm while she tottered over the gravel in her high heels. I shook off Ron's hand and walked in on my own. The music was loud, too loud, even from the far end of the parking lot. The pounding in my chest reminded me of a heart attack, and as soon as we walked through the doors I could feel a headache coming on.

It was much darker inside than out and it took a few minutes for my eyes to adjust to the gloom. The grad dance committee had settled on "Under the Sea" as their theme and split the decorating budget eight ways by the looks of the place. An old fishnet filled with balloons hung from the ceiling with streamers dangling down, and the tables were covered in blue paper with the overhang cut into upside-down waves. Stubby candles on scallop shells, sticks of driftwood, and glass bottles of coloured rocks, the kind you put in the bottom of a fishbowl, were set on the tables to round out the scene.

"What are these supposed to be?" yelled Ron, pulling on a streamer. "Fish turds?"

He and Jimmy went for punch, and I seized the opportunity to take a good, long look around the room. I checked out every table, scrutinized the small groups by the wall, and craned to see past figures on the dance floor. There was no Darek Dąbrowski. There was no one interesting at all. The evening would be a write-off, a complete waste of my time. If I hadn't promised Sandra, I'd go back home and finish de Beauvoir.

Ron set a Styrofoam cup of punch on the table in front of me, but before I had a chance to lift it to my lips he was grabbing my elbow and pulling me out on the dance floor. I followed along like a girl with no sense, when it suddenly dawned on me: they were playing a slow song, and I froze to the spot.

"No!" I jerked my arm out of Ron's grasp and retreated to my seat. I was not ready to slow dance. Just the thought of touching Ron or vice versa made me sick to my stomach.

Sandra kicked me under the table. "Don't be an ass!" she hissed. She grabbed Jimmy's hand and they both stood up. She lowered her head for a quick drink of punch, whispered, "Just do what I do," and then walked away, pulling Jimmy behind her.

I stayed where I was and watched from the sidelines. Sandra wrapped her arms around Jimmy's neck, and he put his hands on her hips. Then she closed her eyes and laid her head on his shoulder while he buried his face in her neck. They started turning in circles, a sort of stiff-jointed, Frankensteinish turning in circles. It was the most ridiculous thing I'd ever seen and way more body contact than I could ever endure with the likes of Ron—that is, unless I was bubble-wrapped or wore head-to-toe chain mail. Lucky for me, I'd watched Lawrence Welk as a kid and knew about other options, options that were still gruesome, on account of I was dancing with Ron, but slightly less so.

"All right." I stood and walked out to the dance floor where I gingerly took one of his clammy hands in my fingertips and tried to ignore the one on my waist, although I could feel the sweat seeping through the dress to my skin, and it made me want to scream. Then I sucked in my gut to maximize the distance between us and thought about *The Blood of Others* and Helene standing by silently as the Germans snatched a Jewish child from her mother.

The second slow dance was no better and the third even worse. By eleven o'clock Ron's breath reeked and it wasn't from punch. He seemed to be mistaking me for someone else, someone who liked him, because he kept inching his chair closer to mine, and on our last slow dance I had to remove his hand from the curve of my backside.

"You know I'll be a rich man in a few years?" he said at the table, leaning in close and breathing his polluted breath into my face.

"You wish." I moved my chair a good two feet away.

He pulled a rectangular something or other out of his shirt pocket and slapped it down on the table. I pretended not to notice. "Go ahead, pick it up."

I hesitated, but finally took it to shut him up. "Wayne Gretzky?" I said, holding the card to the light of the candle and squinting to make out the words.

"A Wayne Gretzky rookie card," he announced with triumph, pounding his fist down on the table and making my hand shake so that a corner of the card tipped into the fire. Flames danced around Wayne's head. I blew on them, a giant breath—the way you blow out candles on a birthday cake—but to no effect. Then I waved the card with short, quick turns of my wrist. The fire burned brighter. Now Wayne had no head and was well on his way to losing his jersey, with the flames edging closer to my fingertips. I threw the card on the floor and stamped on it with both feet. Plumes of black smoke climbed the skirt of my dress and drifted to the ceiling, a few random balloons popped, and people all over the room tipped back their heads to sniff at the air.

"It's okay! Everything's under control!" I said, but no one could hear me over the riffs of electric guitar. I knew the answer to the question the Clash was singing: Go! As fast as you can! Run for your life! I picked up the charred card, now punctured with holes from my pointy high heels, and noticed a band of orange creeping up my shiny, pink hem.

Ron snatched the card out of my hand and pieces of black broke off in his fingers. "You owe me $50,000!" he moaned. That's when the fire alarm went off.

I looked at him. Big, fat tears were rolling down his cheeks. I looked at my dress. The band of fire was spreading out in all directions, wider at the bottom than at the top, like a fiery triangle used for animal tricks at the circus. At the edge of the flame, where the dress was still whole, the fabric glowed red, and then all the little fibres curled in on themselves and disappeared like magic.

"Fire!" I yelled. All I could think was to take off the dress. I screamed and stumbled onto the dance floor, fumbling for the zipper in the back. The tab was in that no man's land between the shoulder blades, which is impossible to reach whether you twist your arms behind your head or reach up from behind your back. I had the floor to myself. Everyone just stood back and stared. It was quite a show, I presume, what with me screaming and fighting to get out of my dress and, as a sideshow, Ron on the floor crying his eyes out. So entertaining were we, it seemed like forever before someone had the bright idea to take the punch bowl and empty it down the front of my dress. There was a loud hiss, like air escaping from a hole in a tire and then thick clouds of smoke.

It didn't take long for the firemen to arrive. They burst through the doors as the last few members of the Class of '83 doused me with their punch. "Out!" they yelled. "Everyone out!" Their eyes darted in all directions, in search of some smoke, a spark or an ember, the smallest flicker to extinguish so they wouldn't feel their trip across town was for nothing.

There on the dance floor, I was an easy target, so I quickly joined the crowd and inserted myself in a line for an exit. I stayed close to the wall and walked like a crab scuttling for shelter, with the back of my dress, the intact side, facing the room. I prayed to God I'd get out the door without my dress reigniting.

The air outside was clean and fresh, and I gulped it down, though every breath hurt like a knife to my chest. The night sky was cut up in a million silver x's, which was probably God's way of telling me what a big mistake it was to come here, and the moon looked down with a mocking grin. The one good thing—there was no sign of Ron, and I had a feeling he was gone for the night. The dance resumed on the stretch of grass outside the hall with the music playing so loud it made the fire alarm sound like background percussion. The rotating lights on the fire trucks painted the dancers with queer red streaks that made them look crazy and out of control, and I felt like the only one with a frontal lobe in a clan of Neanderthals.

No one showed the least concern for me. My flaming dress was history and their minds had moved on to other things. Even Sandra had abandoned me. Out of the corner of my eye, I saw her disappear with Jimmy into the darkness behind the hall.

I borrowed a quarter and went to the pay phone on the corner. The hem at the back of my dress trawled the asphalt, coating the ground with a glistening trail. I called my father to come take me home. He wouldn't come to the phone. He was watching the ball game. It was the top of the eighth and the bases were loaded. He told Jude to tell me it might be a while.

I waited on the grass under a street light, squeezing punch out of my dress, swatting mosquitoes, and wondered why life never went the way I planned. Was it going the way God planned? I had no idea.

After a while a pair of legs emerged from the crowd. They zigzagged across the lawn, smoothly navigating prehistoric man and his creepy contortions and then cut straight across to the parking lot before suddenly making a detour and heading my way. I observed all this in a state of semi-detachment, more concerned with the goings-on in my head than with those in plain sight. I absentmindedly noted those legs had a good four or five inches on other legs in the vicinity—more flagpole than stovepipe and topped by the slimmest hips around. They moved with a purpose, not once pausing to talk or sway to the music. But it didn't register just whose legs they were until they stopped right in front of me, the toes of those shoes mere inches from mine.

"Where is your friend?"

My head jerked back and hit the pole. I blushed a deep red, assuming Darek (Darek, by the way, in a t-shirt and blue jeans with Irving Oil coveralls over his arm; Darek who never came to the dance because he works Saturday nights) referred to my fugitive date. "He had to leave," I said, suddenly taking great pains to rearrange the skirt of my dress to make it look whole.

"No, no. I talk about Kundera. Your friend, Milan Kundera. Or perhaps tonight you have some other friend. Perhaps Tolstoy or Camus?"

I continued to adjust already-adjusted parts of my dress while my mind stalled, trying to think of something witty to say.

"But you are not reading now," Darek said, dropping his work clothes on the ground and reaching for my hand. "So, I think you will dance with me." He pulled me to my feet.

"But I'm soaked." I peeled the dress away from my legs, and under the street light the punch stains made my dress more red than pink.

"I can see this."

"You'll get wet."

"It is a minor problem."

"I don't know how to dance."

"I know." He winked. "But, I do. Come." He laid a hand on the small of my back and pulled me close. The smell of cigarettes and gasoline enveloped us, making me feel heady and very close to danger. One of his legs was advancing, pushing through the wet folds of my dress, and I held my breath in anticipation. He pressed his thigh between my legs, but I didn't pull away. I told myself I'd never see him again. That this was the very last time. That made it all right. That made it desire that never conceived; desire that never ripened into sin. We moved together in slow circles, our bodies close, our movements soft as lapping water.

Just as I was getting up the nerve to lay my head down on his shoulder, someone tapped me on the back. "Your father's here."

I closed my eyes and pressed closer to Darek. My chin was inches from his shoulder, my nose skimming the curve of his neck, hovering over the pale skin that showed above the collar of his t-shirt. I breathed deep, wanting to penetrate the outer layers of gasoline and tobacco to the true scent underneath—his scent. I could smell the metallic odour of sweat, but also the cool, clean scent of what I thought might be dill, but could just as easily have been parsley or oregano. My herb know-how was practically non-existent—all we used at my house were salt, pepper, and vinegar.

Darek pulled away first. "I think it is time you must go," he said. "Your father is waiting."

I stared at him. The street light drenched him in an orange-pinkish glow that made him look like a celebrity—a rock star perhaps or a Hollywood actor. I thought about how he had seen Communists and life in a police state. How he had seen violence and tyranny, but courage and conviction too. Then I thought about how, with those very same eyes, he saw me. It seemed too incredible to be true. I looked deep into those eyes and tried not to think about kissing his lips. I counted the reasons it was wrong to be Catholic in no particular order and I prayed for God to give me strength.

"You do not want to go." He smiled and pushed a stray strand of hair back from my face. "It is all right, Eleanor. We have time. I will see you in the summer, if you like it."

Summer. He'd said summer. Sandra was wrong. He wasn't moving away. We had the whole summer ahead of us. Maybe fall and winter, too. Maybe he had no plans of leaving Lampeq and would be here forever.

Suddenly it was like someone had turned off the power to the whole world. There was no music. No fire alarm. No flashing red lights. Just Darek's voice calling out to me over what seemed a great distance. My heart was pounding in my chest. "I can't," I said. "I have to go."

✽✽✽

JULY 22, 1983

My legs turned to pudding the moment Mr. Gillis told me my mother was on the phone. To appreciate my reaction, you must know my mother never calls the gas station. My mother does not use the phone at all. The phone at home is in the kitchen and she prefers to lie in bed or sleep in her chair, and so it is a gruelling journey into the kitchen, particularly for a woman who has nothing to say.

My mind raced through possible reasons for her call. Did my father lose a leg to a chainsaw? Or get pinned under a tree? Perhaps he'd had a heart attack and was dead before he hit the ground? I forced one foot ahead of the other all the way to the office, willing firmness into my knees and ankles, keeping one hand on the wall as an added precaution. Inside, I sank into a chair and carefully picked up the receiver with both hands. "Mama?"

"Darek, listen. You must come home for supper. I have a splendid surprise."

"What...?" She'd already hung up, but hearing those few words had sent my hopes soaring. I cradled the dead receiver and told myself not to be stupid. How naive to think a sentence or two from my mother could mean she was better. Hadn't I seen her that morning? She was still in bed with the blinds closed and her clothes from yesterday heaped on the floor. And when I told her goodbye she'd said nothing in reply, although, I knew she was awake, her hands working the sheet like she was counting on a rosary. My theory was that she rationed her energy, saved it for what was absolutely necessary, going to the bathroom, for example, or sipping her tea. I accepted her behaviour, considered it good strategy for handling a commodity she held in short supply. My father had come to accept it, as well. He'd given up his staff-sergeant approach a long time ago. He finally could see that it wasn't effective. "To be homesick is a terrible thing," my father insisted when he and I were alone. "But, it does not last forever. If we let her be, it will pass." So we dutifully prepared the meals, taking her a big plate to eat in her chair—although she only nibbled at the edges—kept the house clean, and watched her face for signs of progress. We watched in top secret, seeking out her reflection in the black screen of the TV, peering at her over newspapers and hot cups of tea, and studying her from the window with the curtain pulled as though we watched the street. It was not easy, maybe worse than waiting for the letters from my father.

But my hope hinged on more than the words that she used on the phone. It was how she had said them. There was life in her voice. The slow, dreary monotone was gone and, in its place, her old voice was back—her bird-flitting-through-trees-first-day-of-spring voice. My heart was leaping in my chest.

The next hour crawled, but I could not stop moving. I washed the shop windows, swept out the office, and, emptied the waste cans. I pumped a dollar twenty-six too much unleaded fuel in a Ford half-ton pickup. Finally it was time to go. I hung my coveralls on a hook inside the garage and told Mr. Gillis I'd be back at six.

"Not eating here tonight? I thought I saw your lunch box in the fridge."

"Yes, but my mother's made supper. She wants me at home."

"Some special occasion, is it then?"

"I hope so." I didn't tell him my mother was like the prodigal son—once dead, but now alive; once lost, but now found. I didn't say it, but in my heart I believed it was true.

"Well, take your time. There's no rush. Nobody's buying gas tonight, anyway. The weather's good and the forecast calls for better. Everyone's gone to their camps for the weekend." He gestured toward the cash register. "Your cheque is ready—do you want me to cash it?"

"Yes, sir." I had been working full-time since school ended and earned $300 every two weeks. Fifteen dollars I put in my wallet for cigarettes, but the rest went in the bank. I had over a thousand dollars now, counting the money I'd made before school ended. It was money-in-waiting. Money for plans that would happen sooner, not later, if indeed my prayers had been answered and my mother was better.

I got home and stood a moment inside the back door, revelling in the smell of roast pork with caraway seeds. Pork is my mother's specialty. In Poland, she served it at Christmas and Easter, but not once had she served it in Canada.

My father was already home. He'd left his rifle propped inside the back door. He, too, must have been overcome by the amazing aroma or he would have put his rifle away first and showered later. But today, on what was turning out to be a most astonishing day, people were behaving in unpredictable ways, and my father was indeed in the shower, his strong baritone ringing out over the sound of the water, while his rifle waited outside, unattended. He was singing a Willie Nelson song, one of Big Country 97's finest, and so I presumed Bill had just dropped him off.

Bill had a coyote problem at his place in the country. He said their yellow eyes glowed in the bushes at sunset, and in the daytime when his kids were out in the yard, the coyotes would skulk along the edge of the treeline and sometimes sit in the tall grass and watch them play. One of the bigger animals had dragged the family cat into the woods, the cat's tail sweeping the ground like a grass snake while the children yelled and threw rocks. The coyotes were the reason they had spent the day hunting.

I took off my boots and went into the kitchen. My mother was setting food on the table: dumplings, mushrooms in sour cream, dill pickles, and mixed beans and carrots with a crumb topping. She floated between the counter and table in what looked to be a brand-new dress. Its long, flowing skirt and loose sleeves disguised her thin frame, and the tomato-red shade was flattering, making her face look vibrant and strong. Her hair was clean, but less blond than brown from lack of sun. She wore it braided and pinned across her head like a crown.

"You look beautiful," I said, and kissed her lightly on the cheek.

She set a champagne bottle at my father's place and then turned to kiss me on both cheeks. "Don't just stand there, kochanie. Wash your hands. Tonight we celebrate."

My father entered the kitchen in an undershirt and blue jeans with his wet hair slicked back off his forehead. He slipped an arm around my mother's waist and kissed the nape of her neck. She slipped out of his grasp and continued with the preparations. As she turned back to the stove, her gaze settled on his face and then scrutinized his body. She put down the dishcloth and left the room. A moment later she returned with a dress shirt in hand. "Please, Andrzej," she said.

He took it without comment, obediently pushed his arms in the sleeves, but couldn't pull the material beyond his bulging shoulders. "I guess I need to go shopping," he said, making light of the matter. He threw the shirt aside and sat down at the table, buttering a slice of bread like he was mortaring brick. "First, you must think like a coyote," he said to me, as my mother carried in the roast pork, but I wasn't really listening, my interest more in the meat, in the dark crust and the glistening fat and the juice running down. "You must know where he sleeps, where he eats, where he drinks."

My mother set down the platter and then settled into her chair on my father's right side while I took my place on his left. She spread out her skirt and then smoothed down her hair with both hands.

"Second is patience, because you must be willing to wait for a very long time. Coyotes are clever and very careful. They never let down their guard and can smell a man from two hundred metres away."

My mother handed him the bottle of champagne.

"Coyotes are smart, but a sly man can trick them." My father absent-mindedly pulled out the cork and filled the flutes my mother offered him. "Bill's trick is to cry like a wounded fox." My father set down the bottle, brought his hands to his mouth, and whined in a way that sent chills down my back. "The coyotes are fooled. They approach, hoping for an easy supper—a coyote's version of fast food." My father laughed at his joke, jostled the table and the flutes of champagne. The white tablecloth turned grey where it soaked up the spills.

I studied my father, completely bewildered. He was acting as though nothing was out of the ordinary, as though this wasn't the first supper my mother had prepared in half a year or the first time she'd worn a dress and put on makeup in even longer. And this talk of coyotes made no sense at all. My father had shown no interest in coyotes before. Why was he filling the room with this nonsense? Still, I wasn't overly concerned. The important thing was that my mother was happy—and that the food looked delicious.

My mother placed her hand on my father's arm to silence him and then lifted her glass. "To Poland," she whispered, tears filling her eyes. "To the end of martial law. To going home, at last." She clinked her glass first to my father's and then to mine, and then put the rim to her lips and drank it down in one swallow.

I glanced from my mother to my father, my arm frozen in mid-air. *Martial law was over?* My father was not drinking, either. His arm trembled as he lowered the glass to the table. His hand fell away from the stem and lay there palm up, as though in surrender. "Please, don't do this, Teresa." His voice quivered. "I am the head of this family and I ask you to stop."

"I will not stop." My mother poured herself more champagne and tipped her glass to my father before drinking. "Listen to you talk. Coyotes, of all things! What has become of you? What has become of us? I will not live in this frontier town. My son will not live in this frontier town. We are from Europe, Andrzej. We do not belong here. If God provides an opportunity, it is our duty to go back."

"No!" My father pounded the table. "We cannot go back. It is impossible."

My mother's eyes flashed. "I will go back. Alone if I have to! And I will take Darek with me."

My father stood up abruptly, his chair crashing to the floor. He shook a finger in her face. "What kind of woman are you? What kind of mother? You care nothing for your family. You think only of yourself." His face was red and his eyes feral. Her defiance was like a match to tinder, igniting a year's worth of rage and frustration. I grabbed the knife and moved between them, my hand carving jagged slices of the pork. My father had never touched my mother before, except in love, but this anger was an unknown entity. I was afraid what he might do.

My father hesitated, his nerves taut as guitar strings, but then withdrew. He marched to the door, slamming it so hard behind him the glass shook in the windowpanes.

My mother had aged ten years in that moment of time. Her lips and eyes drooped at the corners and deep grooves cut the skin on both sides of her mouth. She laid her head down on the table and cried. I hid the knife under the edge of the platter and then put my arms around her. "It'll be all right, Mama. It'll be all right." I stared at the pork, my mouth dry as bone.

My mother would not be comforted. She retreated to the bedroom, where her quiet weeping turned to howls. I slumped down in her chair, weak and defeated. I didn't know who I hated more at that moment—my mother for her manipulative ways or my father for his brutal logic. I wished my father had stayed away from Solidarity. I wished we'd never had to come here. I wished I'd never been born. I could see myself in ten years' time—my mother in her orange recliner and me in the kitchen responsible for a lifetime of suppers and dishwashing. I'd never make it to America. I was stuck here forever. I heaped food on my plate: piled on the meat, covered it with sauce, added some dumplings and a scoop of every vegetable. When the plate could hold no more, I sat down to eat. My upper lip curled. The pork tasted like wood. I spit it out on my napkin and tried a mushroom. It was different from our Polish mushrooms, the ones with brown caps and bulb-shaped feet that grew in the forest and tasted like almonds. These mushrooms were grey and tasted like nothing, worse than nothing—like paper. I picked at the food, ate what I could, and then left for the Irving.

I did not walk, so much as drag myself, back to work with my eyes on the sidewalk and my mind deep in thought. My father liked it here, I had no doubt. I think he saw himself as a kind of modern-day cowboy, similar to the ones he watched in Westerns when he was young, a cowboy in a mostly untamed land where people did as they liked, and took their freedom for granted.

My mother was different. Her life would not transplant here, would never transplant here until pears could grow on a willow. In Canada, she was no one special. A woman could survive here without elegance or charm. She didn't need to lavish others with attention, do them favours to get ahead, or work a complicated social network to locate good kielbasa.

In Canada, the stores were full. You just walked in and filled your cart. You could even use credit if you didn't have cash. Or you signed up for welfare and went to the food bank. My mother would die if she stayed here much longer.

I pushed my hands deep in my pockets. My fingers closed around the bills I'd forgot to leave at home. Suddenly, it occurred to me—a solution. I would make a present of my savings to my mother, and she would orchestrate the greatest triumph of her life. My mother would return to Poland. She would cross the ocean, and leave my father and me behind.

✸ ✸ ✸

JULY 23, 1983

I learned the news at Needham's Grocery. I'd gone up for cereal cream, took my bike even though it was close, less than a two-minute walk if I hurried. Mum had supper on the table and there was rhubarb crumble for dessert. We liked to eat it hot from the oven, and the cream was important, not just to keep it from burning your mouth, but also to even out the lumps so each spoonful went down silky smooth and even the bits of rhubarb became soft enough to flatten on the palate.

Needham's was small: two short, narrow aisles with a cash register by the door, cigarettes under the counter, and movie rentals in the back where a freezer used to be.

I put the cereal cream on the counter along with a couple of fuses I picked out of a sale carton. My Pot of Gold box didn't have any fuses. I figured they'd make a nice addition.

Two people were in line ahead of me. The man with the carton of Export A was through in a jiffy, but the woman with a two-litre bottle of Fresca and a bag of Mrs. Dunster's doughnuts planned to be a while. I could tell by the way she leaned across the counter, oblivious to the fact her massive bosom was resting on a tray of homemade date squares and squashing them flat. She got right to the point.

"Did you hear about that Polish woman? She's dead—killed herself!"

The clerk froze with the Fresca bottle raised in mid-air. "My soul!"

"Shot herself in the head." She straightened up, held an imaginary gun barrel under her chin, and pulled the trigger. "Imagine! The boy found her last night when he got back from the Irving."

I stared at the woman, took in her flushed cheeks and bright eyes, the fat trembling at the backs of her arms, heard the thickness of her speech through her saliva, and smelled the musky odour of her sweat. I stood there not moving for what seemed like forever, until my entire body started quivering, the epicentre somewhere in my chest, then travelling along fault lines to my fingers and toes. My hands knocked the fuses to the floor and then, one of my elbows winged out and sent a box of Pixy Stix sailing through the air. The paper tubes arced across the counter in a show of rainbow colours. I stabbed at them with hands like lobster claws, but succeeded only in pushing them onto the floor. "Sorry," I said, "I'm sorry," taking a few more stabs, but, finally giving up and staggering to the door on discombobulated legs, the cereal cream abandoned on the counter. My ten-speed was propped against the front steps. I climbed on and pedalled as hard as I could.

Mrs. Dąbrowski is an only child, the daughter of an aged widow. Her mother cries non-stop for two whole days when she hears her daughter is leaving Poland. After that, every day for two weeks, her mother begs her to stay. She wraps her cold hands with their paper-thin skin around the hands of her daughter and presses them to her heart. "Mama, I must follow my husband," says Mrs. Dąbrowski, fighting back tears. Two months after her arrival in Canada, her mother gets ill. She writes her daughter every day. The letters are short and to the point. They say, "Please come home." Mrs. Dąbrowski argues with her husband. "We have no money," he says. "We came here with nothing." The letters keep coming. The writing deteriorates, but the message stays the same: "Please come home," and then just "Come." Time passes. Mrs. Dąbrowski can't sleep. She can't eat. She cries all day long. But they still have no money to fly her back across the sea. One final letter arrives in the post. "We regret to inform you..." Her mother is dead.

My body was on automatic. By the time I got my bearings, I was already outside Lampeq and on the highway that leads to Saint John. Pulp trucks and transports whizzed by as well as campers and motor homes with Ontario plates headed for Prince Edward Island and points further east. I took the turn-off for Fishtail Light and kept the pace up a long incline.

The screen door slams behind Darek as he enters the kitchen. The first thing he sees is a long twist of apple peel dangling over the edge of the table. Then his high-tops slide out from under him. He grabs for the counter, his legs treading the sticky floor. Blood splatters his jeans, black stains on blue denim. His body caves like a cardboard box as his eyes take in the scene, record the terrifying images like snapshots. He opens his mouth, but no sound comes out.

I heard the crash of waves before I saw them and knew it was high tide. Throwing my bike into the bushes, I stumbled down to the water, my feet sliding on the rock. Images bombarded my mind, each one more vivid than life. I saw Mrs. Dąbrowski with her movie-star hair and hard-working hands. I saw Mr. Dąbrowski with his hands on her shoulders. It occurred to me his posture was all about power. He towered over her, keeping her down. I saw them both outside of St. Gertrude's. He was holding her close, dragging her around like she was a hostage or a wayward child.

Scooping up fistfuls of pebbles, I flung them into the air and watched them pelt the water like a hard rain. The gulls close to shore rose up like a screeching mob. Water leaked from my eyes and nose as I pulled off my sneakers and waded into the frigid water. My bare feet stung, partly from cold and partly from the prick of jagged rock.

Darek hears his parents arguing as he gets home from work. His father is yelling, but his mother just cries. His mother wants to leave, has been threatening to leave for years now. His father begs her to stay, promises to be better. Darek gets a drink of water in the kitchen. There's an empty vodka bottle on the table. Quietly he puts it in the garbage, and then, retreats to his room and shuts the door. The argument escalates. His father has progressed beyond pleading to threats. There's an explosion and the house shakes. Darek runs to the front room. There's an overturned suitcase on the sofa and clothes that belong to his mother strewn all over the room. Then he sees his mother. She's on the floor beside the coffee table, blood streaming from her mouth. Her eyes stare straight up at the ceiling, and he knows even before he puts his ear to her blood-drenched chest that she's already dead. The screen door swings in the wind and his father is gone.

A breaker was barrelling to shore, and I stepped out to meet it. It crashed on the rock, unleashing its white foam against my body and forcing me off balance. The cold cut my body like a thousand knives. In seconds, my entire body was stiff and numb, and the images in my mind were growing fuzzy, blurring like the rock and seaweed that lay beneath the rippled surface of the waves.

JULY 29, 1983

I thought about Darek all the time: washing my hair, doing dishes, walking the beach. Even when I was thinking something else, he was there on the fringes, a constant like the white noise of an air conditioner, the dull ache of a cavity, or the shadow of a tree on the ground. Nighttime was worst with its barrage of images: Darek eating his lunch done up in wax paper; Darek walking down Main Street in winter, his head bent against the wind; Darek in a t-shirt and blue jeans with his Irving Oil coveralls slung over his arm. But mostly I imagined him at the instant he discovered his mother. I wondered who cleaned the room after they took her body away. I prayed all the time it wasn't Darek, but in my mind I saw him there on his knees with a rag in his hand.

I wondered if blind people have nightmares. I wondered if they drive themselves crazy painting pictures in their minds. Or do they not see at all, not even in their minds, and create solely from their other senses? I assumed that'd be less painful. I mean—how does death smell? How does it feel? How does it sound, other than silent? Sometimes I wanted to poke out my eyes.

I biked by Darek's house on the way to the beach. It was out of my way, but I took that route every time. The curtains were closed and no one was ever around. I gave up going by the Irving. He didn't seem to work there anymore. I was afraid he'd left Lampeq. I was afraid he'd gone somewhere far away.

✻ ✻ ✻

The right whales avoided the Bay of Fundy that summer, with only twelve sightings reported by Labour Day. The other whales came back in full force, the fish-eaters like the humpbacks and fins. The right whales don't eat fish, only plankton, remember? Fact number two: 4,400 pounds of it a day. Could that be the reason? The scientists thought so. They said the Bay of Fundy was a hotbed of red tide and they hypothesized that the plankton might be contaminated or just taste so bad the rights couldn't stand it and so they left, retching and gagging, in search of better feeding grounds.

Red tide looked beautiful in a *National Geographic* I found at the library—artistic sweeps of rusty red in dreamy seas of green and blue. I sat at Fishtail Light and scanned for similar waterscapes, but without success. To me, the Bay of Fundy looked exactly the same as it always did: a deep, brooding black.

One of the twelve whales sighted out in the bay was a dead calf. The residents of White Head Island found her washed up on Battle Beach. She had deep gouges down her back and a fluke slashed to ribbons. The scientists recorded her cause of death as contact with a ship propeller.

I don't know how the scientists are so sure that it's red tide keeping the right whales away and not the massive tankers that cut a path straight through the right whale feeding grounds. I'd put my money on the tankers. I'd hypothesize one of the whales finally got smart and said, "Why are we eating in the middle of a highway and risking our lives and the lives of our children?" And the other whales clapped and whistled and some hollered, "Screw this," and others said, "Let's go," and they all turned en masse and swam out of the bay.

PART III

I couldn't think of a good reason not to go to Maritime Bible College—that was the problem. If God had let me in on his plans, it might have opened the door to other options, but, at that point, as always, his will as it pertained to me remained a mystery.

I knew what I wanted to be—a marine biologist who specializes in whales. I also knew that my wants and God's will were rarely the same. Actually, I figured the fact that I had wants at all was like getting the amber light before the red, like getting a mid-term report card from God on how I'm doing in life with all my marks D's. It went without saying that I needed to smarten up or else fail the semester. But how to sit on my hands and will myself not to want? How not to want when every cell in my body was wanting and waiting? And not just for me but for Darek Dąbrowski. How does one even begin not to want without wanting? We're supposed to be content whatever the circumstance—that's what Paul says in Philippians. He says God will supply our needs, but that's as far as he goes. Our wants are not guaranteed. Start listing wants and you're wasting God's time.

But, why does God have to keep everything secret? I felt like I was doing my part—praying for direction, asking for a sign. A whale bursting up through the waves at Fishtail Light would have been a clear indicator. Baleen on the beach would have worked for me, too. It's the silence that's frustrating. I doubt myself. I doubt God. Hey, God! Are you out there? Can you pick up my call?

I can't wait forever and I'm afraid to take risks so I fall back to something safe, something certain—"missionary," for example. I figure I can't go wrong with missionary. I'm not big on travelling and I hate heat and mosquitoes, but I'm sure missionary's a winner as far as God is concerned. And I'd prefer not to be outside of God's will if I can help it. Think Adam and Eve being kicked out of Eden, the destruction of Sodom and Gomorrah, the drowning of the Egyptians in the Red Sea—fall outside of God's will and the effects can be devastating. Or think of Jonah and the whale—step outside of God's will and he'll drag you back kicking and screaming. Better to do nothing at all than set out on one's own. Better to be safe, than sorry. Especially if you're someone like me, someone who's in no position to push my luck, not after my uttermost failing with Mrs. Dąbrowski.

I dreaded meeting my roommate. I was afraid she'd be one of those beauty-queen types—the kind who shampoos twice a day and then follows up with conditioner, styling gel, a blow-dry, and hot curlers before cementing her coiffure in place with VO5 hairspray; the kind of girl who gravitates toward fine washables; the kind who likes picking out paint colours and sewing up curtains; the kind who gives Maritime Bible College its bad name—*Maritime Bridal College*. I always worry about the wrong things.

"Hi! I'm Patricia Tanzer," she said, sticking out her hand when I walked in the dorm room the very first day. "But my friends call me Patty. I play goal."

Posters of professional players in Montreal Canadiens jerseys were lined up shoulder to shoulder on the wall over her bed, staring at me with brazen eyes while a haphazard pile of sticks lay in the corner. But the unmistakable smell of body odour was what really got my attention: the putrid smell of a hundred locker rooms that emanated from the hockey bag at the foot of Patty's bed. My stomach did a triple somersault, but I managed to hold my ground.

"Look, Walter!" said my mother from the doorway. "Eleanor's roommate likes hockey!" She swallowed hard and took a determined step over the threshold, but, then her hand flew to her mouth and she beat a hasty retreat back into the hall.

She hesitated, but then veered right, committing herself to the east wing in a mad dash for what I could only surmise was the bathroom.

"Hi Patty," I said, leaving the door open to let in fresh air. "Pleased to meet you." I extended my arm and gave her a "Let's get off on the right foot" kind of smile. Then I looked out the window over her shoulder to where the curb met the grass in an improvised horizon, focused on breathing through my mouth, and pretended not to hear what sounded like my mother retching her guts out a few doors away.

"Bit presumptuous of you, isn't it?" said Patty, who resembled a fully dressed hockey player even in street clothes. "I'm only joking." She laughed hilariously, like she had just told the funniest joke in the world, and punched me in the arm. "Of course you can call me Patty. We're roomies, aren't we?"

I forced a chuckle that sounded less like a laugh and more like a cat bringing up a hairball, then excused myself and went to join my parents in the hall.

"I guess you'll get used to it after a while," my mother said, breathing deep from the vial of toilet water she keeps in her purse and holds to her nose when we drive past the paper mill in Utopia on our way to the States. After that, my parents couldn't get away fast enough. Once the last of my boxes were deposited outside the door of my room, they were on their way to the car.

I bid them farewell over the revving engine and then marched back to my room alone. "Maybe there's a special room in this place for storing hockey equipment?" I suggested to Patty, who was sprawled on her bed, propped up by pillows, and reading *Sports Illustrated*.

"There's a special room, all right," she said without looking up. "It's right here where my bed is."

"Come on, Patty—it smells rank."

"Au contraire. That is the smell of hard work and success." She eyed me over the cover of her magazine.

"You got to be kidding. The entire room reeks!"

"Give it a week or two and you won't even notice."

"Are you telling me that hockey bag is a permanent fixture?"

"It's $800 worth of equipment. I can't leave it out in the hall."

We argued back and forth while I emptied my boxes onto the mattress. The Pot of Gold chocolate box was at the bottom of the last carton and tumbled down the mountain of sweaters and corduroys to lodge itself at the foot of the bed. I pulled it out and searched its contents. Matches, Band-Aids, fuses, batteries, but nothing for unbearable stench, and now my head was starting to throb. I resisted the urge to stickhandle her hockey bag to the window and heave it through the glass and instead pushed all my clothes to the wall side of the bed, flopped down beside them, told myself that stench was good, and tried to breathe deep and practice not wanting. When Patty finished her first *Sports Illustrated* and started in on a second, without so much as a glance my way, I went outside for fear I'd do something drastic.

The parking lot was full of teary-eyed mothers, stony-faced fathers and hunchbacked progeny weighed down with cartons. I checked out the neighbourhood. There was a trailer park across the road, a 7-Eleven beyond that, a smattering of houses and lots of trees. Trees as in forest, not, flowering ornamentals. Apparently MBC was twenty minutes from the city—driving, not walking—and since I had no car and the bus schedule was almost non-existent, I didn't expect to get there much. No big deal. I'd survive. But one thing I definitely needed was ocean. To calm my nerves and preserve my sanity, I needed regular visits to the bay. The bay wasn't an option. The bay was my lifeline. But how did I get there? I knew it was south so I set off down the main road, took the first road that veered south (Marina Drive, so it couldn't be wrong), and then continued to pick roads that showed promise, confident I'd reach the bay before long.

I ended up at a river, a wasted river that bore a striking resemblance to a stagnant pool of raw sewage. Thankfully, there was no smell of waste—human or other—only wet earth and night crawlers, and I crossed a field to get closer, still hopeful, still positive, although not quite as hopeful as I'd been at the start, before an hour of midday sun had beat down on my head. The river must empty into the bay if I followed it to the end. My feet stirred up hornets and grasshoppers and I walked quickly, waving my arms like a windmill to keep the bugs off my skin. Nearer the river, the grass disappeared and there was only mud, sun-baked mud that was crisscrossed with fissures like overdone cheesecake. And when I crouched down and looked close, there was the gleam of iridescent wing and the nonsense circling of insects on spindly little eyelash legs. I cringed and kept going. If only there was a breeze or the sound of a current and not just this steady drone of insects. And then I was at the edge and could see the river continued on straight a great distance with no bay in sight; I stood there, arms crossed, and took in the view. No secrets here; mud and bugs in plain sight.

I stood there defeated and feeling more homesick than I'd felt the whole day. Why had I come to this place? Why had I come to the college at all? I walked back to the dorm with my shoes caked in mud.

Patty flashed me a Cheshire-cat smile when I entered our room. Her hockey bag was nowhere to be seen, and the only smell was the smoky aroma of hickory sticks.

❋ ❋ ❋

The college had part-time jobs for students. No cash payouts, but a modest discount in room and board in exchange for labour. My job was cleaning bathrooms in the girls' dorm—twelve toilets, six showers, three tubs, twelve sinks, and three tile floors. It was hard work, but I performed the chores with a peculiar relish. I scoured tiles and porcelain with my bare hands until my skin cracked and the smell of Javex radiated from my pores. I worked like it was cruel punishment, until it seemed my back would break and both my arms fall out of their sockets. The gleaming surfaces of a job well done, however, did nothing to allay the guilt I had hoped would fade away once I left Lampeq.

Not that I was a stranger to guilt, but this guilt was like no other. It never let up. It weighed on my heart and lungs like a stone on my chest. When I woke up in the night, it was there, suffocating me so I could barely breathe. I hardly knew Darek. I had no idea what his life was like at home or why his mother took her life the way she did, but I admit it was my fault. I didn't pull the trigger, but I know I was to blame.

I wrote letters to Sandra and poured out my grief. Sandra wrote me back that I was crazy. She said I had absolutely nothing to do with what happened at Darek Dąbrowski's house that night in the summer. She was right about one thing. I did absolutely nothing. How could that be okay?

※ ※ ※

I wanted to like it there at the college. Really I did, and no one had more determination than me. I tried my best to focus on the positive. It wasn't hard. On the surface things looked great. We had daily chapel, impromptu prayer meetings, and talks about God over every meal. Unfortunately, I'm not a person who likes to hover at the surface. I have to peel back the edges to see what lies beneath. Then I grab a shovel and go down even deeper. It's a gift I have or maybe a curse, depending on how you look at it. Sometimes I feel like an archaeologist working away in a corner section of the site grid, digging, scooping, brushing, sifting; hoping to turn up something significant, something precious. I also like to pick at scabs.

What turned up, inevitably, was disappointment. What showed up in the light, when the soft morning sun was seeping like honey around the curtains in the girls' lounge, was a carpet strewed with popcorn and the odd sock or shoe, a coffee table coated with the sticky rings of pop bottles and the latest dog-eared issues of *Vogue* and *Cosmo*.

What turned up were bathtub rings, shit stains on toilets, long blond hairs with inky roots, and if you were the one who cleaned the bathrooms in the girls' dorm—empty blister packs of birth control pills at the bottom of the trash.

So by the time I walked into theology three weeks into the semester, I had resigned myself to the only reasonable conclusion: Jesus didn't live in people's hearts, not in mine, not in anyone's. And God, if he was out there, was retired or on some extended vacation.

I slipped into a left-handed desk close to the front, pulled out my binder, and opened to a bright, clean page. "September 28, 1983," I wrote with painstaking neatness in the upper right-hand corner of the paper, crooking my hand above the words so as not to smear the ink. Then I moved back to the centre, wrote "Theology 102" and underlined it twice. I stared at the page. The perfectly spaced, uniformly sized letters filled me with disgust. I crossed them out with broad strokes of my pen, but those, too, displeased me. The lines were too straight, too precise, and so I took my pen and covered the page in scribbles. The result looked like the work of a two-year-old, but I liked it much better. It suited the way I was feeling inside. On a roll, I took out my Bible and opened to the title page. Beneath the words "Holy Bible," I added "A Work of Fiction" in bold black print and then closed it quick and put it back in my bag.

A solemn-looking boy was the last one through the door. I'd never noticed him before—he must have started the semester late. He nodded to the professor and then paused, his eyes scanning the thirty or so of us mostly crammed into the back of the room. As he stood there, just inside the door, a shaft of sunshine showered him in a golden glow. He stared into the light without squinting or batting an eye, the rays glinting off the metallic end of the pencil that poked through his hair. With the sun trained on him like a spotlight, he crossed the room and took a seat alone in the front.

Dr. Connor, punctual to the point of anal, glanced at his watch and then went to the blackboard and wrote "NAMES OF GOD" across the top with the long side of the chalk.

"In our twentieth century Western culture, personal names are little more than labels to distinguish one person from another, but it hasn't always been this way. In ancient times, names carried special significance. To primitive peoples, the name of a god was magical. It called up the character of that deity, not only in the imagination of the supplicant, but also in the here and now. To say the name of a god out loud was to release the power of the god." He paused to straighten an empty desk beside the aisle while I got a head start on my list and wrote "#1. In absentia."

"The names of the Christian God we find in scripture are also very significant. Each name is like a miniature portrait that captures a particular face of God. In essence, to know God's names is to know God." He raised an eyebrow, then turned to the board and wrote out the letters YHVH. "Now then, let's get to know God a little better, shall we?"

He began to pace back and forth, both hands sliding up and down his tie like the stripes were strings on a bass stick and he was practising a number in the privacy of his basement. I wondered how many times he had given this lecture. Fifty? Five hundred? Elohim, Adonai, Theos, Kurios, Despotes... the list of names went on and on. My empty page quickly turned into a mess of ink smears and scribbles. My eyes darted between my paper, the professor, and the boy in the front row. He listened intently to the lecture, but wasn't writing down a single word. He didn't even have paper out on his desk. No sign of a tape recorder, either. I stared at him a moment, baffled, and missed out on the next four names.

Twenty-some names of God later, Dr. Connor smoothed his tie flat against his chest. "Any questions? Comments?"

I dropped my pen with relief and circled my right thumb into the back of my writing hand to massage the cramped muscles. The boy in front put up his hand.

"Mr. Carpenter?" The professor cocked his head to one side and folded his arms across his chest.

I stopped rubbing and leaned forward to hear.

"You haven't included 'Mechoqeq' on your list, sir."

"Define 'Mechoqeq' please, Mr. Carpenter."

"Mechoqeq is a Hebrew word used throughout the Old Testament. It translates as lawgiver or judge and conveys the idea of God's absolute sovereignty over his creation."

I sat up straight in my chair and studied the boy. He still looked to be glowing, but not from sunlight, because the sky had clouded over and it was raining outside. Don't get me wrong, he wasn't glowing like neon or with the clean, white light of a fluorescent bulb. No, his was a subtle glow, like the translucent petals of a ghost plant or the glow in the dark dial on my alarm clock. Otherwise, he seemed perfectly ordinary, although lacking in fashion sense in these striped train overalls and red suede Puma sneakers, clothing Sandra would have called ridiculous but which I considered possible marks of a higher man, a man who'd set his mind on things above, not on earthly things.

Dr. Connor smiled for the first time all class. "Well done, Mr. Carpenter. We shall add Mechoqeq to our list." With a flourish of his arm, he squeezed the word in along the bottom of the chalkboard. "Everyone take that down before you go."

Carpenter was the first one out the door. By the time I reached the corridor he was gone. "Who is that Carpenter guy?" I asked another girl from class.

"John Carpenter? He's an MK."

"An MK?" I raised my eyebrows.

"A missionary kid. He was born in Canada, but has spent

the last few years in Timbuktu. Or is it Kathmandu?" She shrugged her shoulders. "I don't know. Somewhere far away. His parents are missionaries there." She paused. "I hope he doesn't think he was doing us any favours in there." She jerked her head in the direction of the classroom. "Twenty-three names of God are plenty, if you ask me."

※ ※ ※

John Carpenter and I shared one other class—Synoptic Gospels. He had a penchant for motorcycles. Peach yoghurt was his favourite, but he would settle for vanilla when the peach ran out. He showered before breakfast, worked in the library Monday through Friday between seven and ten, and preferred Coke to Pepsi. He did dish duty in the kitchen three nights a week. It was all evidence I committed to memory, possible clues to a type of person I had never known the likes of up to now, a person I didn't think existed anywhere in the world, a person who was truly good.

When I was four or five, my mother and I would play this game on her bed. The rules were simple. I'd say, "One day Mum laid on me," and my mother would roll over on me. When I struggled and moaned she'd roll off. The relief was exhilarating. I made her play it again and again. Finding John, felt almost the same way. Suddenly I could breathe again. The panic was gone.

I still thought of Darek, just not as much as before and after more than two months of insomnia, I was finally sleeping through the night.

※ ※ ※

By October, there were still major gaps in the John Carpenter puzzle, although searching for pieces was my new, favourite pastime. I was always on the lookout. My big break came at Student Union. John avoided Student Union as a rule, so the minute I saw him I knew it must mean something big. I moved closer to the front and judiciously picked a chair that would give the best view.

The first issue raised was the budget surplus. MBC had the biggest enrolment ever, which meant the Student Union had money coming out the yin-yang and was looking for input on how to use it. There was no shortage of suggestions from the floor, and the Student Union secretary listed all the options on a giant writing tablet with black marker.

"Pizza party."

"New books for the library."

"A Nautilus machine."

John's right temple began to throb.

"Invest it in equities and at the end of the year distribute the assets."

John couldn't contain himself. He sprang from his seat, and catapulted through the crowd to the very front of the room, where he raged like a hurricane, the rest of us cringing in our seats. "Don't you people read the newspapers or watch the news? Don't you know about the famine in Ethiopia? Two hundred thousand people have already died of starvation. Another eight million are this far from death's door." He held up a hand with his index finger a hair from his thumb. "Maybe you live in your cozy, Christian cocoons oblivious to the outside world. Or maybe you know and just don't care. Jesus said we are his brothers and sisters if we hear God's word and put it into practice." His eyes were like high beams searching out every section of the room. "I don't see any of Jesus' brothers or sisters here today."

The room was quiet and you could hear the buzz of the fluorescent lights overhead. John waited a moment and then walked straight down the aisle and out the main door. The lights flickered and sizzled as he passed underneath them.

My heart was pounding so hard it felt like any second it might burst through my chest and plop onto the red carpet at my feet. "I second John's motion," I said in a trembling voice, my sweaty hands slipping on the cold metal back of the empty chair in front of me.

"What motion?" murmured Rooster, the Student Union president, staring at the swinging door with a stunned look on his face like he didn't know what hit him.

"The motion to donate extra money to Ethiopian famine relief." My face and neck, arms and chest—every inch of my body—were burning up, and I pulled on my collar to let in cool air.

He tore his eyes away from the exit and scanned the crowd. "What good is pizza if a man loses his soul?" he said with a wan smile. "All right. All in favour of the extra money going to famine relief, raise your hands. Opposed?" He waited a moment, but not a hand went up. "Looks like it's unanimous. Motion carried."

✳ ✳ ✳

I was conceived in sin and out of wedlock, which were two marks against me right from the start. My mother denies the latter. She says I was born three weeks early, but I don't believe it. I came out of the birth canal weighing a hefty ten pounds, twelve ounces. And I've seen my baby pictures. There's one of me asleep in the hospital bassinet with pink barrettes holding down great clumps of brown hair and my swaddled body squashed between the two sides. If I'd been born any later, I'd have had baby teeth and been started on solid food. But that's my mother's specialty—rewriting history to support her sunny view of the world, and who am I to begrudge her a few, basic facts, especially when her version of events gives her such pleasure. I don't see the point so long as I know the truth and God doesn't mind.

The first memorable event of my life was the arrival of my brother, Jude. I wasn't quite three, but I remember the details—namely the overwhelming sense of betrayal. I was underneath the Christmas tree at the time, flat on my back and staring up through the branches at the tinsel and admiring its shimmer and how the effect was much the same as falling snow beneath street lights. I jumped up at the sound of my mother's voice. She was standing in the doorway of the living room with her winter coat still on. Jude, who was bootied, capped, sleepered, sweatered, snowsuited, hooded, and not very happy, was making his debut. One glimpse of my mother with that screaming infant in her arms and I ran straight to my father, immediately aware that life as I knew it, had definitely taken a turn for the worse.

My mother secured the squirming bundle under one arm, eased herself onto the couch with the other, and then motioned me over. I buried my face in my father's legs. "Honey," she called, and promised me a new book for my "Adventures" collection.

The Adventures of Old Mr. Toad? I was not above bribes. She nodded and I sidled over, my lips in a pout. She pressed a stick of Juicy Fruit into my hand. I removed the foil, folded the gum into thirds, and popped the whole thing in my mouth. My tongue floated in squishy sweetness, but my heart stayed hard and bitter.

"Lennie, this is your brother, Jude." She pulled back the blanket like she was opening a present and didn't want to tear the paper.

I was appalled. Jude was the ugliest creature I'd ever seen, all red and wrinkly, with a mouth like a goldfish. "Take him back!" The force of my words shot the gum out my lips and straight at my brother, where it attached to his head like a blood-sucking leach. I admired the effect with unbridled glee, and would have been captivated for hours if my father hadn't spanked me hard and sent me to bed without any supper.

Hating Jude was only one of a long list of sins that would mar my childhood self. I picked my nose and wiped it on the couch; said "shit" and "bastard" in my mind, chipped paint from the windowsills (lead-based to boot), trick-or-treated in the middle of summer when my mother refused to give me money for candy, and sometimes when I was alone in my room, I'd pleasure myself with objects stuffed in my underwear—foam curlers worked best.

Since then not much has changed except for some 750 Sunday-school classes, 250 youth group meetings, 1,600 church services, 300 junior choir practices, 16 weeks of camp, 60,000 prayers to God, and two complete readings of the Old and New Testaments plus Genesis and Exodus for the third time around. Oh, and my list of sins has grown even longer. I divide them into categories: the sins of omission and the sins of commission. Sins of omission are my specialty. They're the things you know you should do, but don't. The really bad ones are recorded in my head in bold type. The worst ones are recorded in all caps, bold type, and highlighted in chartreuse marker. Darek's mother's suicide is lit up with red lights because I could have taken all my money and bought her an airplane ticket back to Poland. I could have helped her pack a suitcase and delivered her safely to the women's shelter. When Darek asked, I could have agreed to see him in the summer. Then I could have done something. Then I would have known.

✳ ✳ ✳

After Student Union, I was too scared to do anything more than steal glimpses at John from across a room and Patty wouldn't stop hounding me about it.

"I'm tired of watching you worship this guy from afar," she said one night after we'd both gone to bed. She'd woken me when she got in late from her hockey game too excited to sleep. Our team had played the Wesleyan college and won 4-3. She'd stopped thirty-seven shots on goal and suddenly felt like an expert on everything. "If you ask me, you're going about this all wrong. I've had a few boyfriends in my life so I think I know what I'm talking about."

I rolled my eyes in the darkness. "Boyfriend" was such a juvenile word. It didn't begin to describe the relationship John and I shared in my mind. "It's not a boyfriend I want," I told her.

"What?" She was silent a moment. "What do you want, then?"

"Oh, I don't know. A meeting of minds, a meeting of hearts; to know in full and be fully known."

She hemmed in disgust. "Would you please speak in English. Anyways, I can tell he's interested in you, so let me give you a word of advice 'cause you are blowing this big time. When there's an empty seat beside him, take it. Don't walk by like you're the Queen of Sheba. And when he sits beside you, talk to him for Pete's sake. Don't get up and leave. And go to his volleyball games, why don't you? It's almost the end of the semester. Time's running out. Why won't you go for it?"

I turned on my side and lay facing the wall. There was a whole list of reasons that only got bigger with each passing day. "I'm not good enough, for one thing. Can't you see how good he is?"

"Good? He's not even nice."

"No, no. He's not nice-good. He's truth-good and justice-good."

"How 'bout we fill the bathtub and see if he walks on water?"

"Patty!"

"All right, just tell me something," said Patty. "What did you ever do that was so bad?"

I didn't answer.

"Oh yeah, I keep forgetting. You're a mass-murdering psychopath."

I shrugged my shoulders under cover of the blankets. Close enough.

"Lennie!" She grabbed a slipper off the floor and threw it at my bed.

"Oww! Would you leave me alone and go to sleep?"

"You know I'm right. You'll be sorry if you don't do something."

I rolled onto my back and watched the shadows of passing cars slink across the ceiling and walls. It took me a long time to fall asleep and in the night I had a dream. I dreamt there was a terrible storm with artillery-like thunder and the kind of lightning that turns darkness to day. Meanwhile, I was asleep in the hold of a boat. I knew nothing of the storm and was oblivious to the wrenching of the small vessel on the waves. Suddenly hands seized me by the shoulders and gave me a shake. I awoke to find Dr. Connor, Pastor Martin, and Darek Dąbrowski all hanging over me with wild eyes and pinched faces. "Are you the one who's brought us this trouble?" they cried out in one voice. Before I could make my defence, they seized my arms and pushed me up the ladder to the deck. Together, they hoisted me overboard. My brain shut down the instant I hit the water, my muscles stiffened, and my blood froze. Down, down, down I went. My arms fanned the sea in search of a warm, wall of flesh; my fingers probed for a handhold, a knob of crust on smooth skin; my toes strained, not for the sea floor, but for the springy surface of a fat tongue. Thoughts drifted through my mind like icebergs, barely reaching my awareness. Thoughts of nothing: blackness; silence; cold; and desolation.

Suddenly a strong hand closed around my wrist, pulled me straight up out of the water and set me down on solid ground. I coughed and wiped the water from my eyes to find John standing beside me, John standing firm in a field of water with whitecaps breaking against his thighs. And me, right next to him, steadfast as a column of rock rising out of the sea.

✳ ✳ ✳

The first Thursday in November was perfectly normal, as was the whole week, and I was expecting nothing out of the ordinary as I sat in the dining hall eating my supper. Actually, I expected the meal to be downright boring as I was there way before the time John typically eats. But it couldn't be helped. I'd skipped lunch to cram for a theology test and my stomach refused to suffer the pangs of hunger any longer, and so, unless I wanted to pass out from low blood sugar, on this one occasion, there'd be no dragging out my meal until he arrived, no eating my peas one at a time, no peeling my orange, eating it section by section, sucking out the juice before chewing the pulp, no seconds of dessert, and then once he arrived, no watching him eat like a machine, dutifully shovelling the food into his mouth, barely stopping to chew, let alone taste or smell, as though eating was no more than a chore that he wanted to get through as quickly as possible.

As I bent my head for a spoonful of soup, a figure loomed across the table. I hesitated, spoon hovering in mid-air to look: John. The spoon slipped from my hand and back into the bowl with a clatter. Tomato splattered my blouse. I pulled some napkins from the holder and dabbed at the stain until the paper disintegrated and stuck in pieces to my front like a tissue collage. I gave up at that point and tucked the remaining shreds under my plate.

John said grace while I turned my attention to the Salisbury steak. You'd have thought I was doing brain surgery the way I was cutting up that hamburger with such intensity and precision and all the while racking my brain for something to say, something acceptable that John would approve of, because if John liked me it would change everything. If John liked me, I would take it as proof that I wasn't so bad and I was desperate for proof, because, I had decided that being saved was more complicated than I'd always been led to believe. I was beginning to think that having Jesus come live in your heart might be something akin to selling a house and putting a 'for sale' sign on the front lawn was only the beginning. Maybe Jesus didn't automatically buy up each property that goes on the market. Maybe he gets to pick and choose. Maybe his acceptance comes with conditions, say the number of bedrooms or the surface area in square feet; perhaps whether or not there's a finished basement or a pool in the backyard.

Maybe he doesn't like a place that needs too much work. One thing was for sure, there was more to being saved than I had been taught at church.

John opened his eyes and started buttering his bread. "Have I offended you in some way?"

"No, no. Why would you say that?" My eyes were glued to my plate. How small to cut Salisbury steak before I looked like a moron?

"Because I get the feeling you're avoiding me."

I put down my knife and fork and gazed at the inspirational poster on the wall over his shoulder. It showed a solitary skier in a vast plain of white with Proverbs 3:5-6 printed across the bottom. I took a deep breath and forced myself to look him straight in the eye. "Will you cross-country ski with me on Saturday? I hear there are some good trails around here." My fingernails were digging into my palms beneath the tabletop and I could feel trickles of blood running down. Or else it was sweat.

John looked at me thoughtfully. "All right. After lunch? About one o'clock?"

"Good." My fingers relaxed, tapped out a lively rhythm in my lap. I didn't own a pair of ski boots, had never strapped a pair of skis to my feet. They seemed like minor details at the time.

✻ ✻ ✻

I looked through the window as the first light of dawn strung itself across the horizon in salmon-coloured crepe streamers. But my attention was less on the sunrise and more on my bowels as I pondered the need for a third trip to the bathroom in less than an hour. I always get diarrhea when I'm nervous and this was the most nerve-racking day of my life if I didn't count the time in grade three I got home from school to find no one at home and a mixing bowl and dry ingredients laid out on the counter. My mother was always at home so an empty house could mean only one thing: the rapture had come and I'd been left behind. I spent an agonizing two minutes contemplating whether or not I should take the mark of the beast when the Antichrist rose to power, and then my mother walked through the door with a carton of eggs. But that was only two minutes. This was two nights, one and a half days so there's no real comparison.

I still couldn't believe I had a meeting with John. "Meeting" was the word I finally settled on—"date" seemed too presumptuous and "appointment" suggested money changing hands. "Meeting" was nice and neutral, while at the same time, completely accurate. I didn't see how I could go wrong with a word like "meeting."

I filled those last five hours as best I could. Cleaning the bathrooms took up a big chunk of the morning, which was also convenient, in light of my bowels. After that I changed my bed and did the laundry. By noon I had painted all the runs in my pantyhose, sewed two buttons onto a blouse, pushed back my cuticles, plucked my eyebrows, trimmed my bangs and got my library books renewed. It was my most productive Saturday morning ever.

I skipped lunch out of deference to my bowels and started to dress at twelve twenty-five, although, truth be told, I didn't dress myself so much as let myself be dressed by half the girls on my floor. I don't think it was an act of Christian charity so much as an attempt on their part to justify this momentous event—the most eligible bachelor at MBC was going skiing with Eleanor Hansen. I had to look worthy of his attention or they might have to think and rework their world views. I tried to convince them they were wasting their time; that looks were irrelevant and John only cared about the inside, but they wouldn't believe me. And so, there I was in pink ski pants and a coordinating pink jacket, courtesy of a girl two rooms down, a fuchsia scarf, hat, and gloves donated by three different sources, but all perfectly matched with painstaking care, and make-up slathered on with a trowel by a girl who spent her spare time at cosmetic counters getting free makeovers and whose room looked like a kindergarten art class with paint by number trays of blush and eye shadow laying around.

I kicked everyone out at ten to one and inspected my reflection in the mirror. I looked like the Snow Queen meets the Sugar Plum Fairy meets the cover girl of Vogue. I scrubbed my face clean with a wet towel. Then I noticed the way my long hair puffed out beneath the brim of the toque—make that Snow Queen meets the Sugar Plum Fairy meets the Indian princess. I pulled off the hat—no more Indian princess—and searched Patty's closet for the Russian fur cap with earflaps she'd picked up at Frenchy's. It didn't match the outfit, but it made me look exotic in a secret agent sort of way, which was more to my liking, and would also ward off hypothermia as an added bonus. Five minutes to one—time to go. I pulled Patty's skis out from under her bed and went to meet John.

As I rounded the main building, he came into view. I stared at him unabashedly, soaking in every detail of his appearance as excitement danced pirouettes inside my stomach. He wore a navy sweater tucked into bright yellow ski pants with the suspenders down and swinging back and forth as he worked over a ski with firm strokes of his arms. Suddenly a small, white bird no bigger than a sparrow swooped down from a tree and lit on his shoulder. I squinted to see better. It was definitely a bird. There was no mistaking the little curve of its head and the gently rounded back. It spread its wings and then neatly folded them, tucking them in against its body. I watched for a moment and then tentatively moved a foot forward, setting it down ever so slowly, ever so softly. Then the other. Right, left, right, left. My footsteps echoed like a marching army across the hard snow and the bird flitted away.

John turned around. "Excellent skiing weather!" he called. "The snow is perfect—firm and smooth."

"Hey!" I said, coming up alongside him. "What's up with the bird?"

"What bird?"

"The one that was just on your shoulder a minute ago."

The corners of John's lips twitched. "You got to be kidding." I shook my head. "No. It was a bird. I saw it." My eyes searched the nearby trees for a flicker of white feather.

John looked at me with a funny look on his face. "It's a bit blustery here next to the building. You must have seen the wind blowing the snow around."

"I know what I saw," I said, driving Patty's skis into a snow bank.

"I'm telling you, there was no bird." He shrugged his shoulders and turned back to his skis.

I opened my mouth to reply, but stopped myself just in time. There was no point in arguing with him, just like there's no point in arguing with God. You can only lose. I kicked a chunk of ice into the brick wall. It shattered into sparkling diamond.

"Do your skis need wax? You can use mine." He pointed to a wax cylinder on the same picnic table that supported his skis.

I didn't see how wax could hurt and on the off chance it might help, I pulled a ski out of the snow and went to work.

"Hey! Don't wax the ends. Just the fish scales." He stopped waxing and put a hand on his hip. "You've never waxed skis before, have you?"

I hung my head. "No. To tell you the truth, I've never actually skied. At least not until yesterday when Patty gave me a quick lesson out in the soccer field." I hadn't planned on telling him that, had hoped that with my natural athleticism I could pass myself off as a seasoned skier, but, now, in his presence, I found myself forced into utter transparency. I resumed waxing, but this time just the fish scales and with my body angled away from him to hide my red face. John didn't go back to his waxing. My peripheral vision wasn't picking up any movement from his direction at all. I imagined him standing there, his lips a tight line and a pulse throbbing at his right temple. When the suspense got unbearable, I turned to face him square on. "You mind, don't you?"

"Mind what?"

"That I've hardly skied."

He gave me a sharp look. "What I mind is being misled."

"Well, excuuuse me." I grabbed the skis in one hand, the poles in the other and backed away from the table. "I'll give you a call once I qualify for the Olympics."

"Wait!" he said. "That's not what I mean. Anyone who can walk can cross-country ski. What I mean is this isn't about skiing, is it?"

I stopped in my tracks. "What?"

"I don't intend to hurt your feelings, but there's something you need to know about me."

I stood there immobilized, barely daring to breathe for fear of missing out on a word, no a syllable, of his confession.

"When I agreed to ski with you today, it was because I like skiing, that's all. I'm not looking to get married."

I stared at him, my lower jaw hanging down around my knees. "Me, neither," I sputtered, which was technically true, but, only because I knew we had no future together. We were totally different, two distinct species, like the little mermaid and the handsome prince or Albert Einstein and an anencephalic, but, no sooner were the words out of my mouth than an image popped into my mind, a picture of me walking down an aisle in a long, white dress. The bodice was tight, but the skirt draped over my hips in soft folds and my legs pushed through the rich fabric like they were wading through water. And the man waiting for me at the end of the aisle? None other than John, his face aglow with adoration. How could I not love a man who put honesty first? And now, more than ever, I wanted to know him. I wanted us to be close, close enough for truth to surround us like a shield.

He pulled up his suspenders and slipped on his outer shell. "Good, because God has bigger and better plans for each of us.

Come on. It'd be crazy not to ski on a day like today. And don't worry about waxing. Your skis have a no-wax base."

I dropped Patty's skis on the snow and stuck my feet in the bindings. It took me several tries to zero in on the first latch because my hands were shaking so badly. By then John had whizzed past the tennis courts and was halfway to the woods. When I had the second one fastened, John was a yellow beacon at the tree line.

"How far do you think you can go?" he said when I finally caught up to him.

"Who knows? I can handle forty-five minute runs, if that means anything."

"You should be able to manage the loop, then. It's about five kilometres the whole way around; winds through the woods to the power lines and then follows the railroad track back to the college. There's one steep hill, but you don't have to ski down it."

I trusted his judgement and followed along like a faithful old dog while he forged a path through the unbroken snow. The trail hadn't seen any traffic since our last snowfall—a big one, too. The spruce and fir boughs were still weighed down with the stuff and the snow muffled all sound just like thick, heavy drapes. Even the swish-swish of the skis sounded far, far away and I felt transported to some ancient cathedral with the tree branches forming a high arch overhead and sunlight breaking through in straight lines to dissect the shadows.

"Eagle's nest." John pointed to a crown of sticks propped atop a towering tree.

Yes, but, no sign of an eagle, although I dutifully scanned the treetops in search of one. I don't know my birds like I know my marine mammals. I didn't ask if eagles fly south for the winter. Sometimes it's better to say less than more. Not to mention that I doubted my ability to talk and ski at the same time. I was already short of breath trying to keep up and sweating profusely beneath my Russian fur cap.

"I need to get my heart rate up for this to count as an aerobic workout," he said about fifteen minutes into the woods. "I won't be long."

"OK. Don't let me stop you." But he didn't hear. He was already way ahead. Then I blinked and he was gone, which made me realize that what I was doing was in fact closer to plodding than skiing and probably nowhere near as fun. I lifted a foot and tried to run. The front of my ski came off the ground, but then dropped clumsily onto its mate. I tripped and fell sideways into the snow. I got up and tried it all over again. Then again. And again. Finally, it dawned on me—skiing was like skating, not running and I was no novice to skating. I had skated every winter all through elementary school. In fact, I'd even earned some skating badges. Well, not exactly, but reasonable facsimiles copied with painstaking precision by Deanna, my best friend before Sandra, who moved away in grade eight, took figure skating from the time she could walk and wore furry blue skate warmers. She always got the best part in the end of season figure skating shows. In Snow White and the Seven Dwarves—she was Snow White. In The Wizard of Oz—she was Dorothy. But she never rubbed my nose in it. On the contrary, with unfailing patience, she taught me everything she knew, or at least, as much as I was capable of learning. Last I heard she was with the Ice Capades—a six of clubs in an Alice in Wonderland number. She was Anglican, not Baptist. Yes. Now, I was getting it. My body was settling into a rhythm. Arms and legs moving in harmony. Kick, kick, kick, kick. Faster, faster. I was a symphony of movement, and it felt amazing. Then my hip muscles caught fire and I reverted to a walk.

When I caught sight of John's yellow jacket darting through the trees, I resumed my new-found talent, only, with considerably less vigour, hoping to amaze him. Apparently he didn't notice, or, noticed but didn't care, because all he said was, "The trail gets better up ahead" which made me want to kick my ski into his ankle or whack him in the back of the head with my ski pole—if only I'd had the speed and could keep up. "Am I doing this right?" I called.

He stopped and looked at me, his eyes scrutinizing me from top to bottom. "Looks like skiing to me."

"Real skiing?" I asked.

"What other kind is there?"

I punched him in the arm, momentarily forgetting his special status, and broke ahead. We started to alternate back and forth between walking and skiing, with me setting the pace.

At the first major incline, John stopped and dug his poles into the snow while I resisted an urge to fall on my knees from utter exhaustion. Five K runs had been no preparation for this gruelling workout. I should have been running marathons in lead boots.

"The best way to climb a hill is to sidestep your way up," he said.

I shaded my eyes and looked up, way way up, to the top of the hill. Did I say hill? It was actually more like a mountain. "Which way to the ski lift?" I was serious.

"You can do it." He turned his skis perpendicular to the hill and demonstrated the technique. Looked easy, but when I tried to do the same, my feet resisted and were bent on doing the opposite of what I told them. The skis wavered, crossing first in front and then in back. When I gingerly lifted a ski to detangle myself, my weight shifted and sent me slip-sliding back down the hill. Great—now I was comic relief.

"Keep trying," he called, already at the top.

Keep trying. I rolled my eyes and wondered what had ever possessed me to ask him to go skiing in the first place. We could have played badminton in the gym and I might have won. We could have walked circles around the trailer park. We could have gone to the library and read Dietrich Bonhoeffer on the Trinity. We could have gone to the dentist and had all our teeth pulled or any one of a number of other activities all of which would have been less painful than this. Never mind. I would make it to the top of that hill if I had to crawl up on my hands and knees and I would do it wilfully and in blatant disregard of proper ski etiquette.

Five hundred thousand sidesteps later, not to mention the two hundred or so leg splits and a few dozen falls, I reached the top. The skis couldn't come off quick enough.

I dropped, bum first in the snow and lay flat on my back in snow angel repose. Snow had worked its way down my neck, up my sleeves, and into every possible opening in my ensemble, including under my ear flaps and I wondered, but only briefly because I was too exhausted to worry properly, about the risk of hypothermia. Every muscle in my body yearned for a hot pack and I dreaded the morning when I knew I'd wake up covered in bruises and my arms and legs locked in the fetal position. I'm not complaining—just underscoring the pain and humiliation I was willing to endure for the sake of John's company. Although to be honest, by that point my enthusiasm was beginning to wane and I'd have sold my birthright for a drink of water, if I had a birthright—I was pretty sure I didn't.

John skied over and stopped like a hockey player, showering every square inch of my body in a blanket of snow. I grabbed his pole in retaliation and almost pulled him over. My sense of humour was wearing thin.

He went back to racing end-to-end across the hilltop while I recouped and thought about surgical suites and how they weren't much different than this—white and cold, but, with beeping, not bird chirps. Not that I'd ever been in a surgical suite in real life, but I always watched St. Elsewhere and even Trapper John on occasion.

"How do you like it?" John asked, coming back when I pushed into long-sitting. He spread his arms wide to encompass the ridge. "I call it Checkmate."

I stood up to see what he was talking about. The top of the hill, long and narrow like a football field, had been crisscrossed with ski tracks so it looked like a checkerboard. So that's what he'd been doing while I was struggling up the mountain: playing etch-a-sketch in the snow. I studied this work of art as I stood there rubbing my hips and wondered what it meant, beyond the obvious—that he was bored and I was wasting his time. "It's lovely," I said. Why hadn't I asked him to collect bottles for missions or peel potatoes for the soup kitchen? God knows that's probably how he spends a typical Saturday afternoon. Or why hadn't I kept my big mouth shut and never asked him to do anything at all? What was I thinking? I must have been out of my mind.

"Come on," he said, motioning me to follow. "Now's your chance to ski downhill. You do know how to snowplow on skates?"

I should have called it quits then. I should have listened to my aching limbs, plugged my ears and followed our tracks back to the school, but no. My paranoid mind had to misconstrue his probably innocent and in no way ill-intentioned question as a challenge. Snowplow on skates? Was he kidding? The forward snowplow was a requirement for CanSkate badge number two. It was one of the first things Deanna taught me—without the advantage of boards, it was the only way to stop on the river. "Come on. Let's go."

John went first, proficiently wedging his way down the slope in a way that looked so slow and so safe it was boring. At the bottom he did another one of his hockey player stops, this time shooting snow way higher than his head in a manoeuvre that amazed from even my vantage point. "Now it's your turn!" he said.

Now that I'd been on my feet a few minutes, my legs were quickly coming unhinged. I tried not to think about them disconnecting at the hips and leaving me a torso neck deep in the snow; tried to imagine them as sturdy two-by-fours screwed into my pelvis; I also blocked out thoughts of a hot bath, hot chocolate with marshmallows, and cinnamon buns hot from the oven. I was cold. What can I say? I eased my way to the edge, crouched forward like an Olympic skier at the starting gate, and then gingerly pushed off with my poles. I achieved what seemed like breakneck speed in a matter of seconds, with my head fighting to stay on and my arms and legs flailing in all directions. My poles became weapons of self-destruction, two sticks circling my head and threatening to take out both my eyes or penetrate my skull for an instant lobotomy. I wrestled them to the ground and plunged the tips into the snow, holding them down as though driving spears into a man-eating shark. They finally surrendered to their fate at which time I threw in the snowplow to clinch my survival. "Piece of cake," I said at the bottom, with a small bow and flourish of my poles. I felt great and completely pain-free. I guess my near-death experience had released some endorphins. Calling it quits and heading back to the dorm was suddenly the last thing on my mind.

Ten minutes later the trail spit us out on a cliff and I was berating myself once again for my horrible judgement. I should have known the worst was yet to come; that we were still on the mountain, that the little slope we'd come down before was a mere hiccup en route to the bottom, and that sooner or later we'd have to make up the distance.

"We're at the halfway point." John beckoned with a sweep of his arm. "And the way down's over here." I followed him to the back of the ridge where my eyes bugged out at the sight of the hill. The slope was a killer, steep as a soft-serve with a vertical rock face on one side and a drop-off on the other. "There's a sharp turn to the left about a hundred metres down, but then it's straight going the rest of the way."

I was already taking off my skis. I wouldn't ski down that hill in a hundred years, not for a million dollars. He nodded as though to say he supported my decision. "I'll be waiting for you at the bottom." I watched him work his way down the hill. He wasn't wedging this time. He was flying. Not me. I was tottering down the slope like an arthritic granny with my skis in one arm and my poles in the other. The crust was hard and icy so I dug in my heels, stayed low to the ground and progressed at a rate of one step per minute. I was doing just fine until about halfway to the turn when my bindings caught on some alders and pulled me off balance. Before I knew what was happening, I had slipped backwards and then, I too, was flying—on the slippery seat of my ski pants. Shrubs and trees whizzed by in a blur. Skis and poles became flying projectiles. Just like that, I was off the trail and over the side leaving a path of devastation in my wake—broken branches, flattened shrubs and grasses pulled out by the roots. It was all over in a matter of seconds. In the end, all I could do was close my eyes, and pray not to hit the giant spruce that loomed larger than life and seemed to stand in direct line with my path, no matter how my path wavered. Sure enough, I hit it feet first and crumpled like a front end bumper.

    I laid there, eyes closed, and waited for the bright light to come take me. No bright light, though I counted to a hundred—slowly. So I wasn't dead yet, but I had to be injured. How could I be intact hitting a tree at sixty miles per hour? It'd be a minor miracle—right up there with Jesus calming the storm. I started at the top and went through a checklist. Head—still attached, but spinning so fast I had to close my eyes to shut out moving tree and cloud. Neck—I moved it up and down, and, side to side. It seemed OK. Back—upper back fine, low back not so much. Still, my fingers and toes were moving so I couldn't be paralyzed. And the low back was more of a localized pain, like the feel of a bedspring poking through a worn mattress. Probably just a stick or a spruce cone. No big deal—nothing life threatening, but annoying that I couldn't quite angle my arm the right way to remove it nor get off it because my scarf, snagged on something or other, prevented all sideways movement. The best I could do was edge my hips a little to one side. The pain in my back shifted to my left buttock and now my ankle was throbbing.

"John!" I yelled, although, it came out sounding more like "Shong" because of a mouthful of spruce needles. I spit them out on my sleeve. "John!" Tears pricked the corners of my eyes. I probably had a broken ankle. Maybe even a fatal flesh wound. Maybe this very instant my blood was leaking into the snow and staining it red all the way to the ground. "John!" I strained to hear his voice or the sound of his skis on the snow. The cheery bird chirps had stopped and the only sound was the indignant caw of a crow perched high in an adjacent spruce. Would he find me in time? I imagined John coming as I took my last breath, my hair spread out around me in a glorious fan and my face white as the snow that pillowed my head. I took off my gloves and ran my fingers through my hair to untangle and arrange it to best effect. Bad move. Spruce needles pierced the skin under my fingernails and blood welled up in tiny beads.

"Eleanor!"

"Down here!" I pulled my gloves back on, grabbed a branch, shook it hard enough to attract his attention and shower more needles down on my head.

Seconds later John was pushing his head through the branches. "Are you all right?"

I searched his eyes. Maybe he knew something I didn't. Maybe things were worse than even I had imagined. No. He knew nothing. That was quickly apparent as he circled me on hands and knees, looking me over like a second-hand car. He noticed my snagged scarf immediately, tried to free it from where it was caught on a spruce branch, but quickly gave up and cut it loose with a penknife. I watched his efficient manner and had an urge to lean forward and kiss the lines between his eyebrows, to slide my lips down the bridge of his nose and press them to his mouth, to make him suspend all judgement and see something in me that he liked. Instead, I sat up and gingerly stretched out my legs. "Ooooh!" Moving my ankle was agony.

"What?"

"My right foot—I think I sprained it."

He was up and standing behind me now. "I'll pull you out so we can take a look." He hooked his arms under my armpits and dragged me into the open. Then he knelt at my feet and honed in on my boot.

"I'll get it off," I said, but in the seconds it took for me to take off my gloves he was already on the job, his long, slender fingers making great loops of the laces, loosening them all the way to the toe and freeing the tongue to create a great hole my pre-injury foot would have slipped through as easily as a hand through an open car window. Not this foot. He pulled the sides wide and tried to inch off the boot. My foot wouldn't budge, though I grit my teeth and clenched my fists to bear the pain. In the end he took his knife and split the seams. The boot peeled away like a banana exposing my foot in all its glory. There was obviously something very wrong with my ankle. It was turned in with a peach-sized bulge on the outside that was quickly approaching the size of a grapefruit. He pulled down the sock, an old wool sock that fit like a potato bag. My foot was all purplish-red, like a peony in full bloom with a white glimmer of bone poking out through the skin. The look of it made me lightheaded and nauseous. John pulled up the sock and then touched my shin in a gesture I couldn't be sure was intended to comfort or was even deliberate. "There's no way you're getting back to the school on foot." He looked around, his eyes finally settling on an old, ragged stump. "Here." He reached for my hands. "Get up."

John did all the work. I planted my good foot and rose up like a water skier. A moment of awkwardness ensued—he and I face-to-face with hands locked, but an arm's-length between us, and me teetering on one leg in the uneven snow.

"Hold onto my shoulders and you can hop to the stump."

I tentatively wrapped my arms around his shoulders and with his arm supporting my waist, we did a three-legged shuffle to the stump. I hadn't been this close to a boy since my dance with Darek Dąbrowski—Ron didn't count, except as torture—and I couldn't help but notice a disturbing trend; that brushes with death and/or serious injury preceded any close contact I had with a boy, at least boys that I liked.

John rolled a log close to support my right foot. "I'm going back to the college." He slipped into his skis. "I'll be back with a snowmobile." I watched his broad back and strong thighs as he muscled his way up the bank. I watched the herringbone pattern his skis left in the snow. He was so calm, so capable, so decent and true. No one could disapprove of him. Not even God.

"Twenty minutes, max," he called from the top.

"Wait!" I said. "Just tell me one thing—will I be all right?"

"Just keep your foot elevated and don't try to walk on it."

As soon as he dropped out of sight, the pain in my foot quickly skyrocketed to a ten out of ten and I couldn't resist pulling down my sock and sneaking peeks at my ankle, watching mesmerized as the redness worked its way up my leg to my calf and then knee and my skin swelled out like a water balloon. *What's the worst thing that could happen?* I asked myself, in an attempt to stem the rising panic. *I could die.* Not exactly the answer I was looking for. Still, I had to be realistic. People die every day. Why should I be an exception? People cross the street and get hit by trucks. People drown in undertows. People suffocate in burning buildings. But do they really die from broken ankles? Truth be told, I wasn't sure. I asked Jesus into my heart one more time, just to be on the safe side. I took the tattered scrap of wool from my neck that was all that remained of my scarf and draped it over my foot to block out the view. I pretended the foot had nothing to do with me, that it was a renegade foot that belonged to a stranger who would be showing up soon to take it back home. *Relax*, I told myself. *Everything's fine. There's no need to worry.* I pretended to believe myself and turned my attention to the giant snowflakes that had started to fall, drifting to the ground like chicken feathers.

I tipped my head back and they lit on my face, combined into clumps that cooled my forehead and cheeks. I closed my eyes and let the snowflakes fall, felt my face go numb.

Minutes later the drone of an engine carried from the distance. I sat up straight and scanned the treeline. It couldn't be John. Not this soon. Still, I was hopeful—lame made to walk/blind made to see—when you've been brought up on Bible stories, the off chance of a miracle springs eternal in your mind—and eagerly sought out the source of the noise until two snowmobiles ripped out of the trees. A startled pheasant in some nearby cattails flapped his wings and rose into the air. The bird flew low over my head, fanning snow from my hat and eyelashes, before disappearing over the hill. Neither rider was John in his yellow suit so I hoped for the next best thing—a doctor or maybe a paramedic. Even a high school dropout with some Tylenol 3's would be better than nothing. The machines raced across the field several times at top speed and then did a slow tour around the perimeter before turning toward me. They parked alongside the cattails and stood up—two men, one a full head taller than the other. The taller one was solid too, like an upright freezer or a sidewalk plow. He was definitely the boss—I could tell by the way he swaggered around and kept shooting his mouth off. "Goddamn four wheelers fuckin' up the trails again. Need their cock-suckin' heads kicked in." Any fuckin' beers left in your box?" "Give me a cigarette, would ya."

I've heard people say there are two kinds of drunks—belligerent drunks and friendly drunks and this guy belonged to group number one. Beer in one hand, cigarette in the other, he headed toward me. Not the other guy. He stayed back.

"What's a pretty girl like you doing all alone out here?" His glassy, unblinking eyes looked like those of a herring and his face was pockmarked like he'd had wall-to-wall chicken pox as a kid and picked every scab.

"Waiting for my friend to get back," I said, trying very hard not to look scared, because he was very scary and I was all alone and you know what they say—that if an animal senses you're afraid it's game over—you're dead. I assume it works the same way for all predators—even the human variety. One minor problem, I didn't know what to do with my eyes. I couldn't remember if the experts say to stare an aggressive animal in the eye or look away.

The jerk studied the path the seat of my ski pants had worn down the hill and let out a guffaw. "I think you're feeding me a line," he said. "I think you're really all alone out here. Lance and I, we've been riding these trails since morning and haven't seen dick all—other than you, that is."

I kept my eyes trained on a power line in the distance, going with the averted gaze to start with, and focused on breathing and not peeing my pants.

"You seen anyone around here, Lance?"

Lance was leaning against his Ski-Doo, head down and mouth clamped around a cigarette while his hands hovered close with a lighter. He took a quick puff and then snapped the lighter shut. "Nobody, man."

"You calling me a liar?" I said, looking him square in the eye and working the aggressive tack. "Because all you have to do is look. See—two pairs of footprints in the snow. Well, two and a half." I pointed out the messed-up trail John and I had made from the tree to the stump and then unveiled my foot with a sweep of my arm, which, judging by my ten-out-of-ten pain level, promised to be big as a watermelon.

He took a good, long look at my foot and whistled. "Jesus fucking Christ," he said, the ash building on the end of his cigarette. For a moment at least, I thought I'd done the right thing and, at the very least, bought myself some time with the shock value. "You got yourself quite the fuckin' boo-boo there." He took a long drag on his cigarette. "I guess those are the risks you take when you're a woman all on her lonesome and out of her element. I guess I'd say you're real lucky we happened along."

Lucky wasn't exactly the word I had in mind, but I didn't say anything. I figured I could take the aggressive tack only so far before it backfired on me.

"Cat got your tongue?" he said after a moment during which time the only sound was of him guzzling beer and me grinding my teeth. I swear I could hear the rise and fall of his Adam's apple with each swallow. Also the sound of gurgling from his abdomen, which raised the possibility that his internal organs might be drowning in alcohol and anytime now he might be passing out face down in the snow. He held out his beer—what little was left of it. "Here," he said. "For the pain."

"I don't have any pain," I shot back which was a total lie, but, possibly a lesser sin than accepting the beer, although I couldn't be sure.

"Then to quench your thirst or because of the taste. Shit—just for the hell of it. Who in fuck needs a reason to drink?"

"I don't want it," which I immediately realized was the wrong thing to say when his face turned deep purple and his lower jaw jutted out like the blade on a bulldozer.

"God Almighty—I'm trying to help. You don't have to friggin' bite my head off." He finished the bottle and fired it at a rusted out skidder that must have been abandoned exactly where it broke down. The bottle missed by a mile and sank bottom first so that only the small round opening showed in the snow. Then, like a man doing magic, he pulled a new beer from one of his pockets.

"On second thought, I guess I'll take one," I said. Better I have it than him. He was already wasted and if I could keep the alcohol from one less beer out of his system, I figured I'd be doing us both a favour.

He hesitated, but finally handed it over and then waded back through the snow, forging a new set of prints as he couldn't coordinate his feet to follow the old, to the Ski-doos. In no time at all he returned with a beer, still, I'd had enough time to pour out half my bottle while his back was turned.

"Cheers," he said, clinking his bottle against mine. I put the rim to my mouth and tipped back my head, but with my lips pressed together. The beer smelled like cat urine and I wasn't letting a drop of it down my throat. It was all I could do not to gag. If God was watching, surely I would score points for that.

The psycho straddled the log at my feet, yanked off my hat, and held it over his head like we were both in grade five and it was afternoon recess. "There should be a law against hats covering hair like that." He took a strand and stroked it in his fingertips. "Smooth as silk."

I cringed and pulled away. In the few minutes I'd known him, those fingers had been in his nose, through his grease-laden hair, in his mouth, and scratching at red welts on his neck. I didn't want them anywhere near me.

"You don't seem so happy to see us. I hope you're not the stuck-up kind." He reached a hand into the front opening of his snowmobile suit and held it there in that classic "I've got a gun and I'm not afraid to use it" pose you see in gangster movies. "Maybe we just got off on the wrong foot. How about we start again? Take it right from the top. My name's Jase and this here's Lance." He pointed to his companion, who was taking long drags on his cigarette and pacing figure eights around the snowmobiles. "Now it's your turn." He nonchalantly pulled a hunting knife out of his suit and plunged it into the log, not six inches from my foot. The knife had an ivory and brown streaked handle with an eagle's head carved in the end. "What'd you say? I can't hear you." He leaned forward, cupping a hand to his ear.

I swallowed hard, trying to keep my heart from scaling my windpipe and leaping out my mouth. "Eleanor," I whispered.

"I'm very pleased to meet you, Eleanor." He stuck out his arm and shook my hand.

"Come on, MacDonald!" Lance called. "Let's go."

"Shut the fuck up!" he shot back, his eyes bulging so they looked poised to dive off his lower lids in a tuck position. "Can't you see Eleanor and I are making friends?" He closed his eyes and took a tremulous breath; laid both his hands on his knees. "I just know your friend's not coming back—it's my instinct, you know—so let me make you an offer." He was trying hard to control his voice, to keep it quiet and calm. "How about you come back to the camp with Lance and me?" His hands were clenched so tight the knuckles showed white. "We'll make a fire and tend to your foot. Heat you up something warm to drink. Hot chocolate sound good?" Then to Lance, "We got a first aid kit back at the camp, don't we, buddy?"

"Can't you see you're wasting your time?" said Lance. He lit another cigarette, his fourth or fifth since they'd arrived. "She's scared shitless. Twitching like a bunny. To hell with her—she's not our kind. I bet she's from the Bible college down the road."

The psycho stared as though seeing me for the first time. "Is that true, Eleanor baby? Do you love Jesus with all your heart and not give a fuck about people like us? You love your neighbour, but, you'd never spread your legs for a guy like me? I bet that's the deal, isn't it, sweetheart?" He put a hand on my ankle and gave it a squeeze.

Flames shot through my limb. I was sure if I looked my foot would no longer be attached to my leg, but hanging from that degenerate's fist like a prize winning bass. That's when my body took over, showed me it could act on its own without any direction. My arm pitched the beer bottle straight at his head. He moved, it missed, and my legs sprang into action.

"Fuckin' bitch! Get back here." He was right on my heels.

"Hey, man! Whatcha doing? You said you wouldn't hurt her! You said..." A snowmobile engine started up. "You're crazy, Jase! I'm out of here!" The machine accelerated with a roar and then faded away in the distance at full throttle.

Halfway up the bank, my bad foot gave way and the psycho got close enough to grab the boot of my good leg. My leg pulled free, minus my boot, and then my entire body did a one-eighty and I was flat on my back. There was no good leg or bad leg, just a steady barrage of punches and high kicks. I took special aim at those parts that are most prone to injury—the groin and throat. I especially tried to poke out his bulging frog eyes, but the strikes had no more impact than the snowflakes that were sliding off his snowmobile suit. He towered above me, shaking with laughter, then in one quick move, he hit me in the head. I sank into the snow, my head heavy and limbs limp.

My body was levitating off the ground, which didn't make sense because the psycho was on top of me, holding me down. His face was tight as a fist and so close to mine I could smell his bad breath. Blobs of spit quivered on his chin. I focused on that spit. My world was reduced to those blobs of spit—they were like flecks of white foam that sometimes wash up on shore, like the froth from a rabid dog.

"You think you're something, don't you?" the psycho said with a sneer. "A real heartbreaker in your fancy ski suit. Or maybe Lance had it right, and you're a child of God. Are you saved, Eleanor? Does Jesus live in your heart? Come on, bitch. Answer me." Spit rained down on my face.

"Do you still love God, Eleanor?" He held the cold blade of the knife to my cheek. I felt a rush of heat and then tasted blood in my mouth. "Does he still love you? Do you feel his love? Right here, right now?" He ripped open my clothing, pulling off buttons and splitting seams. "You're no child of God." He drove a knee between my legs. "All you are is tits and cunt. A whore." Cold metal was pressing into the bare skin of my abdomen and he was ramming himself into my crotch, pushing again and again until he plunged through flesh. My insides were tearing apart, and still he pushed deeper, pulled back and pushed deeper.

I stared at the snowflakes falling through the deep, deep sky and prayed for it to be over. When darkness closed in, forcing the light into the centre, I wasn't alarmed. When the light got smaller—squeezed to the size of a keyhole—and then went out, I felt nothing. Nothing at all.

One hundred and twenty-seven days ago my mother killed herself. In the beginning I didn't believe in softening the truth. I refused to say "passed on" or "crossed over." I avoided the word "died." "Took her life" was my least favourite euphemism because to me the words were misleading. They suggested her life was her own and she had the right to take it, which is complete and utter bullshit. My mother's life was not her own, leastways, not hers alone. She shared her life with my father and I. We were all three together; the way it'd been since the day I was born. She should have talked to us first. She should have told us her intentions.

My mother used a gun to kill herself. She laid on the floor with the muzzle under her chin and pulled back the trigger. One hundred and twenty-seven days later I still don't understand it. This much is certain: a gun is not a cry for help. It leaves no room for second chances. A gun is a quick, sure finish. A final solution.

My mother was always one to know what she wants and with the drive to accomplish it. What better pairing for success? I presume the same virtues applied to this, her most powerful act. "I'm killing myself and no one can stop me." Was that what she thought before pulling the trigger? Was hers an act of revenge? Or was it a cry of despair? Or a last break for freedom? I don't know why I need to understand. It won't bring her back.

At first, I was raw nerves operating at the level of cause and effect. I looked at what moved, answered when spoke to, and did as was told. Then, after the initial onslaught of horror and panic—the blur of sirens and men in dark uniforms, and of course my mother's body on the floor, arms neat by her side and legs pressed together, the skirt of her dress smooth over her thighs as though she'd taken great pains to arrange it that way and the only sign of disorder her braid, which had come undone and lay in long, winding pieces, and, of course, the blood, and the hole in her head—subsided to numbness, my father and I took one long look at each other and went separate ways, each wandering the streets like he was fevered and coming back to the house only to sleep. Or to lie on our beds our bodies rigid as boards; coming in the back door to reach the bathroom and bedrooms and in the front door for the living room and always, always avoiding the kitchen. If the phone rang, neither one of us answered it. The phone was ignored now, located as it was on the counter by the breadbox in that part of the house that didn't exist. We didn't bother with food, certainly not anything that required refrigeration, heating or any kind of preparation. We survived on stale bread, peanuts and Willocrisps. And for liquid refreshment we kept a case of Pepsi in the living room as well as boxes of vodka, which we drank from the bottle.

Later, when our bodies insisted, my father picked up takeout from the canteen down the street. We came in the front door and ate in the living room. We sat on the couch, he at one end, I the other. We chewed our hot dogs silently, our eyes fixed on the TV and never, never veering to the left where my mother's chair loomed in the corner. I went out the front door and came in the back to go to bed. My father stayed in the living room and sometimes remained there through the night. We were, neither of us, normal.

"This is crazy," my father said one night as I was going out the front door on my way to the back. "We should think about moving."

"We can't move," I said, quickly coming back in the house and securing the deadbolt, as though prepared to hunker down for the duration.

After weeks of meticulous kitchen avoidance, the practice became habit and it was as though our house had never had a kitchen and was cut off in the centre, until one evening the unexpected happened: the phone rang and my father simply got up and answered it. We were in the middle of Wheel of Fortune—a show we had taken to watching without fail. The sound of the wheel paired with the vodka lulled my father into a kind of senseless docility, besides which he took comfort in the fact that Pat Sajak had a Polish father. "Slavic face," said my father. "Look at his cheekbones, his eyes."

Truthfully, Pat Sajak was our closest connection to Poland in Lampeq, which shows how far from Poland we had come, and I guess when life goes wrong it's the familiar one craves and so my father ignored Vanna White in her long evening dresses and projected his grief on to Sajak. Is it any wonder that in his state of semi-drunken wheel-driven lethargy, the phone was able to short circuit his memory and temporarily override the part that remembered Mama and what happened in the kitchen.

He showed no hesitation. The phone rang and he stood up, turned right at the arm of the couch and disappeared into the dingy hallway that leads to the kitchen, his bare feet slapping the linoleum and me, a silent witness, too shocked to stop him. Then there was a clunk followed by several smaller thuds which I could only assume was the receiver dropping to the floor and then swinging against the cupboard as it rebounded on its cord and next my father's heavy breathing as he manhandled the unit to his ear. "So?" he said. "Wrong number." And he returned the receiver to its cradle with a decisive clatter. Then, more footsteps, the sound of the fridge door as it opened and closed and then back to the living room with some pickles in brine; settling into the couch as though nothing had happened when in fact what had occurred was a turning point of gigantic proportion.

He didn't break down in tears or pull his hair out in chunks— both acts I would have understood without question. No, he gathered up his frayed and tattered remains, wound them into a tail, tucked them into his pants and got on with his life—a response I couldn't understand at all. Baby steps first: a shower, clean clothes, a pot of coffee, a trip to the store for some milk and bacon for the fridge. But as he resumed his old habits, it seemed the structure they provided gave him the strength to do more. In a matter of days he was bringing home paint, unmarked boxes, and giant bags from Home Hardware and taking them to the kitchen. I watched his comings and goings through the living room window, all with a growing sense of unease. My father was starting a job, that much was certain, and I knew only too well that once he gets started there's no way to stop him. Meanwhile, I continued with my practice of avoiding the kitchen and divided my time between the front of the house and the back.

When the work was done a month later, he called me in for a look. I wouldn't go. He said I would like it, that the kitchen was different from before, that I would be comfortable there and not feel afraid. I said I wasn't afraid, that I'd never been afraid. We didn't belong there. It just wasn't right. Then he tried to bribe me with red borscht and sour cream. I could hear the metal spoon scrape the pot as he filled up the bowls, but remained defiant. He ate supper alone. I was sure he'd bring my bowl in eventually, when he saw there was no changing my mind. He didn't. I remained on the couch, my stomach aching, and not just with hunger.

He stayed on in the kitchen a long time that evening, even after Wheel of Fortune came on, although I turned up the volume and knew he could hear it. He sat very quietly. No buzz of hand tools. No pounding of nails or scraping of primeval floor glue. Finally he got up and walked to the phone. "Bill? I must back to work. Yes. Is time. Doesn't matter is Friday, I must back tomorrow. No make you trouble? Thank you, Bill. Thank you very much."

Quietly, quietly, I went out the front door, came in the back door, slipped into my bedroom and shut the door. I dropped onto the bed and stared at the ceiling. If I was afraid, then what was it that scared me? Usually this was as far as I got. A flood of words and phrases would rise up in my head, dashing themselves against the walls of my mind as though in a panic, turning any real thought to chaos...and then, click, I'd shut down. The screen would go black. But this time was different. I was calm and the words were coming to me, one at a time like precious stones on a necklace, and I had the presence of mind to consider each one, to order and thread them, to assemble the string through to the end.

Was my father right and I was afraid of remembering? No, that was impossible. The image of my mother was imprinted on my mind for all time; every pore, every eyelash, every detail of her body enlarged a hundred times over and in clear, vivid colour, her fingers curled up in her palm and the sliver of teeth between her lips. I could replay every second of that nightmare, from the moment I turned on the light and saw her there on the floor to when the ambulance attendants took her away on a gurney.

Then, was I afraid of forgetting? I shook my head. The very thought was ridiculous. Then what? Long ago conversations I'd had with my father popped into my mind; him talking, me listening, lecturing me on the subject of life after death. I allowed them a toehold, although my heart took to pounding. "What do you remember from before you were born?" he would ask. "Nothing," I'd say. "And it's the same when you die. You don't think; you can't feel...you no longer exist." He spoke with authority, as though his perspective on the afterlife was general knowledge and left no room for debate. His summary statement was always the same: "Heaven's a fairy tale and hell is here on the earth."

I knew he was wrong, though. The dead did exist. I'd seen them myself—the little girl beneath the willow and the men hanging from the tree at Pawiak. He'd seen them, too—I was sure of it— back when he was a boy, but had turned a blind eye so long they stopped being real. Isn't that what we all do? Ignore the painful to make living easier? And so, instead of existing, the dead blend into the concrete, they disappear alongside the trees and the traffic and the trappings connected to everyday life.

So was I avoiding the kitchen for fear of what I might find there? Perhaps my mother perched on her chair in her peach coloured dress with arms folded, legs crossed, eyes narrowed and cold? Then, as I watch, her right arm extends, a curled finger straightens and jabs a hole in my chest. I ran to the bathroom, bile burning my throat.

By the time Bill pulled in the next morning I had made my decision. The time was right. I would enter the kitchen. I felt hollow inside, like my middle had been cored and the insides scraped clean, but I was ready to face the truth and hoped strong enough to bear the consequences.

My father barrelled out the back door in his steel-toed boots, his lunch bucket banging the screen door, oblivious to the possibility I might still be asleep and disturbed by the noise. I threw off the blankets and rolled out of bed, forced myself to turn left at my bedroom door for the first time in months. In the doorway to the kitchen I fumbled for the light switch, buried my face in the crook of my elbow until my eyes adjusted to the light and then entered the room holding my breath.

My father had overhauled the room completely. Now it looked less like the place where my mother had killed herself and more like the diner on upper Main. My eyes briefly registered the changes—the linoleum had been replaced with black and white tile in a checkerboard pattern, the cupboard doors painted red with red curtains to match, the wallpaper gone and the walls painted white—but didn't focus on them, more concerned with scrutinizing the spot close to the stove where my mother had lain. I stared at the place, straining with all of my senses, hoping to see her or hear her or breathe in the scent of her Pani Walewska, but my mother was absent. I went to the living room and came back through the hall door. She wasn't there. I was alone. I pulled out a chair and sat down to wait. If she didn't show up...I exhaled a long, tremulous breath. Now that was a possibility I'd never considered, that was the worst outcome of all.

When my father got home, I was slumped in the chair with my head on the table. He whistled coming in the door, bent down to remove his boots as the door slammed shut behind him. A pleased smile crossed his lips when he looked up to find me sitting in his newly renovated kitchen. He set a thrift box of Dixie Lee down on the table. "Supper tonight is complements of Bill," he said. "Save me two legs. I'm taking a shower."

There was a slight, almost imperceptible spring to his step as he started for the bathroom—a stranger would not have noticed at all, but to me, a son familiar with his father's gait, it was unmistakable. My head started to pound, a thumb-sized spot between the eyes. Suddenly, it occurred to me that everything was my father's fault, everything that was wrong with my life could be traced back to him; everything, up to and including my mother's death as well as every miserable day since. And now he was getting on with his life, carrying on as though nothing had happened; rewriting history as though she'd never been born. He was as bad as the Communists, maybe worse. I got to my feet, scraping the chair legs across the new tile on purpose. "You could have flown Mama back to Poland!" I cried, the anger unfurling in my chest, catching the air in my lungs like a spinnaker. We were all three together. It was my father who broke that bond the day he signed up for Solidarity. "It was you they didn't want. They would have taken Mama back. You didn't ask because you didn't care. You wanted her to die—that's why you left the gun out!"

My father turned, his thick socks soiled and coated in spruce needles. His whole demeanour had changed. He looked like a befuddled old man with no idea where he was or how he'd got there.

"Mama's gone," he said, almost too softly to hear. "We can't bring her back."

"You're glad she's dead. You didn't love her."

Tears were squeezing out the corners of my father's eyes. He tried to blink them away to no avail. My father was crying and I didn't care. My father was crying for the first time in my life and I turned my back on him and walked away. "Darek," he said. "Darek." I went in my bedroom and closed the door.

✳ ✳ ✳

Most dead whales end up on the bottom of the sea. There are hundreds of thousands of them down there—a used car lot of carcasses. They lie like shipwrecks on the ocean floor, the long, sleek bodied fins alongside the galleon-shaped sperm whales. They may float for a while before they go down, but sooner or later, most of them fall. Not straight down or hard and fast like a 747 plunging out of the sky, but back and forth in the currents, graceful as dandelion fluff in the breeze. Some end up in the most desolate parts of the ocean, the equivalent of an underwater North Pole or Gobi Desert, where their bodies are received with much fanfare; their coming considered a cosmic event, like having a spaceship touchdown in your garden or a massive Big Stop with food galore, calories enough to sustain life for a hundred years delivered to their back door.

But not all whales fall. The healthy right who's been rammed by a tanker's prow or repeatedly struck by a cruise ship's propeller—she does not fall. She's too fat to fall. All that blubber, remember? Instead, she floats on the surface like a barge of garbage, birds pecking her flesh from above while sharks feed from below, her suffering plain for all to see.

Sometimes the tides wash her ashore, where, given any nearby population, the whale becomes an instant attraction. People come from all over to see. Call in sick to work and make it a day. Parents call it a chance of a lifetime and pull their children out of school to make the trip. Entrepreneurs grill hotdogs over open fires on the beach. Sell Cokes out of coolers. Anyone with a camera brings it. Those without find one to borrow. Hang them around their necks. Use up all their film.

Kids race across the rocks to be first. Some sprain an ankle, their crying barely heard above the crashing of the sea. Tentative fingers touch a flipper. The more aggressive ones peel off strips of skin. Poke a stick in its eye. The adults approach slowly, holding their noses. "How big!" they all say. A boy picks up a rope of seaweed, swings it at the deep cuts that cross the whales back, pretending he's responsible for the whale's wounds. "Stop that," says his mother. "You're spraying water everywhere."

"Poor thing," says a woman with a chihuahua in her arms. "Survival of the fittest," says another. "Didn't have the brains to stay out of the way." A man with a jackknife cuts off a strip of baleen. His personal souvenir. Two little girls start to circle the carcass with mayweed, but the wind keeps blowing the flowers away. Ever resourceful, they lay rocks on the stems to keep them in place. They search the whole beach, but run out of flowers before they've made it halfway.

Seagulls squawk atop the whale's back, their backs arched in outrage. Then, as night falls and the people go, other scavengers take their place: foxes, rats, raccoons, and ermines. Any animal with an appetite.

The professionals arrive when their schedules allow: the marine biologists, conservationists, and people from the Ministry. They confer in hushed tones behind closed doors. The government people wear suits. The government wins. The whale must go. But how to remove it? There's no burying the behemoth. The beach is solid rock. And no way of getting a backhoe down the cliff to dig a hole, anyway. Blowing it up's not an option. That's been done before, not here but away, with disastrous results. They decide to tow the whale out to sea. Volunteers cut the body into pieces—there's more help than they need—and fishing boats haul the pieces to sea. The government says, "Take them so far out, they can never come back." They mean never back to New Brunswick. They salvage the skull for the museum, but not the skeleton. That would require too much manpower and time. The government doesn't have the money for such extraneous projects. And the NGO's don't have time to fundraise.

The fishermen release the lines where the Bay of Fundy becomes the Gulf of Maine. The whale bobs on the waves, a collection of red granite boulders defying gravity.

Fast forward a few months to when the bones are picked clean. Surprise! Even the bare bones float. A dead right is in limbo. Land and sea both reject her. She has nowhere to go, nowhere she belongs.

✳ ✳ ✳

Nine whole days I was in hospital, drifting in and out of a drug-induced stupor. My parents came and went. Dad had work and Mum had Lucy, Jude, and Michelle so mostly I was on my own. The people from church sent me cards with tranquil nature scenes or paintings of Jesus holding a lamb. A few made the trip from Lampeq, not on purpose just to see me, but because they happened to have a specialist's appointment in the same hospital or had long ago booked time off for Christmas shopping in the hub city and considered it their duty to stop in for a visit between malls. The ones who put in a live appearance gave me Gideon testaments or wooden plaques decoupaged with Psalm 23 or inspirational poems like the one about the single pair of footprints in the sand because God had been carrying the person who could no longer walk for himself. Nobody stayed long or said much. I guess they weren't sure what to say. Or they were afraid of saying the wrong thing. I guess they figured it was safest to let God do the talking. I could understand that. I didn't know what to say to them, either. For instance, I didn't let them know God wasn't carrying me, that I felt like I was being dragged down gravel roads on my head.

Sometimes I'd get to worrying that the girl who'd loaned me the pink ski suit would show up wanting it back. She wasn't the type to take no for an answer. I had no idea where it was, nor did the nurses. If the shape I was in was any indication, I suspected it was in no condition to return and had gone to the incinerator or else was collected as evidence by the RCMP. I wondered how I'd pay her back.

Patty stopped by whenever she could, sometimes twice in one day and she never stopped talking. "Hey!" she said on her first visit, tossing a bag of licorice babies onto the bed and waking me up with a voice like a megaphone. "Have they found that bastard, yet?"

"Who?" I said, my medicated mind clawing for the surface like a man caught in an undertow.

"The son of a bitch who landed you in here—who else?"

I stared at her through heavy eyelids. "Oh yeah," I said. "I keep forgetting." I remembered parts, like going skiing with John, falling down the bank and hurting my foot, but everything was a fog after that. I was relieved in a way, although I might have been immune even had I known the details of the assault—the pain meds made it impossible to take things personally or get worked up. They made me feel like my life was a movie I was only half-watching while I flipped through a National Geographic with the radio blasting after weeks of no sleep.

I kept looking for John. I hoped he could make sense of things. I thought he might squeeze me in between his last class and supper or between supper and the library, but he never came. I stared at the phone and willed it to ring, but he never called. I memorized his number, but I couldn't make the call. My hands shook so that dialing the numbers was hopeless. Even the RCMP abandoned me after a couple of visits, once they realized my mind had taken all memory of the assault and hidden it away somewhere even I couldn't find it. I had nothing they could use: no eyewitness record of events, no description of the suspect, no names or direct quotes. All I had for them was myself, my wreck of a body and my blood work and x-rays.

I could tell they were frustrated. Even the crime scene had failed them miserably. By the time the detectives got there, snow had covered all the clues. Apparently, they still went through the motions, cordoned off the area with yellow tape and took a gazillion photos. One detective said my friend who had made the 911 call reported seeing the tracks of a snowmobile when he first arrived on the scene. He watched me closely as he said this, as though he thought that tidbit might be enough to set off a landslide of memory. I shrugged my shoulders, sad to disappoint him. "Oh, well," he said and gave me his card. "We'll be in touch."

I heard from one other person while I was in hospital—God sent me a postcard from Punta Canta. It said, "Get well soon."

❋ ❋ ❋

On day eight the doctor came to my room. She stopped just inside the door like I might be contagious. "Miss Hanson." She flipped through my chart and made marks here and there in black pen. "The latest CT of your head looks excellent, your Mini-Mental score is normal, the x-rays of your ankle show good alignment, and there's no reason why your doctor in Lampeq can't take out your stitches. Will you please call your parents to come take you home?"

"Now?" I asked. Lampeq was two hours away and it was already nightfall.

Dr. Murch looked at her watch. "I guess it could wait until morning."

"Are you sure I don't need to stay longer?"

She wrinkled her forehead. "We're not a hotel, Miss Hanson."

My father showed up at eight the next evening. By that time, I'd been relegated to the patient lounge, to make room for a gallbladder.

"Sorry I'm late," he said, "but I had to work until five. We've got this promotion at the store—no money down and no payments for six months. The furniture was nearly running out the door."

Some nurses came out of the staff lounge to say good-bye. "Good luck," they said through mouths full of peppermint bark. "Merry Christmas! Happy New Year!"

I missed the hospital with its sterile sheets and gleaming floors, its fluorescent lights over the bed. I belonged there with the special cases: the sick, the injured, the falling apart, and the dying; where nobody cared if you stayed in bed all day and meals were brought on a tray and the most you had to do was hold out your arm for a blood pressure or open your mouth like a baby bird to swallow some pills. At the very least I belonged with the ones who were waiting—the little old ladies in their terry cloth housecoats with aluminum walkers who weren't safe to go home. Or the ones who'd been in car accidents with all their wiring undone and hanging loose in their heads like a tree in the ditch all tangled in tinsel.

Some people find comfort in things that are soft, a stuffed bear, for example, or a rag doll or blanket. Not me. My hands yearn for something solid, a hardcover book or something cold and metallic—a cast iron pan, a shovel, a pipe wrench. Straight edges are good and also sharp points.

If someone had asked me what it was like, once the pain meds ran out and I hit rock bottom, I would have said it's like coming home to find the front door kicked in and everything you hold most dear scattered in pieces across the yard: fistfuls of pages ripped from your diary and strewn across the lawn for all to see; your books and letters charred to ash and photographs gouged beyond recognition.

You drop to your knees and a scream crouches in your throat, but you can't get it out. How could God hate me this much? The question is blazoned across your mind in neon letters under spotlights, because, maybe if you knew the answer to that question life would make sense and you could find the will to keep on going. You could change and do things different. But no one's giving you an answer. Maybe there is no answer.

※ ※ ※

My solution was to be invisible. I locked myself in my room for forty days and forty nights; used my wastebasket for a toilet and emptied it out the window like they did in the Middle Ages. My mother slid pancakes under the door, bacon and eggs, slices of pizza, and Freezies to quench my thirst. She wasn't concerned that I slid the plates out untouched. I was in the Lord's hands after all. Why should she worry?

Lucy slipped pages from The Sears Wish Book under the door, pictures of Cabbage Patch Kids, Care Bears and My Little Pony. She scrawled "To Lennie" at the top and "From Lucy" at the bottom. She used a different crayon for every letter in the same colour order as the rainbow. I turned her wishes for me into paper airplanes and flew them across the room. I pretended I had a window seat and watched each one do exactly the same loop to loop and then crash to the ground.

※ ※ ※

On the forty-first day I was ready to do something. I gathered up every lump of the soft, quivering glob I'd become and turned it into something sharp and solid, something that felt a lot like rage. It was the only way I could survive. I was a black hole imploding into a pin dot and if things didn't turn around I would disappear completely.

※ ※ ※

"And Michael McBride was back home by Thanksgiving," said Sandra between bites of a Caboose Burger. We were at Burger Station, Lampeq's answer to fast food. Decorations were sparse—a life size cut-out of Conductor Joe with a ratty piece of garland strung over his shoulders and a 3D mural of a train chugging over a hill of felt-covered Styrofoam. The felt wasn't white to match the season, but, emerald green for summer. "Oh, yeah." She wiped some ketchup off her chin. "Student loan money ran out. He spent every cent of it. Bought a state of the art sound system and you can imagine what happened to the rest—beer and music, mostly; took the basketball team out for a dinner at The Diplomat. They each had a steak. And you know Mary Ann Jensen? She's turned into a major sleaze. Spends all her time in the boys' dorm—different room every week. She was supposed to be in my psychology class—attended maybe three times the whole semester. Seriously. It'll be a miracle if she hangs onto her scholarship. Oh! Before I forget—Darek Dąbrowski." She smiled slyly. "You may be interested to know he's left town. No one's seen him in months. Not since his mother's funeral. It's like he disappeared off the face of the earth. Rumour has it he's gone back to Poland." She took a long drink of 7UP, her eyes gauging my reaction over her straw.

"I doubt it," I said. "Poland's Communist, remember?" Darek seemed like a hundred years ago now; like someone I knew in a different lifetime.

"Yeah, you're right. He's probably gone to Montreal or Toronto. I can see the headline now: Foreign boy escapes Lampeq. Local girls remain."

We ate in silence a moment, but Sandra can only be quiet so long before her vocal cords go into knots and her tongue starts to spasm. She was just picking at her food, really, taking mouse-sized nibbles of burger and so far leaving her onion rings and hot apple pie untouched. "Isn't there something you want to talk about?" she said finally, throwing her burger down on the tray. "I know what happened, you know. The whole town knows. Everybody's talking about it."

I dipped some potato ties in ketchup and popped them into my mouth.

"Something happened?" I sprinkled more salt on my ties and then sat there, salt shaker poised in mid-air, and pretended to think. "I was beat up and raped. Is that what you mean?"

Sandra nodded, giving me her full, undivided attention.

"I was beat up and raped..." I packed in another fistful of ties.

"Yes?" She inched forward in her seat.

"That's it. That's as much as I know." I unwrapped my second burger and took a bite. The special sauce streamed down my fingers and I methodically licked it off, one finger at a time.

"But how did it happen? What did you do?"

"I don't know," I said, the words thick and unwieldy through a mouthful of bun and ground beef.

"Hey! I'm only asking because I'm your friend."

"That's not why you're asking." I took a third bite, then a fourth, my mouth so full of food I could barely chew.

"You're eating too fast!" She came around and pounded me between the shoulder blades. "You act like you haven't eaten in weeks. They don't believe in food at the college? I suppose they have you living on the Word of God?"

It's true I was starving—forty days without food will do that to you—and now my jaws were pumping like eating was an Olympic sport and I was in training for the gold. Plus her inane questions were making me crazy. I coughed the food onto a burger wrapper and then stared out the window, guzzling pop and blinking tears out of my eyes. It was almost dark. Down the hill about fifty metres the river was tucked in tight beneath snow the inky-purple colour of a bruise. It wouldn't wake until spring.

"You don't have to get defensive, Lennie. Things like that happen; more often than you'd think." She reached across the table and touched my forearm. "It almost happened to me."

"I don't care." I slurped up the last of my Pepsi, slid my straw around the edges and poked at the ice.

"I met this guy in Fredericton—fell madly in love with him. He worked in a government office down the street from my apartment. I'd run into him at the coffee shop in Kings Place. He wore Giorgio Armani suits and Drakkar Noir..."

"I'm not listening," I said and started humming, my hands pressed to my head like bookends.

"Listen up, you need to know. One day Paul—that's his name—asked me out. I was standing at the counter of the coffee shop stirring sugar into my third cup of coffee, just waiting for him to show up, when, there he is; just like magic. We made a date for Friday night. He took me to this fancy restaurant on King Street and then invited me back to his apartment to watch movies. How could I say no? He had everything going for him: a Corvette, a good job, not to mention his amazing good looks. Turned out his apartment was in one of those Victorian houses on Waterloo Row, the one with the turret—another score. He lit some candles, put on the Purple Rain soundtrack, and made us drinks. The drinks were to die for, layers of alcohol in these bright Kool-Aid colours that tasted fantastic. I must have drank six or seven while we cozied up on the couch."

"If you're trying to make me feel better, it's not working."

"I'm not done—just listen. So, I'm curled up on the couch with my head on his chest thinking up some key lines to use when I break up with Jimmy when out of the blue Paul straddles my legs. Prince is singing 'I would die 4 U' and Paul is all over me—pushing his tongue down my throat, unhooking my bra—at least trying to, and driving his knee into my crotch. I push him away, but he doesn't let up."

I slid my tray to the end of the table, half my potato ties uneaten. "I've heard enough," I said. "Let's go."

"Wait! Let me finish. He gives up on my bra and starts in on my tights—tummy control so it's a two handed chore. He's using just the one hand, though. The other one's reaching for a candy dish on the table. He's already off balance so I take the chance to buck him off with all my might. He hits the table, the candy dish crashes and condoms go flying. Guess what he says as he picks himself up off the floor? Besides every curse word known to man. Listen, this is classic. He says, 'Hey! Don't forget who paid for supper.'"

Jerk! I ran to the door, stopping only long enough to pull $20.00 from my purse, which I torpedo at him from the kitchen, and then I'm out of there. I slam the door so hard the windows sound like they might break and then I'm outside in the freezing cold. That's when I realize I left my coat in the apartment. I don't go back for it. I'd have died before I saw that jerk again so I walk up the hill and back to my apartment in a skirt and high heels. Nearly freeze my ass off. I can't even flag down a taxi because I'd given that moron the last of my money. So you see?" she said, picking up a potato tie and bringing it to her mouth with a flourish. "It can happen to anyone."

My stomach felt weird. I rubbed it under the table. "But, what happened to you isn't the same as what happened to me. For one thing, I didn't do anything. I mean, the last thing I remember is sitting on a stump waiting for help with a bone sticking out of my foot. I was wearing a ski suit. I had mitts on and a hat. And I hadn't been drinking; I don't drink, not ever. And I hadn't accepted an invitation to some stranger's house and been fooling around with him on his couch. Oh! And another thing—you didn't actually get raped."

"But I could have been. I was just lucky."

"You could have been, but you weren't."

"Thank God—I could have ended up pregnant."

"But, he had condoms..." My voice broke off as the most horrible thought popped into my head.

"Shh!" said Sandra. She looked around to see if anyone was listening. There was only an old couple in the opposite corner of the dining room sharing a muffin and they didn't even look up.

I slid down the bench. "I'm going to be sick," I said and made for the bathroom as fast as I could. My entire supper came up as I entered the stall, most of it, fortunately, into the toilet, but, an English muffin-sized blob down the front of my clothes.

"Hey! Are you all right?" Sandra called from outside the cubicle.

Beads of sweat dotted my forehead. I wiped off the seat and collapsed on the toilet. When was my last period? Definitely not since I came home from hospital. Not in the hospital, either. That put it at least six weeks ago, probably more like eight or nine.

"Do you think it could be food poisoning?" said Sandra. "I feel a little queasy myself. It must have been the hamburger."

"Just take me home, will you?" I hauled on the grab bar to stand up, stopped at the sink to wipe off my clothes, and then headed to the exit.

"Let me do it," said Sandra, but I already had the door open and was on my way through. Sandra wasn't quick enough for its tight spring hinges and the door clipped my recently healed, but still tender right foot as it swung to. "You're useless!" I hissed.

Sandra got me home in record time, her gaze constantly pulling my way like a shopping cart that veers to the right. "Keep your eyes on the road!" I exploded.

"You did too, do something," she said as she pulled into my driveway. She ran her finger down her cheek to mirror the location of my scar. "You defended yourself. You put up a fight."

I looked at her with raised eyebrows. Defended myself? She was a friggin' idiot and I couldn't believe that we'd ever been friends.

"Give me a call, all right? I'm free New Year's Eve. We could rent movies, order in Chinese. You could stay over…"

I slammed the car door on her in mid-sentence, climbed the stairs to the porch and slumped onto the porch swing. I could feel my toes swelling up like Vienna sausages. It was a minor setback in the big scheme of things, small potatoes compared to being pregnant. Pregnant. I couldn't believe this was happening to me. I sat in the shadows, my mind racing. I remembered popcorn cooking over a burner in a heavy pot, the kernels pushing up the dented lid. I remembered riding a two-wheeler with training wheels. Its metallic blue frame sparkled in the sun and the streamers on the handlebars made the ride like a parade. I remembered driving down Orange Street in the back seat of my father's car and seeing Darek Dąbrowski sitting on his stoop, head bowed and hands clasped between his knees. Lampeq or Poland? Poland or Lampeq? There was no difference. They were exactly the same. A hot tear rolled down my cheek. I wiped it away and went inside.

❋ ❋ ❋

I couldn't believe it. That's not true. The part of me that always expects the worst wasn't the least bit surprised. The pregnancy just confirmed what I'd always suspected, God or no God, the world as we know it is full of calamity and just lying in wait for its next victim.

One thing for sure, it terrified me thinking about this foreign body sinking its slimy tentacles into my uterine wall, drawing nourishment from my body like some fast-growing cancer. All in top secret and without my consent. It was the worst thing I could imagine. I wanted it out and I wanted it out now.

"How are you feeling, honey?" asked my mother as I limped into the kitchen. "Did you and Sandra have a nice time?" She was flitting around with her dishrag, wiping fingerprints off the toaster, but avoiding the jam edged crusts that littered the counter.

"We went to Burger Station." I went straight to the phone, still in my coat and dialed Patty's number from memory. She was my only hope.

"Hello."

"Hey, Patty."

"Hanson?"

"No. Guy Lafleur. Of course it's me. You don't have any other friends."

"Very funny. What's up?"

"There is something."

"They track down that bastard?"

"No..."

"Listen, I'm still willing to take on the case, but I need something to work with, you know, some clues. A composite drawing would help."

"And when you find him? Then what?"

"Vee vill achieve justice."

"And your methods are foolproof?"

"Do not vorry. My vays are very effective. Failure is not an option."

I put a hand around the receiver to muffle my voice. The less my mother heard of my conversation the better. "I'm pregnant," I whispered.

"What?"

"What I said."

"Holy shit! Have you done a test?"

"A what?"

"A pregnancy test. They sell them at the drugstore."

"Why do I need a test to tell me something I already know?"

"Calm down, Lennie. Take a deep breath. Now, listen. Stress can make a period late. Sickness can make a period late. Not eating can make a period late and probably a hundred other things I don't know about. What I'm trying to say is you're probably not pregnant."

"Yeah. Easy for you to say."

"I'm serious."

"Well, I can't buy a test. I buy a test here and the whole world will know about it."

"Come to Riverview, then."

"I'll be on the first bus that leaves in the morning."

"Tomorrow's Christmas Eve."

"Fine with me."

"Marj and Leo don't do Christmas."

"Even better."

"So long as you know what you're getting yourself into."

"Pick me up at the bus station, then?"

"I'll be there."

"Wait! Don't hang up." I shifted the phone to the other ear. "What do I do until then?"

She cleared her throat. "Dr. Tanzer says to stay calm. She says you should take a hot bath, put on your jammies, drink some hot chocolate and go straight to bed."

✳ ✳ ✳

Patty's street was ablaze in Christmas lights. Square inch by square inch it probably cast as much light as the midway during Lampeq Old Home Week. "That house must be yours." I pointed to the one house on the street in total darkness.

"You got it. No lights inside either. Leo reads by the light of the moon."

"Just hurry up and park before I pee myself." I'd bypassed the bathroom at the bus station when Patty said her house was close and she had a pregnancy kit there ready and waiting. Close if you didn't have to take into account the detour for a water main break, maybe.

We went in the back door and walked through to the living room. Her father was reading a paper and her mother was watching Jeopardy with a plate full of pickles on her lap. She cut them into quarters and ate them one piece at a time with a fondue fork.

"Bathroom," I whispered and squeezed Patty's arm.

"This is Lennie," Patty said.

"Pleased to meet you," I said. "Thanks for having me."

Her father lowered the paper and peered at me over the top. "Sorry about your luck," he said and put out his hand. As we shook, I couldn't help but notice his newspaper was in some foreign language that looked like little flames in various stages of combustion.

Her mother smiled. "You're welcome to stay here as long as you like. Pickle?" She held out the plate. "Take a whole one."

"Thanks." I popped the littlest one in my mouth and then Patty steered me out of the room and down a long, narrow hallway. "You told them?" My hands were poised, ready to strangle her.

"I told them your flight home was cancelled due to the weather. They think you're from Winnipeg."

"Winnipeg? The least you could have done is pick somewhere exotic." I squeezed my legs tight to hold back the deluge. "Never mind, just point the way to the bathroom"

She turned in a doorway and flicked on the light. "This is your room and the bathroom's right there." She pointed across the hall, but I had already spied the vanity through the open door and was headed inside.

"Don't forget this." She tossed me a bag. "Pee on the tip and results in three minutes."

At the sight of the toilet, the pee started to flow. I pulled the package from the bag, clawed off the cellophane, extricated the instrument from its protective armour and pulled down my pants all in a matter of seconds. With a little deft manoeuvring I got the wand into the flow without soaking my hand or my clothes. No small feat let me tell you. "You never told me you were Jewish," I called, pulling my pants up with one hand and clutching the stick in the other.

"You never asked," she said from the bedroom, like the subject was closed and there was nothing further to say on the matter.

"Jewish people go to Bible college?"

She sighed deeply, as if that was the dumbest question ever. "Jewish people play hockey. MBC had a girls' team."

I laid the stick on multiple layers of toilet paper and took it back to the bedroom. "A plus sign means I'm pregnant," I said and hunched over the wand, my eyes glued to the window.

"Would you relax?" she said, throwing a pillow at me. "Give the thing some time to work."

"Relax? Are you kidding? If I'm pregnant, my life is over."

She leaned back in her chair and crossed her arms. "You're not pregnant."

"How do you know I'm not pregnant?" My heart was pounding in my throat as I stared at the blank window. Maybe no sign was a good sign. Maybe the instrument couldn't find the hormone it was looking for. Maybe it was searching the same places over and over, opening and closing cupboards and drawers, but coming up empty-handed. I took a deep breath and silently pleaded with God.

"Did John ever call you?"

"No."

"Son of a bitch calls himself a Christian but has all the compassion of an earthworm."

"See! I told you!"

"What?"

I held out the wand. A plus sign showed red in the window; red like the flashing light on a police car or a giant 'F' on a final exam or the fiery gates of hell. "I knew it." I fell back on the bed, weak and unmoving. That was it. For all practical purposes, I was dead; my heart a slab of road kill, my body riddled with bullet holes, blood shooting out of those holes like a fountain. Patty's face hovered above mine. Her mouth was moving, but no words came out.

"Come on," she said, pulling on my arm. "It's not the end of the world. We're going out. Now! She pulled both my wrists with her colossal hockey might and I rose up like a Frankenstein.

"You're going," she said. "And you'll feel better after." She tried to hoist me to my feet, but my legs wouldn't hold. Not on their own. Not with ground control away from the desk and hunkered down in some bunker. Patty ran across the hall, came back with a Dixie cup, and pitched its contents at my head.

"Hey!" I spluttered, cold water dripping off my nose and forehead, streaming down my chin and drenching my vest.

"Get up or I'll do it again, a whole bucket next time."

We went out to the car and drove around for a while. The only place open was the Irving Convenience where we stopped to get movies. Every other woman in the place was pregnant. They walked around with their hands on their bellies like they were showing off prizes on the Price is Right. The sight of them made me feel sick to my stomach, like my head was a tilt-a-whirl and I was about to throw up. I grabbed Cujo and The Dead Zone from the rack at the back, pushing my arm between two tumoured bellies to get them. The rest of the night was a blur. Apparently, we sat on the couch eating ice cream and caramel cakes and watching the movies. All I remember is this rabid dog barking.

❋ ❋ ❋

Patty knocked on the door first thing the next morning. "Lennie, are you awake?"

"Awake? I never slept."

She walked in wearing sweats. "I've been thinking." She sat down on the bed. "I had an aunt miscarriage once. She was lugging a couch up some stairs—total accident. She didn't even know she was pregnant."

"Really?" I sat up and wrapped my arms around knees. I'd spent the night dreaming I had the crevice attachment of a vacuum pushed into my uterus and turned up high like a Mixmaster. Anything that wasn't nailed down in there was coming out. My uterus itself was buckling in places like an old rug.

The little threads of amniotic sac didn't stand a chance. They were pulling away like morning glory stripped off a fence. In my mind, the fetus resembled a baby mouse I'd found in the dooryard one day—just an inch or two long with shiny pink skin and weird little limbs. I just hoped it would all come out in one piece. The last thing I needed was to see a little hand come out after the fact—perhaps bobbing in the toilet or smack-dab in my underwear. Even if the hand was no bigger than a Tic Tac, I'd be a goner; running around with my arms in the air and screaming non-stop until I dropped dead from exhaustion, because baby mice don't have hands. No creature has hands, that I've ever seen, except for apes, I guess, with their opposable thumbs, but they're the exception. Oh! And if man is made in God's image then I guess God might have hands too, for creating of course. Or he's just a big mouth. You know, God as Word. Bottom line, if I got an abortion it'd be the same thing as murder and I'd be headed for hell. Do not pass go. Do not collect $200.00. But abortion is one thing, miscarriage another.

"I need to get a couch up from the basement. Can you help?"

✳ ✳ ✳

The Tanzer chesterfield had a high back, rolled arms and room enough to seat a family of ten. I'm talking adult children, here, and every one of them obese. Patty said it was stuffed with horsehair so it had to be ancient. My guess is that it was there in the basement from the very beginning and the house was built up around it, that if we looked there'd be dirt floor underneath it, maybe fossils from the Paleozoic era.

"I don't know if I can lift this thing, let alone get it upstairs," I said, surveying the monstrosity from every angle.

Patty stared at me pointedly.

"But if I can't, I'll die trying." I laid claim to the far end of the couch. "Where'd your parents go, by the way?"

"They're making rounds of the nursing homes, giving out gifts to the folks all alone. It's their December twenty-fifth tradition. The Christians can't do it—they're at home eating turkey and opening presents. Did you put on the pad?"

"Doubled up on the "heavy protection" ones just to be on the safe side. Feels like I have a pillow crammed between my legs." I got my hands in position. "What time will they be back?"

"Not for two hours at least; depends on the turn-out and if the old folks feel like singing or not."

"Singing?"

"You know, Christmas carols."

"Jewish people sing Christmas carols?"

"My mother's the singer. My dad plays piano. OK, are you ready?" She counted to three and we picked up the chesterfield and staggered to the stairs.

"Anything happening?" Patty said between clenched teeth.

"Not yet."

Patty started up the stairs and the weight at my end tripled at least. I pressed my shoulder to the armrest, sweat pouring off my forehead. Slowly, slowly we went up the stairs, the couch threatening to veer into one wall then the other with each step. At the halfway mark we stopped to rest. My heart was beating an escape hatch straight through my chest.

"OK?" said Patty.

"My back is breaking and my arms are ready to fall off." The words darted out one or two at a time between great gulps of air.

"That's it?

"I might be on the verge of a heart attack."

"You wish," she said and rolled her eyes. We resumed our climb, but this time our bodies out of sync. The couch lurched into the wall. I held my breath, fully expecting the massive deathtrap to take off like a toboggan and ride over top of me, but we managed to regain control, adjusted our hand holds and continued on to the top where we both sank into the cushions and worked on straightening our hook-like fingers.

"Anything?"

"I don't think so."

"Not even some cramping?"

I slipped my hands under my shirt and prodded around my belly button. "Not in the slightest."

"Your uterus isn't way up there, nimrod. At least not in the first trimester."

"Where is it, then genius?"

"My guess is closer to your crotch."

I poked a path down to my pubic bone—no pain in the slightest—and then went to the bathroom to check the pads. I came back totally depressed.

"Hey! Don't give up yet," she said. "We're just getting started." And so we lugged that chesterfield downstairs again. And then back up and back down a few dozen times.

"Well, one thing's for sure—that kid's not going anywhere," said Patty. "He's there for the duration."

I flopped down on the couch and stared at the ceiling.

"Look on the bright side. Once he comes out, you don't have to keep him."

***

I got a job at Saunders' Shoes, a store that sells quality footwear for the whole family. For kids that means leather shoes with arch supports and nonslip soles in sensible colours like black, brown and burgundy. Laces for boys, buckles for girls. No vinyl or plastic. No glitter or sequins. No flip-flops. No fads. If you wanted shiny, pink shoes with princess appliqués or glued on bows or soles that lit up, you went to the Metropolitan where you had to wait on yourself and the shoes were bound together with string and the atmosphere was abysmal. You walked into Saunders' Shoes and you got the rich smell of leather, the stately creak of hardwood floor, and the rustle of tissue paper in cardboard boxes. You walked into the Met and it was the buzz of fluorescent bulbs, the screaming of kids, and the crash of metal as shopping carts met in head-on collisions. To be honest, the job wasn't my idea. It was my father's. All I knew was that I couldn't go back to the college. I spoke to my father in the only language he understands, the language of slothfulness and waste. "If you make me go back, I'll flunk the semester. Doesn't it make more sense to save your money and let me stay home?" Mum was OK with it, but Dad had some issues. No kid of his was going to sit at home doing nothing, not even a kid who was the victim of crime and had major head issues. To give you some background, my father is from a long line of child labourers going all the way back to England and the industrial revolution. He sold papers as a toddler and from there it's been one job after another, usually multiple jobs at once. In other words, he doesn't believe in sitting around. It's not about making money. It's about working hard. It's about using a horse and plough even when a tractor sits in the barn, a shovel instead of a snow blower. It's about perseverance: late nights, early mornings, overtime, bad weather, loud noises, stench, and risk to life and limb. It's about carrying on when the going gets rough, especially when the going gets rough.

My father watched proudly through the frost-covered windshield while he warmed up the car as I set out on foot the first Monday in January with a file of resumes in hand. The temperature was twenty below zero (minus forty with the wind chill), but I insisted on walking knowing it would make an impression. I wore a parka, hat, scarf and mitts—the whole shebang, nonetheless, my fingers and toes went numb within minutes and my breath instantly crystallized on my hair and eyelashes.

Saunders' Shoes was one of the first places I stopped. Old Mrs. Saunders, hunched over her till, was just opening up as I walked through the door. She was a regular at church, sat on the same side as us, only, closer to the front. At that time of morning, the store wasn't much warmer than outside on the street—our breath hung in the air in little clouds. I inched closer to a radiator and waited for her to finish counting the money.

The warmth was creeping back in my fingertips by the time she finally closed the till. I stepped forward. "Mrs. Saunders, are you by any chance hiring right now?"

She looked me up and down with a critical eye. It seemed to me her gaze lingered on my abdomen, although that might have been my imagination because there was no evil to be seen there, not yet, not that was visible to the naked eye. Still, I sucked in my gut and shifted my file folder to cover my stomach just to make sure.

"Aren't you the oldest Hanson girl?"

I nodded. "My name is Eleanor."

"Shouldn't you be back at school?"

"Actually, I'm looking for a job. Do you have any openings?"

"You do the scripture readings at church?"

"Sometimes."

"You enunciate your words like we're all old and deaf."

"I guess," I said, unsure if her remark was an insult or compliment. "The microphone helps."

"We get a lot of seniors in here. Can you start tomorrow, Helena?"

"It's Eleanor."

"What's that?"

"I said my name is Eleanor." I leaned in close and stood directly in front of her in case she read lips.

"Eleanor. Is that it?" She came around the counter and eyed my feet.

"I have shoes," I said quickly.

"No sneakers," she said. "And nothing from the Metropolitan."

"Of course not."

"Nine o'clock sharp."

"I'll be here."

My father was thrilled when I told him the news. Minimum wage plus fifteen percent commission on all sales. I didn't tell my father, but the store is air-conditioned in summer. It didn't get any better than that for a pregnant, college dropout in my town.

※ ※ ※

To be honest, no matter how I turned things in my head, I couldn't make sense of them. Consider the facts:

1. I fell down a hill and broke my ankle.
2. I got beat up and raped waiting for help.
3. My brain blocked out all memory of the assault and there was no witness, which meant the person responsible got off scot-free.
4. I wound up pregnant with the rapist the father.
5. I can't get an abortion because that would be murder and God would send me to hell where I would live out eternity in perpetual torment.

Sound fair to you? Sound loving and kind? Sounds like a nightmare to me. Sounds like a scenario I wouldn't wish on my worst enemy. So how come God let it happen to me? I know I'm not perfect, but what did I ever do to deserve treatment like this? I could only imagine God'd made a mistake, some big-time, major screw-up; like maybe he'd dozed off an hour that one afternoon we went skiing and so wasn't watching over the world the way that he should. And so I decided the only thing left to do was appeal to his finely tuned sense of justice. I wanted to be compensated. I was praying to be compensated, demanding actually. Whining like a child. In the Bible, Paul says to "pray without ceasing." Same thing, I guess. I wasn't being difficult. I didn't expect anything too time intensive or complicated; nothing that required, say, the orchestration involved with feeding a crowd of thousands with five loaves and two fishes or bringing a dead body back to life.

No, I'm talking about the other end of the spectrum here: the cessation of life. I do it myself on a much smaller scale—swat flies and mosquitoes, step on spiders, hit the occasional raccoon and porcupine driving at night. I didn't expect anything fancy. Maybe a little knot in the umbilical cord or a peeling away of the placenta from the uterine wall. Maybe an infection or deadly virus. I'm no obstetrician, but those were ideas I came up with on my own. God, of course, could come up with a good dozen more. It was the least he could do under the circumstances. He owed me that much for sure. And so the scales of justice hung in his hands. He had the power to even the score. The only job left for me was to keep praying and figure out how and when to buy the pregnancy test. Then Patty appeared unannounced the first Sunday in February and I knew it was time.

She'd come upon my Pot of Gold chocolate box back in the dorm room and made a special trip to bring it to me. "There might be something in there you need," she said, handing it over and flopping down on my bed. "But there're no chocolates, if that's what you're thinking. Definitely no cherry centres."

I lifted the lid and poked through the contents. The roll of Beech-Nut black cough drops I tossed to Patty, the mini-flashlight still worked and I flashed it in her eyes and then I dumped box and all in my wastepaper basket.

"Hey!" said Patty. "Don't be so hard on yourself. You can't predict every bad thing that happens or then you'd be God. Now, if you had a big box, say the size of a swimming pool or a two-car garage, you might have covered all the contingencies. Of course a box that big wouldn't be very portable, unless you put it on wheels and attached it to a truck. Or you could just live in a bunker and never come out." She unwrapped a cough drop and popped it into her mouth. "Mmmm, stale licorice."

"That's not the point."

"No? What's the point, then? She got up and started circling my room like a seagull in search of scraps. "Like the ocean, much?" She picked a sand dollar out of my shell dish, took a whiff and turned up her nose. "And you thought my hockey equipment smelled bad?" She returned the shell to its dish and moved on to the pile of cobblestones I'd salvaged from the beach below Fishtail Light. They were the best of the best; five perfect stones; the outcome of hours of painstaking beachcombing. They stacked one on the other in perfect precision. She picked up the top stone and tried to stack them in reverse. Impossible, but she kept trying anyway. "Seriously, I'm all ears. What is the point?"

"The point is God failed me, but he's going to make amends. I've negotiated a compromise."

"What are you trying to say?"

"Just that I'm not pregnant anymore, but I need a test to make sure. Will you buy me one if I give you the money?"

"Are you out of your mind?"

"Just do it," I said.

The drugstore was downtown. Patty left the car running and ran in and then we went back to my house and smuggled the package upstairs in her purse. This time, I stayed in the bathroom to read the results. Alone by myself. I left Patty behind with the seashell collection. There was no way I could risk her negative energy screwing up the results. Me, I was pure positive thinking. Never mind a mustard seed. My faith was big as a coconut. I was Dorothy in red shoes saying, "There's no place like home" and meaning the words with all my heart.

Results took as long as the first time around. I checked for proof while the minutes passed: studied myself sideways in the mirror, slid my hand down my tummy to measure the flatness, and peeled back my bra to examine my nipples. They seemed a shade or two lighter for sure, but no change with my stomach. It could just be fat. Then I took a whiff of the Skin Bracer my father keeps in the cabinet over the sink and—no urge to throw up. Two very good signs, anyway, and I had a mini pre-results show party right there in the bathroom with some fancy foot shuffling manoeuvres between the sink and the toilet.

"What are you doing in there?" Patty called from the bedroom.

"Waiting," I told her. When my status showed in the window, I couldn't believe it. I held the stick up to the light. No, I'd seen right. A bright, red, throbbing plus sign. Nothing had changed. Everything was the same, only worse.

I should have known this was how it'd turn out. If God thought nothing of sacrificing his only begotten son, then, he certainly wouldn't have any problem throwing someone like me under the bus. Breaking news: I had to live out this pathetic life on my own. There was no one to count on; no one rooting for me to win; no one with this great, over-arching plan for my life.

That was it. I was finished with God and his Word. From that moment on, I stopped going to church. I stopped daily devotions and closing my eyes when my mother said grace. I threw my Keith Green cassettes in the garbage along with my praying girl snow globe, Jesus fish keychain and the God is Love necklace I'd made in grade five by pasting alphabet noodles on a circle of tree trunk. It was just me on my own without any hope.

※ ※ ※

Most days the time dragged. On a good day, I might have a couple of sales by noon. On a bad day, I might not lay eyes on a single buying customer until mid-afternoon and earn my money dusting shoeboxes. Either way it was hard not to break into a run on my way out for lunch. At least I had a whole hour. Fifty-seven minutes by the time I got to the library at the top of the hill. Fifty-six minutes by the time I climbed the steep granite steps, pushed through the oak doors, walked past the Maliseet Indian arrowhead display and into the alcove where I settled myself into the same high backed spindle chair that no one else ever used because it was like sitting in some Victorian era torture device, but which I endured for two reasons: first, because of its discrete location behind a potted philodendron and second, because it gave me full access to the 600's section without ever having to leave my seat and so I was working my way through every book with even the most tenuous connection to labour and delivery, reading them like horror stories I couldn't put down, dreaming about red potatoes with knobby hands and feet encased in bubbles like those capsule toys in the vending machines as you go in the Save Easy. Did you know the fetus was now three inches long and weighed almost an ounce? Did you know it had fingerprints? My life remained on its crash course, in a nosedive straight to hell and I had no control.

At five minutes to one, I'd slip whatever book I was reading back on the shelf and head for the store. If I put on my parka as I walked to the door, it left me a minute to stop at the Irving. The pop machine there sold the cheapest Pepsi in town. The only place to get pop cheaper was out at the Save Easy, but only if you bought it by the case.

I'd dig the quarter from my pocket, garage noises closing in all around me and soothing for the most part, except for the erratic screech of the air tools. The mechanics themselves were a quiet bunch. As far as I could tell, they communicated only as the job required, say to shout for a tool or for help lifting a part. I sometimes wondered if any of them had been friends with Darek. Had they joked with him on their breaks? Made fun of his English? Shook his hand when he told them good-bye? I almost had the nerve to ask. If only one would look up from his vehicle or saunter to the door for a cigarette. "Remember Darek?" I'd say. "Where did he get to?"

Or maybe it was the girl at the counter who had all the details, the one who chatted up every customer and wore false eyelashes and long, painted nails. I imagined Darek and she kissing when business got slow, Darek pushing her up against the counter. Her Dici-slung boobs mashed into his chest while his gasoline stained hands ruined her sweater. I hated her, then, with all of my might.

On second thought, maybe cheap pop wasn't the reason I stopped at the Irving. Maybe I stopped there because of Darek. Not that I expected to ever see him again; no, not in a million years, but the place had a certain, je ne sais quoi. Nostalgia? Whatever it was, it was a something conspicuously absent from the Connell Road Irving or the one over on Broadway and so it must relate to Darek somehow. And maybe unconsciously I hoped he might be there which is why I should have been more prepared the day the air ratchet stopped and a certain male voice cut through the sounds of metal and engines and straight to my ear.

"No, no. You must to back up and start again."

I stiffened, my fingers poised at the slot of the pop machine.

"Make straight the wheels. Good. Very good. Now forward, but slowly!"

I stood there, hand poised, but fingers suddenly empty, the quarter having slipped to the pavement and rolled away somewhere near the air machine. It can't be Darek. It can't be Darek. Still... I forced myself to the side of the building, one foot, then the other, almost too scared to look. Even from the back, I could tell it was him; the one boy in town who wasn't built like a refrigerator. I stared, mouth gaping as he directed an old lady into the car wash. If there was one person I wanted to see, it was him; one person I needed to talk to; to be with. My insides were shaking, my hands even worse. I stuffed them deep into my pockets.

"Eleanor? Eleanor Hanson?" He had turned and was walking toward me, wiping his hands on a dirty rag. Less than four feet away now, close enough for me to reach out and touch him. An embroidered badge over his left breast pocket spelled out 'Dąbrowski' in fancy, blue script. He was still tall, but more muscular; still blond, but hair short. And his eyes, his eyes remained that amazing ice blue. I tried to remember the last time I'd seen him. Not since the high school prom. Nine months ago now. Before what had happened to his mother. Before what had happened to me.

"Eleanor Hanson. I am happy to see you." He smiled wide.

I didn't know what to say, how to bypass the small talk and go straight to what mattered. "I had no idea you were still in town, that you still worked here," I managed.

"No?" He raised his eyebrows. "Where did you think I would go?" His eyes searched my face, but then settled on the scar that crossed my cheek.

I turned my head to the side so the scar wouldn't show. "I don't know. Montreal or Toronto?"

He shook his head. "New York is a better guess."

"New York City?"

"America is my dream from the time I am small. But for now I must wait. There is a right way to do things, no?"

"New York is a long ways from here." I felt like a moron as soon as I said it. For someone from Poland, New York was probably like crossing the street. He glanced back at the garage, then, and I was sure he would go. "Darek, how are you?" I hurried the words, packed them tight as a snowball, as though each one stood in for a hundred others, as though there was no Mrs. Saunders back at the store with her eyes on the clock, as though they had the power to make him stay. "Are you doing, OK?"

"Of course." He swallowed, his Adam's apple bobbing beneath the skin like a trapped bird.

I knew he was lying. His mother was dead. How could he be OK?

"And Eleanor Hanson? Is she doing OK?"

"I was raped," I said. "And now I'm pregnant." The words spilled out. I couldn't stop them. We stared at each other like we'd just seen a car crash.

"Where are you going? Soon I have break."

"I'm working," I said.

"Then we will meet when you finish."

***

If my father and I had not resolved our differences in the weeks following our quarrel, we had achieved a working relationship, which saw us treat each other with a marked civility, even engaging in formal, albeit strained conversation when the situation required. Fortunately our schedules facilitated this arrangement. He got up early and worked all day. I worked eleven to seven and weekends and so we had no choice, but to take our meals separately, each one cooking for himself, but willing to give the other any food that remained. I did my laundry and he did his, but we shared the other household chores and split the expenses. He claimed snow removal, groceries, and grass. I took vacuuming, the bathroom, and dishes. If anything, the household was running smoother than it ever had before and if we were no longer a family, no longer a father and son, then at least we were reliable roommates. And if our house was not a home, but more a business, then, we had only ourselves to blame and I was willing to accept fully half of that blame; half, but no more.

To stay angry is very hard work, much harder work than sadness. Sadness is a load strapped to your back that you cannot set down. Anger is a fire in your belly that needs to be fed. It steals the power you need to survive. And so I decided it was time to move on. The past was history. There was nothing I could do to change it. Only the future afforded me options. One thing was certain—I wouldn't be living with my father forever. Lampeq was a stopover, that's all and this house was temporary lodging. As soon as I was eligible, I would cross the border into America and then my real life would begin. This was the soundtrack running in my head through every minute of every day. It was the story I was telling myself the day I saw Eleanor at the garage. She looked like an Eskimo in an oversized parka and boots that reached all the way to her knees and I might have mistaken her for a boy, if not for her eyes, those huge, staring eyes that looked all the bigger in her winter white face. Close up, I saw she still had her freckles, but they were faded and dull like water stains left on paper. The scar, red and raised, was definitely new though and the way she stood there, so stiff and self-conscious like I was a parent and she a bad child; English speaking Eleanor who had probably been born in Lampeq and would probably also die there, too, looked for all the world like she didn't belong. And then later when we talked, I knew she felt all alone. "You understand?" she said and I nodded. One thing I understood for certain: she needed a friend. And so I will be that friend, at least for a while. It doesn't mean I'm changing my plans. It won't stop me from leaving this town.

※ ※ ※

I picked Eleanor up from work the next Friday night. We had planned to see a movie, but she apologized as she climbed in the truck. She said she was tired and would I please drive her home. "Look," she said and lifted her pants to expose swollen ankles that made her legs look like fence posts. "Do not worry," I said. "We will rent a movie instead; watch it at my house with your feet up on pillows." I didn't mind the idea of Eleanor slumped on the couch with her head on my arm. I pictured myself slipping that arm around her shoulder and holding her close, drawing comfort from her even breaths and soft, warm body. I knew my father would be at the Legion with Bill and his band until well after midnight so we would for sure be alone.

Eleanor consented only after I padded my invitation with the promise of dessert. To be truthful, I told her I was an excellent baker and had the most heavenly cheesecake waiting at home. What is important is that I know a pregnant woman feels to eat even more than to sleep. What is also important is that I knew my father had made cheesecake the previous evening.

We went in the front door. She hesitated at the threshold, her eyes absorbing every detail of the room, as though a couch, a coffee table and a television were the most amazing things she had ever seen. Her eyes lingered longest on the crucifix that crowns the doorway to the hall. "So this is how a Polish home looks?" she said.

"I thought this is how a Canadian home looks, no?" I took her coat and hung it on the rack behind the door. "We don't have cable, but we do have antenna. Turn the TV on, if you like, and I will make ready the cheesecake."

I returned to find every light in the living room on and Eleanor perched like a bird on my mother's old chair. I was not prepared for that—I looked twice to be sure I was seeing things right. I never expected anyone to sit in that chair ever again. My father and I never went near it, had thrown a white sheet overtop to mark it off limits, and any outsider, given time to observe us, would have concluded there was a landmine or something equally ominous buried within the chair's innards. I quickly set the cheesecake on the side of the coffee table closest the couch. "Sit here," I said and patted the couch cushion. "It is much more convenient to lift your feet up from here." I grabbed a couch pillow, set it on the coffee table and demonstrated the technique.

"But if you move the coffee table closer I can do it just as well from here." She leaned forward for the plate of cheesecake.

I put out of my hand and blocked her reach. "That chair is forbidden. You cannot sit there." The two bony wrists poking out of her sleeves were bold and obstinate and I grabbed them, one in each fist, and leveraged her out of the seat and around to the couch. She landed none too gently, I'm ashamed to confess, and even in the moment, a part of me knew I was overreacting, while, another, stronger part felt I was defending something important and refused to back down.

"Don't touch me!" she said, rubbing her wrists. "Don't you ever touch me like that again." Her voice quivered and she stared hard at the door like she wanted to leave.

Immediately, I was filled with regret. How could Eleanor know the unspoken rules of the house? The history of the furniture and which chairs were sacred and which for everyday use?

Abruptly she put a hand to her mouth. "It's your mother's chair, isn't it? I didn't think. I feel so bad."

"No, I am the one bad thinking. It is me what is wrong." I dropped beside her on the couch and then shifted my limbs so that our arms and legs touched. She didn't move, but sat extraordinarily still and it seemed to me we both held our breaths waiting to see what would happen next. The onus was on me, of course, but I found I had no courage and lacked the nerve to put an arm around her shoulders, let alone hold her hand or lean in for a kiss. And so it was she who took control by laying her head down on my shoulder.

"I'm not keeping this baby," she said.

"Of course, not. Why would you?" Eleanor has beautiful hair and very nice eyes. If a criminal type had sex with her against her will and planted a baby inside her body, this is in no way her fault. We sat a long time, long after her breathing eased into the rhythm of sleep and it was approaching the time of my father's return. Then I woke her up and took her home.

Baby feet are the cutest. They're pink and pudgy, some as wide as they are long, with rolls of fat above the ankle and little dimples in the toes. And their smell is delicious—a combination of Johnson's baby powder, Ivory soap and rising bread dough. And just like their hands, their feet never stop moving; their chubby legs in constant motion like they're pedaling a bicycle. When they get really excited, their socks fly off and shoot across the room like scud missiles, touching down on an old man's Clarks Wallabee or a La Vallee stiletto. And trying to harness those curling toes and squeeze them into a pair of shoes—next to impossible. Like trapping a toad in a jar.

My favourite shoes are shiny, white high-tops in patent leather. They're for older babies, the ones learning to walk. The newborn shoes are soft leather with flexible soles and sweeps and curls pricked in the vamp. I have a pair on layaway. It doesn't change anything. It doesn't mean I'm keeping the baby.

❋ ❋ ❋

I lifted my shirt and studied my profile in the bedroom mirror. My belly had a bulge that I couldn't suck in and that wouldn't press down. It was barely noticeable under loose-fitting tops, but my jeans wouldn't fasten and I had taken to wearing elastic waist pants. No one said anything. Why would they? My dad's side of the family eats non-stop when they're stressed. They'll say they're OK and then stand at the counter and down a whole tray of date squares; wash it all down with a two-litre Pepsi. My dad must have gained twenty pounds since Christmas. He'd had to buy two new suits for work—alternated between the two. And after all the weight I'd lost while locked away in my bedroom, no one was about to remark on my size. I could swell to a size twenty and my mother would still be pushing the potatoes and seconds of dessert.

Unfortunately, my problem was not one a diet could resolve. My uterus was blowing up like a balloon and even though I wanted nothing to do with this baby and a part of me hated it maybe more than its father, there was a small part of me that felt I should do something. Not much, mind you, but something. It was half-me—that's the problem and so I felt a certain obligation. I just wished we weren't so close. I wished I could scoop it out with a long spoon and raise it in a goldfish bowl at the back of my closet. I'd take care of it—change its water and feed it every day, but the situation would be different. If we were separate I might come to like it. It wouldn't be so personal. It wouldn't be mine.

Don't get me wrong. The fetus deserved a fighting chance. I knew none of this was its fault and deep down I was worried about it. I kept telling myself there was a fifty-fifty chance it would turn out all right. Maybe the two sets of genes that went into his creation would cancel each other out and the kid would turn out mediocre—neither good nor bad. A C average type of kid. So he wouldn't be a doctor or a lawyer, but he wouldn't be a convict either. Maybe he'd be a garbage man or someone who stops traffic at roadwork. Or maybe, with the proper influence, nurture would override nature and the child would excel beyond all expectations. Yeah, maybe the right parents could turn this kid into a superman. Not me, mind you. I would be the worst kind of parent given the circumstances, the kind of mother that can't bond with her baby which psychology has shown is devastating to a child's emotional development and can turn a kid into a psychopath. No, it was my duty to find the fetus some good, decent parents. The perfect couple was out there somewhere. And I'd find them if I started looking. I began a list of prospects:

1. Mr. Caruthers—my grade eight English teacher who wore corduroy pants and earth shoes and had feathered bangs and warm, brown eyes with crinkles in the outside corners.
2. Charles and Caroline Ingalls
3. Atticus Finch
4. Dustin Hoffman

OK, so some of the prospects on my list were fictional characters or unavailable for other reasons, but it helped set the bar.

※ ※ ※

Friday nights at my house became a tradition. We'd wipe our feet on the mat, take off our boots and then hang our coats on the door like an old, married couple; always we undressed in that order and Eleanor always the first because of her emergency need for the bathroom. Then I'd hear the water running in the sink and she'd return to the living room, sit on the couch, lift her feet up on pillows and await my delivery of cheesecake, pączki or whatever dessert my father happened to have in reserve that particular day to satisfy his persistent longing for sweets. She'd stare at the tray a long time and from different angles, but eventually pick out what she believed to be the smallest piece while I manoeuvred the VCR and the movie.

All that movie-watching taught me one thing—one American movie is much like another and exceedingly boring. To tell you the truth, American movies are very much like Soviet movies, which also tend to depict their leading character (a Sasha or Natasha) as a hero out to save the world. Who would believe it in Warsaw? Moscow and Hollywood so much the same.

I think Eleanor also found the movies boring. I think she visited mainly for the Polish dessert and also for the pleasure of my company, although I suppose I might be mistaken on that second count and simply flattering my ego. I know she cut large pieces of cake into quarters, and quarters into halves, but by the end of the evening and with a waning of her willpower, no pieces were left. I know that once she finished eating, she let me hold her hand.

And so we endured the movies to secure other advantages and all was progressing well until the night we walked in to find the family photo album open on the coffee table. I cursed my father the moment I saw it, not because I had the gift of divination and could foretell Eleanor's future, but because it was the third time that week he had left the book out. If he wanted to look at pictures of my mother, that was his right and what could I do to stop him, but why could he not put the book away after? Why did he leave it out for the whole world to see? What would he have me believe? That he was sad and lonely? That he wished my mother was alive and sitting in her chair same as before, heart pumping blood and skin warm to the touch, but her essence somewhere far away? That she was the love of his life and with her gone he had no reason to live? Only an idiot would think me so naive as to entertain such foolishness. I strode across the carpet still in my boots, slammed the book shut and rammed it back in the bookcase alongside an outdated set of encyclopaedias, which pre-existed our arrival. The gesture was a feeble one, I know. I should have undertaken an action much more drastic. Indeed, if I'd had the ability to foresee the future, I would have thrown the album into the stove and set it ablaze.

Eleanor postponed her trip to the bathroom long enough to watch my one-man drama through to the end. I distinctly recall turning around to find her standing there on the mat, one hand in her crotch, the other dangling her coat, and prancing from one foot to the other, great toes poking through her socks.

"Me first in the bathroom," I said, attempting to downplay the significance of my performance as I hurried down the hallway still in my boots with her close behind and protesting vehemently until I veered off at the kitchen and let her pass.

Moments later, when I returned to the living room with a poppy seed cake held high in the air, I found her on the couch, just as expected, but with the photo album, the very same photo album I'd only moments before returned to the bookshelf, out on her lap. This was not as expected and I resisted an urge to snatch it from her hands. *It does not matter*, I told myself. *She is interested in the pictures of me, only, and in how life looks in Poland. She has no interest in my mother.* Nonetheless, I could not help but notice she was ignoring the cake and spending an inordinate amount of time gazing at a studio portrait not of me, but of my parents, one they had posed for twenty-some years ago to announce their engagement. I did not like that—Eleanor looking at pictures of my mother. I thought Eleanor should mind her business and keep her nose out of private family albums. It was wrong for her to poke her tongue into other people's cavities and to pick at their scabs.

My wounds are my own. They are not for public viewing. I put in the movie, fast forwarded past the previews to the main attraction and turned up the volume in the hopes of thwarting her enterprise. She ignored it, behaved as though the television did not exist.

I sat down beside her and tried to ease the book out of her hands. "This album is no good," I said. "Family photographs, is all—Darek and family at Christmas, Darek and family at Easter, Darek and family at confirmation. Very boring, if you want to know."

Her fingers tightened their hold on the album. "Your mother was beautiful."

I shrugged my shoulders. The picture was a head and shoulders pose shot in black and white. My parents are sitting. That they are sitting would not be obvious to a stranger, but I know they are sitting. I know because my mother is a good five centimetres taller than my father, but her height is in her legs. In sitting, their height is nearly the same. In the photo, my mother has her hair in a single braid that she wears on her head like a crown. Her lips are full and shiny and her eyes smolder at the camera. My father looks young and serious. He is in fact a whole year older than my mother, but in the photo looks more like a boy with his slim, frail frame. He looks maybe sixteen, although I know he was older, twenty-three to be exact. I tugged on the album, but she wouldn't let go.

"Don't you think that she's beautiful?"

To be honest, I'd never thought of my mother as beautiful. I'd never thought of her as plain or ugly either. I'd never thought of her as anything other than my mother; someone whose job it was to care for me, to put food on the table and keep the house tidy, to comfort me when I was ill. Still, I could play at pretend if Eleanor insisted. I could envision my mother as a stranger. And yes, with a small adjustment in perception I could see my mother was attractive. What I also could see was how little my mother had changed through the years.

Fast forward to the year before her death and she still had the same perfect skin, the same slender figure, even wore her hair at times in the very same style. But do not think my mother looked old-fashioned. No, hers was a classic elegance that was always in style.

Meantime, my father has changed drastically, even from one year to the next. He puts on weight, grows a beard, adds a moustache, shaves it off. Even his hair colour changes depending on the season. In the summer, the sun bleaches it bone white while winter darkens it to dirty blond.

Eleanor's face was solemn as she studied the page. "Your mother was quiet?" she asked.

"No." I laughed at the thought. "She was invited to every party, the first to arrive and the last to go. My father would be asleep in some corner and she would be clearing tables or in the kitchen washing dishes and all the time talking. Talking non-stop. She loved conversation and knew the value of words and how to talk in a way that made people feel cherished. She was also the best dancer in Wola district. I tell you, she was very popular, my mother."

Eleanor chewed on her lower lip. "Smart?"

"For life, but not books. She had no patience to read and she did not like school."

"She worked hard."

"She worked too hard. She could combinate a television from a doorknob. And our flat was better equipped than some shops. We always had kielbasa, extra lightbulbs and a pound or two of butter in the icebox for emergencies."

Eleanor smiled in triumph. "I knew it. Your mother was just like me."

She turned the page to my parents' wedding picture—an eight by ten portrait that shows them leaving the church. My mother has her hand tucked in the crook of my father's arm and her eyes fixed on his face. She's smiling wide, perhaps laughing, but my father doesn't see. He's in a world of his own.

He stares straight ahead, not at the camera, but somewhere off in the distance, a vacant look in his eyes that suggests boredom, but which I know to be reflection. It occurs to me that this was the difference between my parents—my father theorized, my mother strategized. The grip of her hand on his arm is so tight her knuckles shine white, but my father does not care. His face is serene. He feels no pain.

"Look at how she stares at him! You can tell she's in love."

Love? I shrugged my shoulders. I had no idea. But then, I had an advantage. I'd seen what comes after. Maybe she did love him...then. It was a long time ago. People change. What is true one moment may be false the next. I know theirs is a telling pose: my father, never present to the moment, always looking to the future and on the watch for something better; my mother, his anchor, trying to keep him tethered to the ground.

The next picture was one of my mother and me. My mother lies in a hospital bed propped up by pillows. I'm the babe in her arms, an ugly, naked, red-faced bastard with a startling resemblance to a Shar-Pei. She has the shoulder of her nightdress down and is holding me to her breast, but I'm an unwilling participant, in fact, I'm angry as hell with my hands clenched in protest, my eyes tiny slits and my mouth stretched in mid-wail. My mother watches with the repose of an angel. I could be a harp that she plays from atop a soft cloud of bedclothes.

"How old are you in this picture?" Eleanor asked.

"I'm just born. Look at my eyes. They're closed tight as a kitten's."

"She adores you. Just look!"

Yes, it's true. I am all that my mother sees in that moment of time. I am all that exists in the whole, wide world. Even my father is forgotten. But is what she feels really love or is it something else entirely? Does love turn off and on like water? Or is what she feels a need to possess? Maybe it's closer to greed than love? There's only one thing that I know for certain—you cannot tell the truth from pictures and I'm taken by an urge to seize the book and throw it in the fire. It is a waste of time to speculate and stir up memories. That is my opinion and I believe that it's true.

Eleanor skimmed through the pictures that detail my journey from primary school to the polytechnic; had no interest in the picture of a sixth class me in shorts with a third place ribbon for long jump pinned to my chest. No, clearly she was most interested in the pictures of my mother and she was not disappointed. There were more, many more, certainly more of her than of my father or me. My mother smiles extravagantly in each one. She is the maid of honour beside the bride, the benevolent godparent beaming down on an infant, the doting daughter embracing her mother.

Finally, she reached the last page of the album and gave me her verdict: "Your mother was happy in Poland."

I didn't know how to answer this. Was my mother happy in Poland? I don't know. I'm beginning to think that my sense of history as it pertains to my mother is all wrong. How to look inside and know, really know, what is in the heart of another? "I suppose she was. Come on." I pulled on the book and this time succeeded in slipping it out of her hands. It was a few minutes to midnight and my father would return within the hour. "I'll drive you home."

"Wait." Eleanor pulled the album back on her lap and hunched over a photo. "Who's that there?" She pointed to the corner of a picture where there is a shadowy image of a little girl sitting under a willow with a bun in her hands. "Is that your mother when she was a girl?"

"Your eyes are tired and do not see well. There's no one there. It's just a smudge on the photo."

❋ ❋ ❋

After the weather turned hot, Darek and I swam every day. He'd pick me up after work, the heat pressing on my skin and sucking breath from my mouth as I walked the few steps from the door of the store to his truck.

The first time we went I'd suffered in the heat all day. Mrs. Saunders refused to turn on the air conditioning because it was still early June and technically not summer yet, but she lowered the blind in the big showcase window right after lunch with an extended rant about how the tinted plastic gives the shoes an orange tinge that discourages window shoppers and would kill off all the afternoon business. I didn't feel it was my place to tell her we hadn't had a customer all morning, that the street was empty and anyone with a brain was home by a fan. She, of course, wore her usual heavy wool cardigan buttoned over a long-sleeved blouse with a scarf tucked in the neck and didn't know what we were complaining about because to her the temperature was "lovely."

The baby wasn't moving; hadn't moved in a couple of days, which had me worried. What if it had heat stroke? What if it'd died? If it was dead, was I to blame? I hoisted myself into the truck, spread my arms and legs wide like the limbs of a starfish and tried to ignore the sweat trickling down my back.

Darek opened a Pepsi and handed it to me before starting the engine. "It was cold when I bought it," he said with a grin. I took a long drink and then pressed the tepid can to my pulse points. It wasn't until we crossed the railway tracks down by the Cosy Cabins Motel where the speed limit changes to seventy and the truck stirs up a breeze that I started to feel better. Bruce Springsteen was in the tape deck singing Darlington County and I turned it up because the song was Darek's favourite and he liked to sing along except for he says Darlington candy not County which sends me into hysterics and makes him sing the wrong words all the louder.

"Where are you taking me?" I said between fits of laughter, finally aware that we were driving north and not south and that the further inland we went the hotter it'd get.

"To a place where is cool."

"But this isn't the way. The ocean is that way." I pointed a thumb over my shoulder back toward Lampeq.

"You can't swim in the ocean."

The only place I'd ever swam was in the crowded, noisy chlorine-stinky public pool, but not since I was a kid. Even then, it was never my favourite place to be. "But I don't have a bathing suit."

Darek waved his hand like it was the most ridiculous concern in the world.

We stayed on the old River Road until just before Getapet where we took a side road and then a labyrinth of back roads before ending up on what was definitely a private laneway through the woods. The truck tires found the dirt-worn grooves with a clunk and we inched our way forward, Darek steering carefully to avoid jutting rock. The last hundred metres we had to roll up the windows to keep out the alders and I sat there with my fingers crossed and hoped for no vehicles coming our way.

"You worry for no reason. No one comes here," Darek said with a voice of authority, but I couldn't relax until we reached a small clearing where Darek parked in the grass beside a derelict tractor. "Come," he said, the driver's door open and his feet out and on the ground before I'd even begun to inch my sweaty legs across the seat. Outside the truck, I peeled my shirt away from my back and took a quick look around. Heat rose off the truck in rainbow colours, but the only sign of life was a fat bumblebee suspended like the Goodyear blimp above spikes of lupin and the dull roar of something a long ways off, maybe heavy equipment or a jet to Toronto. I followed Darek who was already striding through the tall grass, stripping off clothes as he went. We pushed through the alders, the dull roar escalating to full-blown thunder, and voilà, just like magic—a waterfall. Nothing close to Niagara Falls, mind you, but magnificent all the same, the water collecting at the bottom in a large pool carved in the granite.

In what seemed a single orchestrated movement, Darek tossed his clothes on the ground, kicked off his shoes, and dove in headfirst. He swam back and forth, the sidestroke, the breaststroke, the butterfly and then he bobbed beneath the falls and let the water pelt his head. I dangled my legs in the water and watched.

Eventually, he shook his head until his hair stood on end, and then swam to a patch of sun to warm up. "Come," he said, kicking water my way, but too far away to generate more than a sprinkle.

And so I did, went in clothes and all that first time in. The baby came to life immediately. I did the back float and admired the perfect blue of the sky through the green leaves of birch. "How did you ever find this place?" I asked.

"I get in my truck and I drive. I am a natural born explorer, a modern day Christopher Columbus."

Darek was first to get out. I treaded water and watched, absorbing all the details that were usually hidden beneath his clothes: the arcs and angles of his shoulder blades, the two dimples in his skin that hovered above the band of his underwear, the milky whiteness of his back and shoulders and the way it contrasted with the nutty brownness of his arms. He lay on a warm, slab of rock to dry off. I stayed in until my fingers wrinkled like raisins and the sun dipped behind the trees. Then, with a chill creeping into my bones, I pressed my back to the rock, pushed through my arms and hoisted myself to the ledge. My blouse clung to me like a second skin. Mortified, I pulled the material away from my bowling ball belly and wrung out the wet.

"The syrena emerges," Darek said with a grin.

I squeezed water from my hair and went to join him, my pant legs flapping around my ankles.

"Do you know this word—syrena? Is it a word also in English?"

I shook my head and sat beside him on the rock, wrapped my arms around my legs to hide my belly.

"She is a fish-maiden with the chest and head of a beautiful woman and the tail of a fish. We have one in Warsaw, but ours is not your everyday fish-maiden. She does not work to lure men to their deaths. No, the Syrena of Warsaw holds a sword and a shield. She is the protector of men, the defender of the city. You look like her in your wet clothes, except her hair is like this. He gathered up my hair, wound it around his fist a few times and pinned it to the back of my head. Then he pulled me close and kissed me on the lips.

That night when I got home, the first thing I did was pull the steno pad out from under my mattress. I grabbed my black pen, the one that writes thickest and added "Darek Dąbrowski" to my list of prospective parents. He was number five, right after Dustin Hoffman.

✸ ✸ ✸

The right whales are back in the Bay of Fundy, forty sightings so far and it's still early on so the scientists are ecstatic and predicting a record number this season. The *Gazette* devoted a whole three inches to the story on an obscure page that I wouldn't have read under normal circumstances, but happened to stumble upon in my frenzied search for the five day weather. Sadly, two and a half of those inches were devoted to a mother-calf pair who had been spotted off the Florida coast in the winter, but were now in Maine waters and likely headed our way. The scientists had given them names and not just any old names, but awe-inspiring, super-hero names: Teela for the mother and Princess Ariel for the calf. I loved the scientists for that, for believing in those whales and wanting them to win.

Teela is entangled in fishing gear. There's no picture, but the article says her head is caught in a gill net and the rope is digging into her back and around both her flippers. The scientists say if it works its way in any deeper, she's at risk for infection.

She's also losing weight because the net is gagging her mouth. Bottom line, the whale is dying a slow, painful death and if she doesn't get free, she won't last the summer. Princess Ariel, however, looks healthy so far. They think she's about seven months old. Unfortunately, a right whale calf nurses into its second year so if the mother right dies, the calf will die, too. They say that with a population of only three hundred, every whale counts and the loss of two females would be a tragedy for the species. The story ends on a high note. Whale researchers from Massachusetts have developed a technique called kegging for disentangling whales whose lives are in danger. These researchers are combing the bay for Teela by air. The bad news—the Bay of Fundy has had one of its foggiest summers on record and the search party is grounded when visibility is zero.

∗ ∗ ∗

Sometimes Darek scaled the hill to the very top of the waterfall, carefully picked his way across the rocks to the middle and dove in headfirst. "I want to do it. Teach me to do it, too," I begged, but he always refused. "Syrenka," he said. "Is dangerous for pregnant woman to jump in a pool; is no good for the baby. You will learn this skill later, after the baby is born." He thinks he's an expert on everything so I back float and pretend to dive in my head. Feet together, legs straight, arms raised to the sky and then I bend at the waist and soar through the air.

After swimming, we dry off in the sun. One day I told him I hadn't lain on my stomach for months and how much I missed it. He poked around for a flat, pointed rock and then, using it like a spade, scooped out a well for me in the moss. So we lay side by side, me on my stomach and he on his back. Sometimes, when I close my eyes, I feel like the Eleanor from before. But then I open them, see him beside me and know that I'm different.

"Why did your mother hate it here?" I asked him once, my eyes on his face. His eyes fluttered beneath their lids, but otherwise he lay perfectly still. "Tell me," I insisted.

He rolled onto his elbow and propped his head on his hand. "What you say is not true. I've been thinking," he said. "She did not hate this place, but she very much loved Warsaw. You see you cannot exist in two places at once. You can try to exist, but you will not be happy. To travel in life, you must leave things behind. If your heart holds tight to the old, how can you embrace what is new? It is not possible, Syrenka."

"But what if you don't like to travel? What if you're happy right where you are?"

He laughed at me and shook his head. "To be alive is to travel."

✳ ✳ ✳

My breasts, now double in size, were hard and round like honeydew melons and overflowed my bra on all sides. Embarrassing didn't begin to describe them. I was ashamed beyond belief as well as surprised that I didn't fall forward and flat on my face every time I stood upright. My wardrobe had been reduced to a few baggy t-shirts and a pair of stretchy waist shorts, which were nowhere near able to surround my great belly and so reached only to my pubic bone in front. Men who wear pants the same way use suspenders. Me, I kept a finger hooked under the waistband to look less conspicuous. I was all about looking less conspicuous from the end of June on. I was about wearing a poncho, standing behind counters, and hanging out in the fridge. It's true. The heat wave just wouldn't let up and so I spent a fair amount of time in the refrigerator. I shifted its contents so I could hold my face in the freezer, my arms straight ahead à la Frankenstein's monster, and my belly propped on the middle shelf alongside the tall drinks: the bottomless pitcher of Kool-Aid and two-litre pop. Mum never told me to shut the door although I'm sure the electricity bill was outrageous. She thought I was eating. Drinking milk from the carton, eating grapes with both hands, wolfing down pickles and sucking eggs from the shell. I could eat us out of house and home and she wouldn't have said anything, so happy was she to think I had an appetite. She had no idea I was pregnant. She blamed my condition on bloating and had banned radish, broccoli, cauliflower and all legumes from the house.

Of course the refrigerator was a poor substitute for the air-conditioned comfort of Saunders' Shoes, but I hadn't worked there since the first day of summer. I had to quit. I had no choice. Saunders shoes was all about customer service and I couldn't do up my own shoes let alone someone else's.

Instead, I was busy counting the days. I'd circled the date on my calendar with the scarlet crayon from Lucy's Crayola box, the red that was closest to the colour of blood. July twenty-ninth. Doomsday. If I could just hang in there four more weeks everything would revert to normal. My regular life would kick into gear. I knew I was only fooling myself. I knew my old life was gone for good.

Corporal Caldwell phoned me once. He asked if I'd remembered anything. To be honest, I didn't want to remember anything. I just wanted this nightmare behind me. He asked me if I still had his number. I said I thought so, but I wasn't sure. He made me take it down again. I pretended to, but had no pen.

❋ ❋ ❋

"Tonight I take you to my favourite place," Eleanor announced, throwing a blanket onto the seat and then easing herself into the truck. The manoeuvre was not easy with her burgeoning belly, but she managed with her new technique: backing onto the seat and then swinging her legs into the cab. I was happy to see she had left her poncho at home. No woman in Warsaw would wear such a poncho; the colours were garish and the style lacking in elegance, still, I could appreciate its usefulness if one was somewhere like the Andes, but to wear it in Lampeq in the middle of summer was clearly insane. Eleanor wore it though—every day once her belly took on cabbage-size proportions and always with her arms crossed underneath and jutting forward so that the poncho hung down in the shape of a yurt. She was a strange and unusual woman, for sure. Why she preferred people think her three hundred pounds overweight rather than pregnant, I did not understand. "What does it matter what people think so long as you know the truth?" I asked. She would not give me an answer. I offered to marry her if she thought a husband might give her the courage she needed to discard the poncho. I laughed when I said it. She did not think it was funny. I was not surprised. I think wearing a poncho in thirty-degree temperatures would make sad the most hilarious girl.

"Where to?" I did not mention the poncho. One word and she would likely run back to the house for it. And I did not want to risk a comment that would spoil her mood, not on our last evening together, not when I had to give her my news.

"Do you know the way to Fishtail Lighthouse?"

"I think so," I said. "It is on the Old Shore Road?" I pretended I was not sure, although, in truth, I could have drove there with my eyes closed. I knew every road in Wolastoq county, but why to ruin her surprise? I also did not tell her that I hated the location; that I found the lighthouse ugly, the coastal climate miserable, and the landscape bleak and desolate. Even the ocean view is not guaranteed because the fog is unpredictable and can rise up like a wall at moments when you least expect it. When this happens, you cannot see the water; you cannot see the shoes upon your feet. I suggest staying clear of the cliff at such times; also the foghorn. The best course of action is to get the hell out and head farther inland. Drive slow, take low beams and watch out for moose.

I parked on the grassy shoulder and we walked to the lighthouse on a path through the heath. I do not know why the trail twists and turns the way it does. The people I know walk a straight path from A to B and prefer not to waste their time walking in circles.

The lighthouse is squat and square and in need of fresh paint. The bare boards beneath the flaked paint are the same grey colour as the cliffs and the rifts in the clouds, the same colour as Warsaw. I touched the worn wood as we walked by on our way to a rocky outcrop, which offers a good view of the cliffs on each side. Eleanor was bravest. She walked right to the edge where the rock had eroded to pebbles and broken shell lay scattered like fragments of dinner plate. The wind blew the blanket straight back off her shoulders like a Superman cape. I caught her arm and pulled her back. "Easy for accident," I said. She smiled at me like one would a small child afraid of ghosts in the closet or monsters under the bed, but let me lead her to a sheltered place in the heath where we sat and waited for the sun to set, I, a little impatiently, because it was cold and I was not dressed for the weather. She, too, was cold; her skin covered in goose flesh, but refused to admit it and gave me her blanket. I wrapped it around both of us and she did not resist.

"There are whales out there," she said, her voice uncertain. Her eyes scanned the water, and so I looked too, but the only life I could see was a man in a small boat tending to a circle of net held up by sticks.

"Have you seen one?" I asked.

She shook her head. "Do you think that might be one?" She hauled herself to a stand and then aimed a finger at some nebulous point out on the water.

How to see the black fin of a whale in a black, moving sea? I do not think so is possible. I wrapped Eleanor's half of blanket across my chest. "I think to see a whale you must abandon land. To make a proper search, you must be in a boat out on the sea. It is not a big problem. I'll find a fisherman to take you."

"Shh!" she said. "Is that a blow?"

"I hear only the wind."

She shivered and walked nearer the edge. "Listen!"

"Be careful," I said.

The sun was trawling the sea with pink and orange ribbons and Eleanor's cheek, the one with the scar, was the colour of amber. "You were wrong about your mother," she said, still staring at the water. "She left *everything* behind." Then, in three quick steps she was hovering on the edge. Her braid was undone and the wind whipped strands in all directions.

There was no time to stop her. Later, the man in the dory said he watched her all the way down. He said she hit the water straight and graceful as a cormorant, like someone who'd been diving all her life. Me, I saw only her straight legs and pointed toes, her sandals flying through the air as her feet dropped out of sight. I stared at the empty air where her feet had been, tried to stand up, but the wind forced me down. Tried again, this time between wind gusts, and then took off, straight through the heath, back for the road where a steep pebbly trail leads down to the shore. In my haste, I never thought to bring the blanket or even to alert the fisherman for help. When common sense finally kicked in, I was already past the lighthouse; a little farther and I'd be at the road. I tripped on a root, fell flat on my face and got up still running. Maybe I should go back. Call to the fisherman for help. Fortunately, just then a boat engine sputtered to life and I convinced myself the man was headed for Eleanor and not back to the wharf, his work done for the day. Yes, the sound was coming closer not fading away.

At the main road, I quickly found the right trail and raced down it riding my heels. My knuckles dredged the ground every step of the way and by the time I reached bottom both my hands were bloody and torn. I feared the worst for Eleanor. I'd seen the rocks rising up through the swells. How could she be alive?

The engine stopped and a disgruntled voice carried over the waves. "Holy-liftin' girl! Take hold of the buoy! Jesus H. Bald-headed Christ! Your arms! Use your arms!"

I shielded my eyes from the last rays of sun and saw the

fishing boat a short distance down shore below Fishtail Light. The fisherman was trying to haul Eleanor on board while she hung there at the side with a weight that seemed close to capsizing the boat. The distance was too far to swim, but I waded in past my knees. The waves drenched me all the way to the shoulders. *Please God make her light as a feather, or, if that is not possible give her fisherman saviour the strength to lift her into the boat.* Yes, she was slowly rising out of the waves. When his arms could reach her pants he pulled her aboard and then steered the boat for the government wharf.

"Hey! Over here!" By some stroke of luck the fisherman heard, abruptly aborted course and headed for shore. I waded in deeper to meet them.

Eleanor was sprawled out on a net on the floor. Her eyes were closed, but her chest was heaving so I knew she was alive. "Syrenka," I said and touched her icy cheek, stroked her inky blue fingertips.

"She needs out of those wet clothes before hypothermia sets in." The fisherman jumped from the boat and we pulled it to shore and together carried Eleanor past the high water mark to the grass. "Take everything off," he ordered and quickly stripped down to his long underwear, while I, hesitating a moment, started to peel off my shirt. "Not yours—hers," the man said. "Take off her wet clothes."

My cold, clumsy fingers struggled to push buttons through the holes of her shirt. "Like this," said the man, exasperated, and he grabbed the neck of her shirt with both hands and ripped through the buttons. Then he pulled her forward so I could slide the shirt over her arms. While the man wrapped her in his coat, I grabbed the waistband of her pants and peeled it over her hips. A pinky-red was creeping up the sides of her underwear and the crotch was solid red. Blood too, streamed down between her legs and drenched the grass.

The fisherman swore under his breath. "She needs a hospital," he said.

※ ※ ※

Penny Lane entered the world at 12:32 AM on the morning of July ninth. She was three weeks early. The doctor said it was one of the fastest deliveries he'd ever seen and he'd seen his share, having delivered a good third of Lampeq over the forty years of his career. He said she slipped through the birth canal like Ty Cobb stealing home. I think he had me confused with the woman in the next room. I swear the baby had straddled my cervix and had her feet braced against my pelvis and her elbows in my sacrum and held her ground for three days before she finally surrendered and came out. She weighed in at seven pounds six ounces and had an Apgar score of eight, normal on both counts as per the books I'd read at the library. The nurse put her in my arms, a red faced, howling, fist-pumping fiend. She was naked and wet and locks of black hair were slicked to her head in a very cool style that was more rock star then baby. She looked outraged, like she couldn't believe the screw-up, like she'd booked a five-star hotel and ended up here. Then she opened her eyes wide, took one look at me, and shut her mouth in mid-scream.

I stared at the infant in amazement. Her fingers were long and slender with perfect creases and nails that glimmered with the pink sheen of scallop shell. Her pursed mouth was a rose bud and her eyes, her beautiful eyes were like twin shiny brown coins. I bowed my head and worshipped her in wonder.

"Penny Lane," declared my mother who had come to the hospital when she got word of my admission and held my hand through the ordeal.

"We don't have anything for her to sleep in," said my father who had come with my mother, but stayed in the waiting room until the baby's grand entrance.

"Look! She's smiling," said my mother. And it was true— Penny Lane's mouth was turned up in a grin.

I looked from one parent to the other. My mother wasn't acting the least bit surprised, like she'd known all along that I was pregnant and had been stockpiling Pablum and diapers for months. And my father was taking it all in stride and not throwing a temper tantrum like I would have expected. I didn't recognize either of them.

"Everything happens for a reason," said my mother. She caressed Penny Lane's fingers and stroked her eyebrows.

"I'm keeping her," I announced, shocking even myself.

My parents looked up in surprise, as though they'd never expected me to do any different. "Of course, Honey," said my mother and my father nodded in agreement.

"She's hungry," said my mother. "Let's see if she'll nurse."

✳ ✳ ✳

I hadn't planned to kill myself. It just happened. Like, when you're not really hungry, but plant yourself at the kitchen counter and eat a whole dozen chocolate chip cookies straight from the oven even though you know they're not good for you and you'll feel sicker than a dog later on. Or when you stay up half the night to read 'The Trial' even though you have school the next day and you know you can't function without eight hours sleep and have a sneaking suspicion you won't like the end anyway.

Standing there on the edge of the cliff, life seemed so heavy and hopeless all of a sudden. The water swirling below was black and mean. Teela was dead. Her carcass had washed ashore on Grand Manan Island. Princess Ariel was doomed and the baby in me didn't stand a chance, either. For one thing, I hadn't found it good parents—proof that I was bad, same as always, and would never be good. To top it all off, I was pretty sure I loved Darek Dąbrowski, loved him so much it hurt—all things that in my lately assumed state of personal Godlessness should not have mattered, but that for some reason seemed to loom larger than ever.

Plunging through the air I changed my mind. I didn't want to die, after all. I wanted to live. Then, I nailed the dive; a clean ten out of ten and as good a dive as any you'd see on TV. I hoped Darek had watched. He would have been proud.

The water was frigid. I started hyperventilating as soon as I went under. Water flooded my mouth, some down my windpipe and into my chest where my lungs absorbed it like a sponge. *This is how it feels to drown*—I thought. *This is how it feels to turn to ice.*

Suddenly, a man's voice exploded over the roar of the waves. "Over here!" Although water in my eyes put my vision on par with the view through a windshield during a downpour, I managed to make out a man maybe eight feet away, a blurry figure leaning over the side of a boat in this warped yellow slicker. At that point I still had the wherewithal to recognize him as the fisherman from the weir, but, only a moment or two later I was a complete idiot and unable to recognize my own hand inches from my face. I guess it was shock setting in. It never occurred to me, for example, to swim the few strokes between me and the boat. (Not to say I was capable even had I thought of it. My arms and legs were like blocks of ice and controlling them like steering an ice floe.)

The man threw me a buoy. I stared at it stupidly. He rowed the boat closer and stretched his arms out toward me. That time his fingertips grazed the back of my hand. A wave pulled me under and then forced me into the side of the boat. The man seized the moment. He lunged forward, grabbed me by the pants, and in one quick movement hauled me over the side, my twenty-pound overweight self in waterlogged clothes with an unwieldy hump of baby sticking out in the front. Did I mention the seaweed wrapped around my ankles and holding me like a bad dog on a leash to the sea floor? The man was a hero and I was an anti-hero, not a villain exactly, more a coughing, snorting, throwing-up-seawater failure. I lay in the boat retching my guts out.

I wanted the fisherman to know I was thankful. I knew I'd been on borrowed time out there. I tried to catch his eye to convey my gratitude, no easy feat in the growing darkness. Then a sweep of the lighthouse showed his face in full view, a middle-aged man with deep lines around his mouth and a body like a chest of drawers. I sought out his eyes beneath the peak of his hat. "Thank you," I said.

✼ ✼ ✼

There wasn't much space for a baby at home. Jude already had a bed in the hall. In the end, we put the mahogany cradle next to my bed in the room I shared with Lucy. I admit it wasn't the perfect arrangement. Lucy couldn't have friends over when Penny Lane was napping and when Penny Lane cried in the night I had to pick her up quick before she woke up poor Lucy who, come September had school every morning. Unfortunately, I was so exhausted by evening I could have slept through a Mack truck idling next to my bed and it was Lucy who always ended up waking first and who delivered a wet and ravenous Penny Lane safe and sound to my bed.

Contrary to how it may sound, life was good; better than ever before, and I'm not just talking the year since the rape. I loved Penny Lane more than I'd ever loved anyone and between diapers, laundry, and feedings, I passed the time in adoration. Everything that didn't have a direct connection to Penny Lane fell by the wayside. Even my guilt and worry were on a hiatus. My world had dwindled to the size of a baby, but it felt vast as the sky.

The day we got home from the hospital was also Jude's birthday. For supper my father brought home a bucket of Dixie Lee chicken and a large coleslaw and my mother made a sheet cake which she poked full of holes, filled in with Jell-O and iced with whipped cream.

The chicken was gone and my mother was in the process of

lighting the candles on the birthday cake (five candles was her record before the paper towel erupted into a burning inferno and required instant disposal in the sink) when I got up to make a phone call that just wouldn't wait. A woman answered on the third ring.

"Hello?" She was in the middle of something and I'd interrupted. It was there in her breathy delivery and in the way she clipped the 'l' and the 'o' in 'hello'. Dinner. She probably had dinner on the stove, maybe rice and black beans, a throwback to their missionary days. She was probably standing there with her hair in a ponytail secured with elastic, pleased to be serving her family a complete protein, but at a fraction of the cost of meat.

"Hello. Is John there?"

"One moment, please." The phone clunked down on something hard, then the clatter of dishes in the sink, hurried footsteps going then coming.

"Hello."

"John, it's me Lennie."

"Lennie?"

"You know—Eleanor. Eleanor Hanson. From MBC."

Dead silence on his end.

I wanted you to know that I'm doing OK." I twisted the phone cord around my finger. "I mean, I figured you'd like to know. You were the one who found me. You were actually there. Five seconds of complete and utter silence. "I just thought you'd like to know, is all."

"Wait. I'm confused. What is it you're trying to say exactly? That you forgive me? Listen, Eleanor. Let's get one thing straight. What happened to you was in no way my fault."

"No, that's not what I ..."

"And if you want to get technical about it—I wasn't there, as a matter of fact. You were the one with the broken ankle. I was the one who went for help. So maybe you need to rethink what you're saying. Maybe you need to forgive someone else."

213

Dead silence on my end.

"Excuse me, Eleanor, but I have to go."

I stood there a moment, the receiver buzzing in my ear. It's hard to explain, but for the first time in my life I felt totally free. I went to the living room where Penny Lane lay asleep on the couch with Lucy's stuffed animals keeping watch on all sides. I laid my hand on her chest and felt the beat of her heart through her terry cloth sleeper.

✻ ✻ ✻

The ladies from church threw me a baby shower in the church parlour. I didn't want one, but they insisted and my mother talked me into going. "Think about Penny Lane," said my mother. "She'll be showered in love." After my conversation with John, I had my doubts about love, but I was sure there'd be a lot of blame.

The room looked like a wedding cake—all pink and white streamers, shimmery pink balloons on silver ribbon and big plates of food arranged on pastel doilies. Everyone was there, even some of the shut-ins who rarely attended church but somehow made it down the full of flight of stairs and through the long concourse to the parlour with their portable oxygen, quad canes, and walkers in tow. The girls from my old Sunday school class all sat together, their foreheads puckered with confusion, their eyes sneaking peeks at my hand for a ring. Only Sandra didn't make it. She had a waitressing job in Fredericton for the summer and couldn't get the night off. Patty made it, though. She was a few minutes late, but made excellent time considering she'd got off work at five and drove all the way from Riverview in her beat-up Ford Pinto. Back at the college, I'd been amazed each time her car made a successful trip into Moncton, never mind a two hundred kilometre trek down the highway.

I was happy to see her. I don't mean to sound ungrateful, but the shower was off to a very slow start. The women who weren't manning the food had found themselves chairs, and so there were little old ladies stranded in chairs with high arms and deep seats, their feet dangling in mid-air and larger ladies with wide bottoms sunk low in chairs with worn springs and soft cushions and everyone else in the hard folding chairs that are used for church suppers. In other words, once a lady sat down it was too much work to get up and so conversation was limited to the people adjacent and even that wasn't certain but dependent on such factors as good dentures, hearing and a flexible neck.

No one said much to me. I had expected questions about how long I'd been married and what my husband did for a living, but there was none of that. All I got were comments about how Penny Lane had my nose and the same neat, flat to the head little ears from the ladies beside me and friendly looks and kind smiles from the ladies in seats farther away.

"Sorry I'm late," Patty said, squeezing between two folding chairs with two big shopping bags held high to avoid spoiling fresh wash and sets. "I have to keep it under one-twenty or parts start to fall off of my vehicle." She headed to the only available spot, the place of honour next to Penny Lane and I on the antique settee. Her loud voice had even the deafest lady's attention. "How are things?" she said and dropped the bags on the floor at my feet and then offered her pinky to Penny Lane who seized onto it with a death grip. "Look at the power in this one, would ja," Patty said, glancing around at her audience. "She's headed for the UN, this one. She's going to rule the world." She casually took Penny Lane from my arms and plopped her in the arms of the woman next to me, a retired missionary who'd spent forty years in the mission field twenty years ago and still went church to church talking about it. The woman, a spinster with no children if I remembered right, immediately went into baby mode, and started talking in this high voice with exaggerated mouth movements. The other women angled their heads like robins listening for worms and "aahed" with approval.

On a roll, Patty rummaged through her shopping bags and surfaced with a fistful of pencils and notepads. "Time to get this show on the road," she said. "I'm Patty Tanzer, best friend to one Eleanor Hanson and her adorable baby, Penny Lane as well as your Master of Ceremonies for the evening. Shall we start with some games?" She sized up the crowd to gauge their reaction and then tossing the paper and pencils aside, announced she was starving and suggested we eat first and play later. No one objected, in fact most of the room broke into cheers with a few of the more feisty ladies pumping their fists. So we made our way to the tables, me first of course, and filled up our plates with mountains of food. All except the ladies who couldn't get out of their chairs without considerable effort and who waited for the food to come to them.

I found I had suddenly lost my appetite and could only nibble at my plate, as Penny Lane made the rounds. She went from one fragile old lady to another, many with their hands gnarled up by arthritis, a few with shaky arms and bobbing heads, and all with hot cups of tea at their elbows. I told myself Penny Lane couldn't weigh more than a communion tray of grape juice glasses and no little old lady had dropped one of those in all the years I'd gone to church. Then I remembered that the little old ladies all sit in the back and never lift the communion plates because the deacon serves them one by one. Penny Lane wasn't scared, though. She nestled into each woman's breast, filled her hands with fistfuls of blouse, and then looked each woman in the eye, blew bubbles and cooed and had them all falling in love with her. I panicked only once—when one of the ladies who'd come with a walker nodded off with Penny Lane in her arms, her elbows suddenly giving way like a cogwheel causing Penny Lane to lurch away from her breast. Fortunately, the ladies on each side—much faster than they appeared—sprang into action and had Penny Lane safe and sound in the next set of arms before she sustained so much as a scratch.

It was your standard Baptist affair. We ate so much and so long that we ran out of time and had to skip the games altogether and go straight to the presents. Patty tied a paper plate on my head and covered it with the ribbons and bows I removed from each package. Penny Lane who had gone round the room full circle and was now back in the arms of the retired missionary stared up at me with big, round eyes.

It was like Christmas a hundred times over. More clothes, toys and linen than any one baby could use in a lifetime. Some of the ladies chipped together for a stroller. Mrs. Saunders gave me a pair of soft sole leather baby shoes in peppermint pink which I know for a fact cost forty-two ninety-five. By the end of it, bows plastered every inch of my body.

"I don't know what to say," I said, ribbon tickling bare skin at my wrists and my throat. "Thank you, everyone. Thank you so much."

My mother sidled up to me as people started to leave. "Did you feel it?" she asked. "All the love in the room?"

"Yes," I said because there was a feeling—a warm, soothing feeling, like when I put on my fleece pajamas with feet after a hot bath and a dusting of scented powder.

One little old lady in a wheelchair caught my hand on her way to the door. "I gave my baby up for adoption," she said. "It was the biggest mistake of my life. If I only knew where to find her, nothing would keep us apart. I would rise up on these rickety legs and run to her and not look back."

❊ ❊ ❊

I loved Penny Lane through the summer and fall. I loved her shiny brown eyes and neat fingers, her baby bird tufts of black hair and chubby, pink bum. I loved securing the tapes of her diaper over the curve of her belly, soaping up her silky, soft baby skin and watching her sleep. I loved when she cried because as soon as I picked her up or gave her some milk or pulled off the socks that were pinching her toes, the crying would stop and she was the happiest girl in the world. My love for her was so excruciating, so great, that sometimes I hung over her cradle and wished her awake.

By the end of November she had doubled her weight and gained four inches in length. During that same period the North Atlantic right whales had come and gone and Princess Ariel was still missing in action. I, personally, hadn't been anywhere near the bay since Penny Lane's birth. I could understand the 'not going.' It was the 'not missing' that had me perplexed.

Darek wasn't around, that much was certain, but I was determined to find him so I packed Penny Lane into her new stroller the day after the shower and we walked to the Irving. The girl in the office said she hadn't seen Darek in a while and had no idea where he'd gone, but she had a pretty good idea why. Then she came around to the front of the counter, gave Penny Lane a pointed look, crossed her arms and stood there glaring at me. I said I highly doubted she knew anything about Darek and why he went where he did, but the Met was selling Playtex underwire bras at half-price and that was something she should know about. Then, I stormed out, slamming the door so hard behind me the windows rattled in their frames. I marched to the garage, a dank, dingy cavern with black stains spoiling every surface and exhaust hanging in the air like shelf clouds. I parked Penny Lane outside the door where I could see her, set the brake on the stroller, and went inside. The mechanics were on break, each with a cup in one hand and a cigarette in the other, some squatting on tires and others leaning against workbenches. "Where you hiding Darek?" one asked.

"You don't know where he is, then?" My gaze went from one man to the next and was met with blank stares or vague shrugs.

"Jumped ship, did he?" the first man persisted.

"Well, I hope he hightails it back soon. I'm starting to miss the Frenchie," piped up a second man.

"Darek's not French. He's Polish," I said.

The man smiled. "Then I guess it's the Polish sausage, you're missing."

Everyone laughed; everyone except me. I picked up a can of motor oil and threw it straight at his head. He stared at me, a stunned expression on his face, and then he dropped to the floor, slow and quiet as a coat falling off a hanger.

That's not exactly how it went. My hand closed around a can of motor oil, that part is true. The can felt good and heavy, solid. And then I zoned in on the idiot's head, lined up the bridge of his nose with my visual cross hairs all in slow motion like the six million dollar man and his bionic eye. At that crucial moment, just after my wind up, but before my release, Penny Lane started to cry. I set down the can without a second thought and went straight back to the stroller. We were halfway across the parking lot when one of the younger mechanics ran up beside me. I'd seen him around. He's always buying three-piece dinners at Dixie Lee, insists all his pieces be ribs.

"Darek quit work a few weeks ago. He's left town, but we don't know for where. His dad's still around though. If you see him he'll have answers."

I didn't want my visit to see Darek's dad to be a big deal. I wanted him to be outside cutting grass or washing the car. I wanted to walk by, spontaneous-like, and call out casually from the sidewalk; something like "Darek around?" or "What's Darek up to these days?" Something off the cuff that didn't sound contrived. Then he'd look up and give me a quick one sentence reply and I'd say, "Tell him I said hi" or "That's nice," or something equally blasé and keep on walking.

No such luck. Darek's dad was inside watching TV. I heard the doorbell sounds from Wheel of Fortune three houses down which meant our exchange would have to be more formal than I'd planned. I'd have to leave the sidewalk, go up the steps and actually knock on the door. It would be a visit rank with intention. I took a deep breath and pushed Penny Lane up the driveway, the wheels of her stroller bumpity-bumping over the gravel. The grass was freshly cut and a hanging basket dripped a steady stream of water just outside the front door. Penny Lane and I stood clear of the drip as I knocked on the glass. I knocked a few times. It would be a visit rank with persistence and intention. Finally, he answered, smelling like Zest and hair wet from the shower.

"Is Darek here?"

"Come in, come in," he said in this deep, booming voice that surged up from his chest like oil from a geyser. "You are Eleanor, no? Darek said you would visit. Darek said when you come I must talk to you everything." He patted Penny Lane's head with a hand like a bear paw and led us inside.

I hesitated inside the door. The furniture was moved around, the couch pushed next to the window and the recliner, sans white sheet, squeezed in alongside. My eyes stared at that chair like it was a crime scene.

"You know what is good," Darek's father said, patting the arm of the recliner. "This chair what you see—it is the most comfortable chair in the house. Please to sit down and I will serve you some borscht. You will like it, believe me. Everybody who eats it, likes it, my borscht."

I gave the chair a wide berth and perched on the couch while he went to the kitchen. "Ukrainian style," he said, back in no time and setting my mug of soup on the living room table. It was the prettiest soup I'd ever seen, a deep, milky pink with red bubbles like rubies skimming the surface.

He settled into the recliner and turned down the TV. "New chair," he said. "Fifty percent off. In this country you are crazy to pay full price for anything what they sell in a store. I saw this chair six months ago for five hundred dollars. I liked it, but I did not need it. I had a chair. I had a couch. We did not use the chair... for personal reasons, but still, it was here. It existed. So, I am patient and wait and wait and my chair goes on sale."

"What happened to the other chair?" I asked, needing to know but dreading the answer.

He stared at me thoughtfully before answering. "It is safe—do not worry. But why to have a chair in the living room what no one uses? It takes up space only and goes on my nerves. I move it to a different room, an empty room where no one goes." He pointed to the TV where Vanna was dutifully revealing the final letters to a puzzle. "I watch every day. I think is good for my English, no?" He grabbed a notebook and pencil from the table beside his chair and dutifully jotted down the answer. "I do not understand this solution. Can you explain what means 'speed demon,' please? Is it noun or a verb?"

"Noun."

"And who is this speed demon?"

"It is the name for a person who drives very fast."

"And is this speed demon a man or a woman?"

"Either one; both."

"And he or she drives European cars, no? Ferraris and Porsches?"

I laughed. "They can drive anything. What matters is they drive too fast, faster than the speed limit allows. For example, in a fifty kilometre zone, a speed demon may go eighty or ninety."

"Maybe even one hundred, no? Maybe two hundred on the autobahn?" He winked at me and made more notes. "There," he said. "See how convenient to have the person who knows English at home?" He put down his notebook and picked up his borscht. "But you did not come here to speak to an old Polish man about the shows he sees on the television. You want to know about Darek." He emptied the cup. "I think you miss my son, yes?"

I nodded.

"It is not very much complicated. This is what happened: His visa arrived and he went to America."

"You mean Calais?" I said. Calais wasn't much different than Lampeq except for gas was cheaper, they had a movie theatre and sold things that we didn't like Almond Joy chocolate bars and red hot dogs. It and Bangor were the only parts of America I'd ever visited. "Around here, we call it 'The States'," I informed him.

"Not 'The States'," Mr. Dąbrowski said like he'd told me a million times already and I should know it by now. "America: New York, Chicago, Los Angeles—America." He spread his arms wide to take in the whole country.

I stared at Mr. Dąbrowski without really seeing him. I was seeing Darek that day in the winter outside the Irving, an old greasy rag in his hands and Dąbrowski in fancy blue script on his chest. Darek had said he wanted to go to New York. I remembered the light in his eyes as he told me. He had wanted to go so he made plans and he went. I didn't take him seriously at the time. Why would I? Nobody around here did things like that.

"His visa came on Friday and he left the next day. Changed the oil in his truck, filled up with gas and was gone. He was too excited to wait. Do you know how long he was waiting already? Since he was a boy this tall." Mr. Dąbrowski held his hand level with the arm of the chair.

"America is a dream in his head. You understand this, yes? Canadian boys dream, too. They dream to play hockey on TV. They dream to be heroes like Gretzky and Schwarzenegger. They dream to be rich. I tell you the true; he could not wait any longer. His visa came, he had to go." His gaze shifted and lingered on Penny Lane. "He wanted me to tell you what he tried to say good-bye."

I stared at the TV, numb with the news. I was re-writing history in my head; telling myself I had been hugely mistaken.

Darek and I had never been close, we were friends—that was all; not even friends. More like acquaintances.

"He stopped at the hospital. The nurses said you were OK, but they would not let him see you. They said it was impossible, visiting hours were only for family. He had to go and not look back. He could not wait another day. You understand this, yes?"

I didn't understand. I didn't understand at all. Still, I pretended to and nodded while I repositioned Penny Lane who, though sliding off my lap, remained transfixed on Darek's dad. She'd been staring at him since we arrived, apparently mesmerized by his loud voice and grand gestures. He finally acknowledged her, warbling at her in baby talk and pulling on her toes. She kicked and flapped her arms in pleasure, drool streaming down her chin and soaking her shirt.

"Of course, nothing is forever," he said, releasing Penny Lane's foot and leaning back in his chair. "Time will show what will be happen. Maybe he will hate it, America. Maybe he will stay there forever. God alone knows the answer."

I imagined Darek camped out in Times Square in the thick of the action and loving every minute of it. I glanced down at Penny Lane. She was sucking her hand the way she does when she's hungry. I finished the borscht and stood up. I felt hollow inside, like the skin of my torso was stretched over bare bone with nothing inside. "We better get going."

Darek's dad stood up, too. "You come again. We will eat cheesecake and watch Wheel of Fortune. You will translate the answers and I will understand everything."

He walked me outside and stood by quietly as I strapped Penny Lane into her stroller. In some ways, he reminded me of Darek. He had the same solid presence, the same watchful eyes. "It was nice to meet you, Mr. Dąbrowski," I said and put out my hand. He pulled me into his arms, wrapped me in a giant hug and kissed me on each cheek. He smelled like spruce trees beneath the Zest. "We have strong characters, you and I," he whispered. "We will for sure survive."

I turned to go before I started to cry and had almost made it to the sidewalk when he asked me to wait. "I have something to give you," he called. "Something what is from Darek." He took the front steps two at a time and returned with a shoebox.

"For the baby," he said and put the box in my hands.

I lifted the lid with trembling fingers. Inside was a pull-toy, an elegant white horse with a golden mane and red roses etched into its saddle. The white paint glittered with flecks of gold. "It's beautiful," I whispered.

"Soon the child will walk and see the world for herself and for this she requires a loyal companion."

I turned the horse in my hands. "But Darek didn't know I was keeping the baby," I said with a catch in my voice and wiped tears from my eyes with the back of my hand.

Darek's dad fished a handkerchief from his shirt pocket and pressed it into my palm. "Do not cry, my kochanie. Darek knows more than you think."

✶ ✶ ✶

Penny Lane was almost four months old when the first postcard arrived. Actually, it arrived before that, but my mother had put it on the fridge for safekeeping and then promptly forgot about it. I didn't blame her. It was hard to keep track of anything beyond the everyday challenges of laundry, dishes and meals in a household of seven, especially with one of those seven a baby. Add the shopping and baking connected to Christmas and I considered myself lucky I saw it at all.

My father had just put up the Christmas tree leaving the house in its usual post-putting up the Christmas tree shambles. Although I don't suppose his performance was quite as exciting as watching a man wrestle a crocodile with his bare hands, there was no denying it held a certain attraction as we all watched from a distance, our mouths hanging open and our hands clasped in prayer. Would this be the year Dad totally lost it and threw the tree trunk first through the front picture window? We held our breath while he lopped off pieces from first the top, then the bottom and then forced the tree into its stand, sap staining his clothes and spruce needles everywhere.

Mission accomplished, my father then threw on his coat, stomped through the kitchen and out the back door to return to the store where he'd probably vent his frustration on some lowly sales clerk until closing. It was as the door slammed behind him that a gust of wind blew the postcard off the fridge and sent it sailing across the kitchen and straight into the cupboards where it then dropped into a sink full of dishes. My mother rescued it and gave it to me. "My soul!" she said. "I completely forgot. This came for you the other day."

I shook off the soapsuds and dried the card on my pants. "Greetings from Florida" it said with a close-up of an orange still on the branch. My heart skipped a beat as I flipped the card to read the back. Nothing. No "Wish you were here. No "The weather is great." The left half of the card was entirely empty. I showed the orange to Penny Lane who promptly stuck the cardboard in her mouth and started chewing on a corner. I quickly salvaged it and took it my room where I stuck it in the mirror.

A second postcard arrived a few weeks later, this one from Charleston. Then a flurry of them: postcards from Chesapeake, Richmond and Philadelphia, Chicago, St. Louis, Sioux City, and Nebraska; my address on one side, the other side blank. I bought a wall map of the United States, taped it to the wall and traced his journey out with tacks.

When he got to Spokane, Washington he started south to Eugene, Oregon and then down to Sacramento. After San Diego he started going east again. There was no rhyme or reason to his path. The route went up down, up down, like the teeth in a jack-o'-lantern.

When I got the card from New York City, I knew that was the end. I knew because he signed his name. Also his address and phone number neatly printed in pen.

※ ※ ※

Things I Know About New York City

1. ~~It has more people than any other city in the US.~~
2. ~~It's divided into five boroughs: The Bronx, Manhattan, Staten Island, Brooklyn, and Queens~~
3. ~~It was founded as a commercial trading post by the Dutch in 1624~~
4. ~~It has many famous landmarks including the Statue of Liberty and Times Square~~
5. ~~Its mass transit is the most extensive of any city in North America~~
6. ~~It's known as "The Big Apple" and "The City that Never Sleeps"~~
7. ~~It's the crime capital of America.~~
8. Darek lives there.

EPILOGUE

I like research. I like controlled variables and experimental studies. I like data I can see and hold in my hand. I like facts written down, multiple sources and footnotes. I like the Word of God in a book in my pocket. I don't always know how to take what I read, but to figure out life one has to start somewhere and I think the head is as good a place to start as any. Just don't hunker down in the head forever. It's a beginning—that's all. Then, you have to move on. You have to test the data with your heart and feel it in your bones. You have to soak in it and let it change you. Because the real story is more than just words on a page. The real story is alive. It is a living, breathing thing.

Princess Ariel defied the stats and survived. The scientists were doing their annual photo ID's of the whales out in the bay. When they compared the photos to their records, turned out one of the young whales was Teela's missing calf. She was with a group of other whales and appeared to be fine.

The same article reported a meeting between the scientists, the fishermen, the government and Irving. The scientists have a proposal. Their research has shown that if the shipping lanes are moved just six kilometres east of the right whale feeding grounds it will decrease collisions with whales by ninety percent. Industry is crunching numbers while the government pours coffee and passes out doughnuts. I'm very optimistic. I think something big will happen.

As for me, I'm taking a trip. Darek sent me an open ticket to New York City and Penny Lane travels free. I have no idea if I'll like it there or how long I'll stay. All I know is that the sun is streaming through the window and there's the smell of lilacs in the air and I've never noticed it 'til now, but way off in the distance where the wind parts the trees I can see the glint of water and what looks to be a tanker on its way out of the bay.

ACKNOWLEDGEMENTS

Many people offered encouragement, suggestions, and practical help as I wrote this book. A huge thank you to Owen Stairs for providing feedback on the early drafts and being my number one fan. Thanks to Laurie Murison, Executive Director of the Grand Manan Whale and Seabird Research Station, and a marine biologist with expertise in all things North Atlantic right whale. Any errors of fact are mine and not hers. Thanks, too, to: Teri Young for indulging me in my quest for that perfect shot; The Writers' Federation of New Brunswick for encouraging me to forge on with the manuscript just as the going was getting tough; Dad, for keeping me in Little Golden Books and Thornton W. Burgess animal stories when I was knee-high to a grasshopper, and my late mother, for tirelessly reading them to me; Malcolm Collicott for fielding my questions on RCMP matters; Jeff Cowen and Billy Dee Paul, of Sarnia Fire Rescue Services, for providing information on fire calls; Michelle, Trevor, Joel, and all my friends around the lunch table at Bluewater Health, for their ongoing support; Denis De Klerck, Stuart Ross, and Mansfield Press, for taking a chance on my manuscript. And last, but certainly not least, thanks to Sławek and Rowan, either of who could have shut down this book writing operation years ago. All my love to you, both.

One book, in particular, helped me understand the Polish psyche at the time of Solidarity and martial law and was an invaluable resource in the writing of this book. It is "The Private Poland" by Janine Wedel.

The population of the North Atlantic right whale has doubled since the early '80s, but the species remain critically endangered. The rights continue to frequent the Bay of Fundy, but their numbers are erratic as the waters have warmed. Go see them if you get the chance. The experience will change your life. And if you're the kind of person who likes to make a difference, check out www.adoptrightwhales.ca

※ ※ ※

Page 39: *The Twenty-Second Demand* was one of the anonymous verses circulating in the main hall of the strike at Gdańsk in August 1980. This version is from *Przestańcie Stale Nam Przeprascac*, (Wydawnictwo im. Konstytucji 3 Maja, Warsaw, 1980)—a collection of some of the strikers' poems issued by an 'unofficial' publisher.

※ ※ ※

Excerpts from *Live from the Underground* were previously published in the *Nashwaak Review* and the *Telegraph Journal*.

Corinne Wasilewski was born and raised in Woodstock, New Brunswick, but now makes her home in Sarnia, where she works as an occupational therapist. Her short stories have appeared in *Front & Centre, The Windsor Review, The Nashwaak Review* and *The Battered Suitcase. Live from the Underground* is her first novel. An early version of the manuscript was awarded the WFNB's David Adams Richards Prize in 2012.

Other Books From Mansfield Press

Poetry

Leanne Averbach, *Fever*
Tara Azzopardi, *Last Stop, Lonesome Town*
Nelson Ball, *In This Thin Rain*
Nelson Ball, *Some Mornings*
Gary Barwin, *Moon Baboon Canoe*
George Bowering, *Teeth: Poems 2006–2011*
Stephen Brockwell, *Complete Surprising Fragments of Improbable Books*
Stephen Brockwell & Stuart Ross, eds., *Rogue Stimulus: The Stephen Harper Holiday Anthology for a Prorogued Parliament*
Diana Fitzgerald Bryden, *Learning Russian*
Alice Burdick, *Flutter*
Alice Burdick, *Holler*
Jason Camlot, *What The World Said*
Margaret Christakos, *wipe.under.a.love*
Pino Coluccio, *First Comes Love*
Marie-Ève Comtois, *My Planet of Kites*
Dani Couture, *YAW*
Gary Michael Dault, *The Milk of Birds*
Frank Davey, *Poems Suitable for Current Material Conditions*
Pier Giorgio Di Cicco, *The Dark Time of Angels*
Pier Giorgio Di Cicco, *Dead Men of the Fifties*
Pier Giorgio Di Cicco, *The Honeymoon Wilderness*
Pier Giorgio Di Cicco, *Living in Paradise*
Pier Giorgio Di Cicco, *Early Works*
Pier Giorgio Di Cicco, *The Visible World*
Salvatore Difalco, *Mean Season*
Salvatore Difalco, *What Happens at Canals*
Christopher Doda, *Aesthetics Lesson*
Christopher Doda, *Among Ruins*
Glenn Downie, *Monkey Soap*
Rishma Dunlop, *The Body of My Garden*
Rishma Dunlop, *Lover Through Departure: New and Selected Poems*
Rishma Dunlop, *Metropolis*
Rishma Dunlop & Priscila Uppal, eds., *Red Silk: An Anthology of South Asian Women Poets*
Ollivier Dyens, *The Profane Earth*
Laura Farina, *Some Talk of Being Human*
Jaime Forsythe, *Sympathy Loophole*
Carole Glasser Langille, *Late in a Slow Time*
Suzanne Hancock, *Another Name for Bridge*
Eva H.D., *Rotten Perfect Mouth*
Jason Heroux, *Emergency Hallelujah*
Jason Heroux, *Memoirs of an Alias*
Jason Heroux, *Natural Capital*
John B. Lee, *In the Terrible Weather of Guns*
Jeanette Lynes, *The Aging Cheerleader's Alphabet*
David W. McFadden, *Be Calm, Honey*
David W. McFadden, *Shouting Your Name Down the Well: Tankas and Haiku*
David W. McFadden, *Abnormal Brain Sonnets*
David W. McFadden, *What's the Score?*
Kathryn Mockler, *The Purpose Pitch*
Leigh Nash, *Goodbye, Ukulele*
Lillian Necakov, *The Bone Broker*
Lillian Necakov, *Hooligans*
Peter Norman, *At the Gates of the Theme Park*
Peter Norman, *Water Damage*
Natasha Nuhanovic, *Stray Dog Embassy*
Catherine Owen & Joe Rosenblatt, with Karen Moe, *Dog*
Corrado Paina, *The Alphabet of the Traveler*
Corrado Paina, *The Dowry of Education*
Corrado Paina, *Hoarse Legend*
Corrado Paina, *Souls in Plain Clothes*
Corrado Paina, *Cinematic Taxi*
Nick Papaxanthos, *Love Me Tender*
Stuart Ross et al., *Our Days in Vaudeville*
Matt Santateresa, *A Beggar's Loom*
Matt Santateresa, *Icarus Redux*
Ann Shin, *The Last Thing Standing*
Jim Smith, *Back Off, Assassin! New and Selected Poems*
Jim Smith, *Happy Birthday, Nicanor Parra*
Robert Earl Stewart, *Campfire Radio Rhapsody*
Robert Earl Stewart, *Something Burned on the Southern Border*
Carey Toane, *The Crystal Palace*
Aaron Tucker, *punchlines*
Priscila Uppal, *Summer Sport: Poems*
Priscila Uppal, *Winter Sport: Poems*
Priscila Uppal, *Sabotage*
Steve Venright, *Floors of Enduring Beauty*
Brian Wickers, *Stations of the Lost*

Fiction

Marianne Apostolides, *The Lucky Child*
Sarah Dearing, *The Art of Sufficient Conclusions*
Denis De Klerck, ed., *Particle & Wave: A Mansfield Omnibus of Electro-Magnetic Fiction*
Paula Eisenstein, *Flip Turn*
Sara Heinonen, *Dear Leaves, I Miss You All*
Christine Miscione, *Carafola*
Marko Sijan, *Mongrel*
Tom Walmsley, *Dog Eat Rat*

Non-Fiction

George Bowering, *How I Wrote Certain of My Books*
Rosanna Caira & Tony Aspler, *Buon Appetito Toronto*
Pier Giorgio Di Cicco, *Municipal Mind: Manifestos for the Creative City*
Amy Lavender Harris, *Imagining Toronto*
David W. McFadden, *Mother Died Last Summer*

To order these books, visit www.mansfieldpress.net